HEART
OF
DECEPTION

ALSO BY M. L. MALCOLM

Heart of Lies

Praise for *Heart of Lies* and M. L. Malcolm

"Fascinating and deftly written. . . . The writing is exquisite, wrapping the reader in another time and place."

—*Historical Novels Review*

"A sweeping saga reminiscent of Jeffrey Archer and Susan Howatch, *Heart of Lies* is brilliantly researched and beautifully written. I could not put this book down."

—Karen White, *New York Times* bestselling author of *The Girl on Legare Street*

"Ambitious, captivating. . . . The expansive plot and rapid-fire pacing are underscored by brilliant depictions of post–World War I Europe and Asia."   —*Atlanta* magazine

"*Heart of Lies* takes the reader on a thrill ride that spans continents and decades, but at heart it's an enduring love story."

—Melanie Benjamin, author of *Alice I Have Been*

"A 'page-turner' in the very best tradition of historical fiction."

—*Midwest Book Review*

© Mark Oxley/Studio 16

ABOUT THE AUTHOR

M. L. MALCOLM is a Harvard Law graduate, journalist, recovering attorney, and public speaker. The author of the novel *Heart of Lies*, she has won several awards for her fiction, including recognition in the Lorian Hemingway Short Story Competition and a silver medal from *ForeWord* magazine for Historical Fiction Book of the Year. She has lived in Florida, Boston, Washington, D.C., France, New York, and Atlanta, and currently resides in Los Angeles. Her website is www.MLMalcolm.com.

HEART

OF

DECEPTION

M.L. MALCOLM

Previously published as *Deceptive Intentions*

HARPER

NEW YORK · LONDON · TORONTO · SYDNEY

HARPER

A paperback edition of this book was previously published under the title *Deceptive Intentions* in 2008 by A Good Read Publishing.

HEART OF DECEPTION. Copyright © 2008 by M. L. Malcolm. All rights reserved. Printed in the United States of America. No part of this book may be used or reproduced in any manner whatsoever without written permission except in the case of brief quotations embodied in critical articles and reviews. For information, address HarperCollins Publishers, 10 East 53rd Street, New York, NY 10022.

HarperCollins books may be purchased for educational, business, or sales promotional use. For information, please write: Special Markets Department, HarperCollins Publishers, 10 East 53rd Street, New York, NY 10022.

FIRST HARPER PAPERBACK PUBLISHED 2011.

Library of Congress Cataloging-in-Publication Data
Malcolm, M. L.
    Heart of deception/M. L. Malcolm.
        p.   cm.
    Sequel to: Heart of lies.
    ISBN 978-0-06-196219-6
    1. Americans—Africa—Fiction. 2. World War, 1939–1945—North Africa—Fiction. I. Title.
PS3613.A433H427   2010
813'.6—dc22

2010022996

11 12 13 14 15   OV/RRD   10 9 8 7 6 5 4 3 2

For John, Andy, and Amanda, whose love and support keep me going when that light at the end of the tunnel seems very dim, and for Alicia, whose wisdom, energy, and kindness keep everything from falling apart.

PART ONE

ONE
TANGIER, 1942

If the city of Tangier had been a woman, she would have been a whore, and a wealthy one. Brazenly straddling the northwest tip of Africa, she brushed one of her sultry thighs up against the undulating waves of the turquoise Mediterranean Sea; the other unfolded west, perpetually teasing the unquenchable desire of the gray Atlantic Ocean. Legend held that her proud limestone cliffs were forged by Hercules himself, when he ripped apart the continents of Africa and Eurasia to create a water-bound kingdom for his newborn son; the splendid bluffs both enhanced Tangier's beauty and granted her patron-of-the-moment a keen view of his many seafaring rivals. For centuries men fought to claim this sun-drenched siren of antiquity: the Phoenicians, the Carthaginians, the Romans, the Berbers, and then, finally, the countries of Europe. For he who possessed Tangier could control the Strait of Gibraltar, the only maritime passage between East and West that did not involve sailing around a continent.

Tangier's charms seduced not only kings, pirates, and warriors, but merchants and artists as well. The merchants came for her magnificent *souks*—grand markets offering spices, silks, exotic fruits, gemstones, livestock, and slaves. The decadent city lured the world's most famous artists with her unique light, a shimmering radiance so bright it could reveal four different shades of green in a single blade of grass, or beguile an unwary soul into a permanent state of lethargy.

But the brightest light casts the deepest shadows, sheltering the creatures who thrive in darkness. Leo Hoffman had lived in sunlight and in shadow for the better part of two years.

He sat at a table in the tiled courtyard of Hotel El Minzah, an unfinished cup of coffee in front of him, watching another customer signal for his check. The man was dressed in a dark wool suit of the type worn only by those new to the heat and dust of the city. "L'addition, s'il vous plaît!" Leo overheard him ask for the third time, the growing irritation in his voice another sign that the man was new to Tangier. One learned patience here. You learned to be patient, or your nerves broke. Then you made mistakes.

Leo was aware of two other men also watching the newcomer. The city was an enormous spider web of intrigue. One small vibration in one isolated corner and out scurried the predators with a thousand eyes, ready to feast on the vulnerable.

He glanced at his watch, drained his cup, left enough change on the table to pay for his coffee, and put on his sunglasses. Time to go meet his new boss.

On the outskirts of the city, where orange sand and scrub brush gave way to the desert, Lieutenant Colonel William Eddy stopped reading long enough to enjoy the sunset. This was his favorite time of day: the magical thirty minutes between the moment the sun dipped below the horizon and the onset of true darkness. He watched as the sky turned a purplish blue, illuminated only by the brightest stars. Lord, how he had missed the enormity of the Arabian sky.

Surely there was some guiding hand at work in his life; just a few weeks ago he'd been president of a small college in upstate New York. Now here he was, back in his marine uniform, heading up America's nascent spy network in North Africa. *If my fate is already written, let the story end here, while I'm doing something more useful than fighting over parking privileges at a faculty meeting.*

The first move Eddy made was to transfer his headquarters from Cairo to Tangier, which in his view held several advantages. The move got him out from under the British, whom he didn't trust. His operation was now a mere twenty miles from Spain, which facilitated communication with their contacts on the European continent. The other advantage was Tangier's near lack of a functioning government. The eight-nation governing council allegedly in charge of the independent city-state had collapsed, and Franco's decision to send in Spanish troops to "protect" the city after the fall of France only added to the confusion. What better place to set up a home base for spies than a city already overrun with them? No one would notice a few more, or even think to complain about commonplace events like car bombings, kidnappings, and bribery.

One of the young marines keeping watch for Eddy stuck his head inside the dilapidated hut. "Someone's coming, sir. On horseback."

"On horseback? Can you get a look at him?"

"Not a good one. Too dark. Looks like an Arab, though."

"That's odd. I'm not expecting any native visitors. If that's not the gentleman I'm expecting, we may have to shoot the poor bastard."

"Sir?"

Eddy shook his head and sighed. "You and Davies come inside.

Flank the door. If he shows any signs of aggression, take him down. Don't kill him if you can help it. A good knock on the head with your pistol butt should do it."

Eddy watched from a crack in the wall as the man dismounted. He stroked the horse's neck and said something into the animal's ear. As he approached the door, he pulled back the hood of his *djellaba*, the long, hooded robe Moroccan men wore over loose trousers.

It was Leo Hoffman, all right. Easy enough to recognize him from his file description. He looked like the Hollywood version of what a spy should be, or one of the agency's Ivy League recruits, excited by the possibility of cloak-and-dagger exploits, with no idea what they were doing.

"At ease, boys. It's him."

Leo knocked. One of the yeomen opened the door.

"Good evening, gentlemen. I didn't see anywhere to tie up my horse. Would one of you be kind enough to mind him? He's not likely to wander off, but one never knows."

Eddy smiled. "There's an old Arabic saying, 'Trust in Allah, but tie up your camel.' Men, go see to our visitor's horse." The two departed with a salute.

Eddy and Hoffman shook hands, openly appraising each other as they did so.

"Have a seat," Eddy said, gesturing to one of three camp chairs, the only furniture in the tiny hut. As he sat down he picked up a file from a small stack on the floor and opened it to reveal Leo's picture, taken when he'd first arrived in London, in December 1939, before his fair skin grew permanently sunburned.

"Don't worry about the files," he commented, as if reading Leo's thoughts. "I'll burn them before I leave here tonight."

"That's comforting."

"And that, Mr. Hoffman, is a perfect example of the type of sarcasm that's noted in your evaluations."

"I assure you, I meant no disrespect, sir, but everyone knows that despite your appointment as 'naval attaché,' you're really here to organize a spy network, just as everyone knows that the American consul in Algiers, Bob Murphy, and those twelve vice-consuls he calls 'inspectors,' are here to gather intelligence. But we little people, the ones crawling around in the dust with our eyes and ears open, we're anonymous, and because I'd like to live a little longer, I'd like to stay that way. Surely you can understand why seeing a copy of my personnel file on display in a poorly guarded shack—"

"The security is adequate for my purposes." Eddy did not plan to interview many of the informants upon whom Murphy and the so-called Twelve Apostles had relied prior to his arrival, but there were a couple of extraordinary cases, and Hoffman was one of them. A real enigma. Eddy wanted to gauge the man's reaction to the information in his dossier to see if he could get a better sense of what Hoffman was all about. He began to read aloud from Leo's file.

"Born in Hungary, 1900. Spent fifteen years in Shanghai as a businessman and banker. And you speak six languages. That's useful. But tell me, Mr. Hoffman, what are the chances that we were shooting at each other during the previous war?"

"Slim, unless you were at the Italian front in 1917."

"Never made it out of France. Went home in 1918."

"With a stack of medals, including two Purple Hearts."

Eddy closed Leo's file and let it drop to the floor. "What else do you know about me?"

"You were born in Syria, to missionary parents. You prefer to eat

Arabian food when you can get it, and you've even been seen riding a camel. Went back to Princeton for your college degree, and got out just in time to go to war, where you worked in intelligence. Injured hip sent you home, and that's the cause of your limp. You've been back in the States since twenty-eight, mostly in academia, and it's said you're the only commissioned American officer who's fluent in Arabic."

Eddy was impressed. "That's pretty thorough, except that it was a bout with pneumonia that sent me home. Hospital infection crippled the hip. So where did you come by all that?"

"As I said, we little people keep our ears to the ground."

The man's sarcasm was beginning to grate on Eddy's nerves. "I expect a man working for me to answer any question I ask him. Why are you here, Hoffman? What made you volunteer for this duty?"

"It's a means to an end, Colonel. And that's to be able to get back to the States, and live a peaceful life with my daughter."

"And how will being here help you?"

Leo pointed at his file. "What does it say in there? That I was recruited in 1939 by the American consul in Shanghai?"

"And that you requested a replacement for your passport. A French passport. That seemed a little strange, given that you claimed to be a Hungarian national."

"Not strange if it's a passport issued in Shanghai. A certain French diplomat there was quite willing to hand out French passports to the right person for the right price."

"Sounds like Tangier."

"The two cities are remarkably similar in many ways. At any rate I was recruited to work for the U.S. Office of Naval Intelligence. But the Americans weren't active in Europe yet, so in light of my language skills I was sent 'on loan' to the Brits, because their Special Operations Executive, the covert angle, was already gearing up. Churchill and company sent me to North Africa as part of the SOE contingent that tagged along with Murphy's American entourage. But unlike the Apostles, I was sent in unofficially, so they'd have at least one clandestine observer."

Eddy frowned. "But how does that get you back to your daughter? I'm missing a piece here."

"I agreed to join Naval Intelligence because I was told that if I served for two years I'd qualify to become an American citizen. Madeleine, my daughter, is already in the States. She went to New York with the woman who was, at that time, her stepmother. An American. I got them out of Shanghai right after the Japanese invasion in thirty-seven. But I couldn't leave."

"Why not? If you were married to a U.S. citizen?"

Leo paused. "I had some complicated business arrangements."

"Of what kind?"

"The kind that make me an excellent spy."

"And then there was that little matter of you being wanted for murder."

"Yes," Leo replied, steadily meeting Eddy's gaze. "There was that."

Eddy was about to push for details, then thought better of it. Self-defense, the report said. Hopefully someone at Naval Intelligence had checked out Hoffman's story before sending him to London. If not, well, he wouldn't be the first man with a violent past to work in espionage. Good spies were rarely Boy Scouts.

"So what's keeping you here?"

"Right now I'm in limbo. Seems my agreement's controlled by a 'wartime' clause that kicked in after Pearl Harbor, so right before my two years were up, the time I needed to serve suddenly became 'indeterminate, until dismissed.' And technically I'm not even in the navy anymore. On paper I'm SOE, covert operations, with an 'understanding' that I'll get U.S. naval credit for time served, however long that is. When I'm released, I'll go to New York."

"Somehow that piece of the tale wasn't in your file. You're listed as an unaffiliated civilian volunteer. No mention of an attachment to ONI, or any other military connection. You're not even on the SOE asset list. My records indicate that you're more of an independent contractor."

Leo's nonchalance evaporated. "That needs to be corrected. The only reason I'm in this game is to earn my citizenship, and get back to my daughter."

"I'll have someone look into it."

"Thank you. I'd appreciate that." Before Eddy could speak again, concern replaced the relief on Leo's face. "But, sir, then who's writing my letters?"

"Your letters?"

"Letters to my daughter. Once I left London I wasn't supposed to write home myself. My chief at ONI assured me that regular letters would be sent home on my behalf, so my daughter would know that I was all right. If I'm no longer with the navy, and not claimed by the Brits, then who's writing my letters?"

"I sympathize with your plight, Hoffman, but I can't even get a straight answer from the top brass about how we're supposed to prepare for a North Africa invasion that may or may not come to pass. I seriously doubt I'll be able to clarify your mail privileges."

Leo stood up, his movements radiating agitation. "I know you don't want to hear my life story. But I wasn't a decent husband, and I haven't been a good father. For the first time in a very long time, I'm trying to play by the goddamn rules, and I'd like some good to come out of it. But it won't mean anything if my daughter thinks I've abandoned her."

"I can appreciate that. So write a letter. We'll throw it in the diplomatic pouch and run it through the censors before it gets to the States. It's no secret to anyone that you're here. Whatever your original agreement was, the only thing that's still a secret is the fact that you're working for us. But the kind of work we need you to do requires complete commitment. If you can't manage that, if you want out now, you have my permission to leave. What that does not give you, unfortunately, is permission to enter the United States."

Leo sat down heavily. "I'll do whatever it takes to get back to my daughter."

"Then work with us. We'll get you back as soon as we can. As soon as any of us can go back."

"Very well. I will. And thank you."

To Eddy's surprise Leo was speaking in Arabic. "How well do you speak?" he asked, also in Arabic.

"Not quite well enough to fool a native for an extended conversation. Not yet. But I can eavesdrop pretty efficiently, and negotiate a deal when I need to."

Eddy slapped his good leg. "That explains how you were able to get the information on those fortifications at the border. You used a native, didn't you?"

For the first time during their meeting Leo gave Eddy a genuine smile. "For the right price, he proved very helpful. I also persuaded him to loan me that beautiful horse."

"That disguise almost got you shot."

"It also got me here unnoticed."

Eddy switched back to English. "Fair enough. Thank you for coming tonight. You'll be hearing from me."

"A pleasure, sir." Leo took his leave.

Eddy took the time to go through Leo's file one more time, making sure he'd missed nothing. "We'll have to watch that one," he muttered, mostly to himself, but Davies, coming back into the hut, overheard him.

"What's that, sir?"

"Hoffman. He could be an excellent asset, but his heart's not in it. And that's dangerous."

"Dangerous?"

Eddy picked up the next file. "A man without commitment can be turned. Become a double agent."

TWO
NEW YORK

Who the hell could that be? Amelia Hoffman lifted her head off the pillow high enough to check the time on the small Cartier clock decorating her nightstand. *Christ almighty.* It wasn't even nine o'clock. Who'd have the energy to be out and about at such an indecent hour of the morning? And why wasn't that stupid maid answering the buzzer? Oh, that's right. She'd fired her yesterday. *Damn, damn, damn.*

The buzzer sounded again. Amelia knew there wasn't a doorman in the building who would dare summon her before noon, not for anything less than a five-dollar tip. That meant the visitor was not only unexpected, he was also the owner of a fat wallet. She threw back the silk comforter, grabbed her dressing gown, and headed toward the intercom.

"What is it?"

"A visitor, Mrs. Hoffman. A Mrs. Bernice Mason is here to see you."

Bernice Mason? The name was not the least bit familiar. "I'm not expecting anyone. Ask her what she wants."

"She says she'd like to talk to you about her niece. Should I send her up?"

Her niece? "I don't know this woman or her niece, and I'm not dressed. Tell her I can't see her."

Amelia barely had time to light a cigarette before the intercom buzzed again. This time the doorman sounded anxious.

"I'm sorry to bother you again, madam, but she says her niece is Madeleine Hoffman, and that the girl is your stepdaughter. I'm not sure that Mrs. Mason is going to leave until you see her, and she doesn't seem like the type who gets tossed out, if you get my meaning."

Amelia stared at the innocuous electronic box as if it had just sprung to life.

"Mrs. Hoffman? Are you there? Should I send her up?"

"Give me ten minutes." *Madeleine Hoffman.* She hadn't heard that name for over two years. How old would she be now? Twelve? Thirteen?

And who was Bernice Mason? As Amelia headed back to her bedroom to change she caught sight of herself in the large art deco mirror hanging on the wall behind her sofa: tousled blond curls, prominent cheekbones, cigarette dangling out of a sensuous mouth. She moved closer to her reflection. She was still slim, and her years as a dancer had helped keep everything up where it was supposed to be. But those small lines around her lips . . . hadn't she heard that smoking causes wrinkles? She grabbed a crystal ashtray off the coffee table and stubbed out her nearly untouched cigarette. She needed to find another husband. Soon. A rich one. Preferably a rich one headed off to war, so that Amelia could mind his fortune until he returned. Or better yet, until she was widowed for the second time.

To improve those odds, I really ought to go back to San Francisco. The government was positively herding eligible men out to the West Coast, like so many cattle lumbering off to the Chicago stock-yards. And Amelia could make a man's last days ashore very, very pleasurable.

She'd used those talents to land her first husband, and then found herself happily single again when he killed himself; among other ad-vantages, being a widow allowed her to marry Leo Hoffman after his pretty little wife died. But then he'd had their marriage *annulled,* the bastard. Amelia kept his name, although legally she probably shouldn't have. True, it hadn't been much of a marriage, but she'd counted on having a chance to make it real. She'd taken his little brat with her to New York, and kept her out of harm's way for two years while he dallied in Shanghai, all because . . . *not now.* She had to throw on some makeup, find something relatively demure in her closet, and slip on a pair of low heels.

Bernice Mason. Was she Leo's sister? Or Martha's?

Precisely ten minutes later Amelia opened her door to see a woman who did not resemble either of Madeleine's parents. This woman's face was almost masculine: long, with thick, unshaped brows, and dark brown eyes hovering over a long nose. She had short brown hair, and her conservative gray suit did nothing to show off a trim figure. She was, in a word, plain.

Yet there was nothing ordinary about the way she handled herself; Bernice Mason seemed to be evaluating everything with scientific pre-cision: the mohair furniture, the satin drapes, the lighting, Amelia's clothes, maybe even the temperature and barometric pressure. The level of scrutiny was unnerving.

"Mrs. Hoffman? I'm Bernice Mason. May I come in?"

She spoke with a distinctly German accent. Amelia recovered her composure and opened the door wide enough for her visitor to enter. "Yes, of course."

Bernice Mason did not offer Amelia her hand before stepping into the foyer. "What a lovely apartment," she remarked, making the compliment seem irrelevant. "May I sit down?" Without waiting for an answer she made her way into the sunken living room, took a seat, and placed her slim leather satchel beside her on the sofa.

Amelia followed, but remained standing. She'd lost the first round, somehow, and wanted to regain the upper hand. She leaned one hip against a credenza on the opposite side of the room and crossed her slender arms in front of her chest. "This is quite a surprise, Mrs. Mason. I wasn't even aware that Madeleine had any surviving relatives, other than her father." *And he might be dead, too, for all I know. May he burn in hell.*

"Where is Madeleine? Is she at school?"

Hmmm. If you thought you'd find her anywhere around here, there's a whole lot to this story that you don't know. The question is, if I fill you in, what's in it for me?

Amelia cocked her head. "Well, who are you, exactly, and why are you here? You're presuming quite a bit, Mrs. Mason."

"Forgive me," she replied, in a tone empty of contrition. "Martha, Madeleine's mother, was my sister. After considerable effort, my husband and I learned that Martha was killed in Shanghai at the time of the Japanese invasion, and that you and Madeleine's father were married a few days after Martha's death. It took more time to discover that you and Madeleine sailed from Shanghai that same day, and to locate you here. But now that we have found you, we are hoping that we have found Madeleine as well."

"Let me get this straight. You've been trying to find your niece for five years?"

"That is correct. Is she here?"

"Where have you been all this time?"

"Mrs. Hoffman, I appreciate the fact that this is a very unusual set of circumstances, but before I elaborate any further, would you please tell me if Madeleine is living here with you?"

Amelia knew the value of a dramatic pause. *Screw the wrinkles. Time for a cig.* She walked over to the coffee table, picked up her enameled cigarette case, selected a cigarette, lit it, and blew out a lungful of smoke before looking back down at Bernice.

"No. She isn't living with me."

"Oh." Disappointment barely registered in the woman's voice. "Then can you give me any information that might help me find her? Is she with her father?"

Amelia went to sit down on a chair facing the sofa. "I'm not sure what I should do. This is really quite a shock, having you appear out of nowhere, demanding information. It's a bit melodramatic, don't you think?"

For some reason the older woman seemed to find this comment amusing. "My life has been nothing if not melodramatic for the past several years, Mrs. Hoffman." Then her humor vanished. "What information do you need from me in order to secure your cooperation? Or may I reward you for what you have to tell me with a check?"

Amelia considered this. She could use a windfall, especially now that she planned to begin husband hunting in earnest. But there was another issue to consider: revenge. She sprang to her feet.

"How dare you imply that I can be bought? I took care of Madeleine for two years because I loved her and I loved her father. I don't know what your intentions are. You've got a German accent, for God's sake. I could be putting Madeleine in jeopardy by letting you know where to find her." She pointed toward the door. "You may leave, Mrs. Mason. Keep your money to pay your private detectives, or whoever it is that's gotten you this far."

Bernice did not budge. "I did not mean to insult you, and I assure you that I have Madeleine's best interests at heart." She tapped her satchel. "I have all the documentation necessary for you to feel confident that I am who I say I am."

Amelia stood her ground. "I'm sure you do. But I also need to know that you'll take proper care of Madeleine."

"My husband and I are well equipped to provide for her every need."

Is that so? Amelia thought. *Well then, the price for information leading to her whereabouts has just gone up.*

"Physical comfort isn't the only consideration. I need to know that Madeleine will be loved as much as I loved her. And, as difficult as this is for me to say because I once loved the man very much, I don't think it would be good for Maddy to be reunited with her father. He would only cause her more heartache."

"How so?"

Amelia sat back down before answering. "Leo was supposed to come to New York with us, but he didn't. He stayed there, on the pier in Shanghai, and never gave me a reason why he wouldn't, or couldn't, get on the boat. It was two years before he showed up, and then he took Madeleine away from me, despite everything I'd done for him—and for Madeleine, of course—and he stuck her in this horrible little boardinghouse. He abandoned both of us. So if her father does eventually reappear, well, in my opinion the poor little thing has been through enough."

"You do not need to worry about that," Bernice replied, with a seriousness that seemed almost ominous. "I want to give Madeleine the life she deserves, and in my view that involves protecting her from any further involvement with the man who is, unfortunately, her father."

"That is very reassuring, Mrs. Mason. In that case, I'm sure we can come to an agreement."

THREE

Margaret O'Connor kept her rosary in her apron pocket. Or hanging over her bedpost, or on a hook on the wall she'd nailed up just for that purpose, for those moments when there were no pockets available.

During the five months that her youngest son had been gone she'd completed the rosary thousands of times, her plump calloused fingers touching each bead as if she were stroking the fuzzy patch of auburn hair crowning his head on the day he was born. She even caught herself reaching for a cooking spoon or a feather duster with her left hand, in order to keep the other quiet in her pocket, moving bead by bead, prayer by prayer, along the sacred circle. She never lost her place. And every time she completed it, she added a prayer of her own. *Holy Mother, I've got no right to ask this, for you gave up your own Son to pay for the sins of all mankind. But I'm askin' ya just the same, dear Mary. Protect my boy. Please protect my boy.*

She'd not had a letter for six weeks—not that the scribbled notes her Jamie sent were proper letters. He had none of the poet in him, that one. But even a few lines about the bad food or his bragging about winning a handsome pot in a poker game was proof enough that he was alive.

Her husband had died so suddenly; there'd been no time to torture herself with terrible pictures of how he might go. He was there one day and then he wasn't, leaving her with five children in a home on the Upper West Side, nearly paid for by the life insurance policy she'd called him an idiot for buying. Margaret piled her family into three rooms and took in boarders. There was no time to mourn. She kept her tears for the pillow, and on many nights was too tired to stay awake long enough to cry. If idle hands were the devil's workshop, Satan would find himself permanently unemployed in Margaret O'Connor's home.

But Jamie was her Patrick all over again, with that crooked smile and his deep-throated laugh, ready to throw a punch when necessary, softhearted when it came to helping anyone who needed it. For three years she'd suffered through Jamie being on the police force, fearing he'd come home with a bullet in his back or his skull cracked open, comforted only by the fact that he was always close by.

And then he'd volunteered. That was the rub. After they'd all seen the newsreels about Pearl Harbor, Jamie had signed up without so much as a by-your-leave: a grown man, all set to fight for his country.

It was her punishment, she knew, for having a favorite. But surely the constant worry was punishment enough. Asleep and awake they came to her: the visions of him floating, terrified and helpless in the cold, dark ocean, surrounded by the screams of his shipmates as the sharks moved in, praying that he'd freeze to death before the beasts got to him. Or she'd see him staring across a ditch at a leg that used to be his, knowing it was the last thing he'd ever see as his blood poured out of him like water. *Hail Mary, full of Grace, the Lord is with thee. Blessed art thou among women . . .*

"Ma! We're home!"

Margaret slipped the rosary back into her apron pocket as her two girls popped into the parlor. "As if I couldn't tell from all the gigglin' and stompin'. About time, too."

"Ma, I told you. We had to put the baby to bed."

"The baby? Merciful heavens, that's what yer callin' it now?"

"Ma, you know what an honor it was for me, a rising freshman, to be chosen as an assistant editor. I can't let the seniors do all the work on the days the paper goes to press." She looked down at her ink-stained hands. "Journalism sure is a dirty business."

"Oh, off with ya both. Get cleaned up and meet me in the kitchen. Potatoes don't peel themselves, at least not in this house."

Margaret watched as the two scampered away. They were closer than sisters, though no one would ever mistake them for blood kin. Katherine, tall and lanky at thirteen, with red hair and an Irish temper to match, would charge into hell to put out the fires with nothing but a glass of water. Half a head shorter and a year younger, Maddy had her father's black curls, but there her resemblance to Leo Hoffman ended. She gazed at the world with her mother's eyes and, Margaret suspected, for she'd never seen anything but a photograph of Martha Hoffman, moved with her mother's grace.

The two girls had been friends for nearly a year before Margaret discovered that Maddy only came around on Thursdays because she'd been using her piano lessons as an excuse to sneak out of the convent school where that awful woman had stashed her, like an unwanted piece of furniture. If one of the good sisters hadn't locked the alleyway door early that day so that Maddy couldn't sneak back in, well then, who knows how things would've turned out? And then Margaret had thought she was doing right by the girl when she'd brought Maddy over to her stepmother's that evening, so that Mrs. Hoffman could sort things out with the school. But when they arrived at that iceberg Amelia called an apartment, and Margaret felt the sadness in the child as she walked through the door, she knew she couldn't leave the poor brokenhearted lass in the clutches of that she-devil. Margaret had taken Maddy in, and never regretted it.

Her father had showed up once, approved his daughter's living arrangements, and then vanished again, to go do something involving the war in Europe long before the Americans piled on. *My Jamie among them.*

Margaret's right hand found her rosary. At least the girls were here, where she could keep an eye on them. Not like Jamie. Not like Timothy or Mark, in the merchant marine, liable to get blown up by a submarine any second, but not, thank God, slap in the thick of the fighting. *Hail Mary, full of Grace...*

Farther down the narrow hallway Maddy and Katherine burst into their bedroom, where Katherine immediately flung herself to the floor, pulled a newspaper out of her book bag, and disappeared under one of two twin beds.

"You know, I think you could go to jail for keeping that stack of newspapers under there. It's not only hoarding; it's a fire hazard," said Maddy, tossing her books onto the same bed and plopping down on the second one, barely two feet away.

"Maddy, I keep telling you. These are for research."

"Researching what? You're not exactly working for the *New York Times*. How much research do you need to do to write about the school field trip to an art museum?"

"But someday I will work for the *Times*," came the muffled reply. "I'll be a famous foreign correspondent, and these files could come in handy."

"If your mum doesn't find them first."

"Why would she look under here?"

"Oh, you know. She has some kind of radar."

"Yeah, she knows everything, all right. Ma Maggie and her Magnificent Irish Boardinghouse. There's days I'd rather take on the Nazis than live here another minute."

"Everyone fights with their mother, Katherine. Just be glad you've got one to fight with."

Katherine's head shot out from under the bed. "I'm sorry. I didn't mean—"

"It's okay. But you know—"

"She loves you as much as she loves any of us."

"It's okay, Katherine. Really."

"I'd go crazy without you around."

"I'm not going anywhere." *Where would I go? There's no one else who wants me.* "Let's get to the kitchen, Miss Pulitzer. Your mum sounded like she meant business."

A few days later Margaret O'Connor answered her door to see a Western Union courier standing on her doorstep, envelope in hand. The color drained out of her face, until it very nearly matched the graying tones of her hair.

"Don't you be comin' to see me," she warned the young man on the doorstep.

"I'm sorry, ma'am." He held out an envelope. Margaret looked at it as if the devil had just tried to hand her his tail. She didn't move.

He jiggled the envelope. "Ma'am," he pleaded, "I've got a lot of people to get to today. I'm sorry."

"Ma? Who is it?" Katherine peered out from behind her mother's stout shoulder. Her eyes locked on to the telegram. "Oh, no."

"It's no one. It's no one for us," replied Margaret, motionless.

Eyes wide, Katherine edged out the door and reached for the envelope. The courier handed it to her and bolted.

Katherine took a deep breath and ripped the telegram open. Margaret flinched. Katherine read the short sentences written there, and shook her head.

"Which one is it, Mary Kate? Which one?" Margaret demanded, looking ready to collapse despite the strength of her voice.

"It's not, Ma. It's not about any of them. It's about Maddy."

"Me?" Maddy squeaked from behind them.

Margaret snatched the paper from Katherine's hand to read it herself while Katherine, her features etched with confusion, explained to her friend, "It's from Amelia. She says . . . she says your mother's sister is here, in New York. She's here and she wants to see you."

Amelia loved traveling by train. What was the point of flying? Why get to where you were going so quickly? Train travel offered so many possibilities.

She took another sip of champagne, savoring the effervescence on her tongue. With the war on, it would soon be damn near impossible to enjoy a glass of bubbly. Champagne was a perfect accompaniment for gloating, and Amelia had a lot to gloat about.

For two years she'd waited, and then, when Leo finally came to New York, they'd spent less than a day together before Madeleine screwed everything up. The stupid girl hadn't listened when Amelia warned her to keep her mouth shut, and Leo had believed everything that whining, lying brat told him about how Amelia had *supposedly* mistreated her during the two years he'd stayed behind in Shanghai. Her outburst ruined the one chance Amelia had to get Leo back. Now Amelia had made sure that Maddy would never get him back, either.

Once Bernice had made it clear that she wanted to protect Madeleine *from* her renegade father, Amelia added another formal layer of untruthful, unflattering information to Leo's dossier, such as the fact that he and Amelia had been lovers for years while Leo was still married to Martha. Leo was the only person who could contradict her, and she doubted Bernice would believe *him*. When Leo came back, if he came back, he'd soon discover that his domestic situation had changed quite dramatically.

Best of all, Bernice Mason knew how to express her gratitude. Amelia got everything she wanted: revenge, a check, and a start on a new life in San Francisco, where men going to war made brides and widows out of beautiful women every day.

She closed her eyes and smiled. Trains, champagne, and a city full of desperate men.

So many interesting possibilities.

FOUR

Margaret called Bernice Mason that evening. She wasn't about to let Maddy meet any woman sent their way by Amelia Hoffman without investigating the whole matter. Who knew what that wretched tart was up to?

"Hello?"

Margaret was startled by the woman's heavy German accent. She knew that Maddy's mother was German, and that her father's family hailed from Austria, which, she'd since learned, was the closest thing you could get to being German without actually having lived under the Kaiser. But Maddy always insisted that she couldn't speak German, and the one time Margaret met Leo Hoffman, why, his accent had been so completely upper crust British, the German aspect of things sort of slipped out the back of her mind. But this woman spoke with the voice of the people determined to see all the O'Connor boys dead.

"Hello?" she heard again.

"Yes, good day. This is Margaret O'Connor. Amelia Hoffman sent me a telegram tellin' us that you were Maddy's aunt."

"That is correct. May I speak to her?"

"Well now, just hold yer horses. We've no idea who ya really are, do we? Maddy's never laid eyes on ya, and, to be frank, we've had enough dealings with that Amelia woman to know she's not the kind of person anyone decent would want as a reference."

"That I can understand."

Margaret thought she detected a note of amusement, but wasn't sure what it meant. Who was this Mrs. Mason laughing at?

"So," she said, clearing her throat, "it seems to me the two of us ought to meet."

"I agree. Are you free tomorrow?"

"No, no. It'll have to be on Sunday, Sunday afternoon."

"I do not mean to be overly insistent, Mrs. O'Connor. But I have waited twelve years to meet my niece. May I at least talk to her?"

The woman's accent set Margaret's teeth on edge. "Not yet. She'll not be havin' anythin' to do with ya until I'm comfortable with the whole situation."

"As you wish."

"Yes, well. Where should we be meetin', then?"

"You are more than welcome to come to my suite at the Regent."

Come into my parlor, said the spider to the fly. "No, I don't think so. There's a coffee shop down the street from your hotel. The Brew Stop, it's called. Look for me there at three o'clock."

"And how will I know you?"

"Oh, it's a small place, and it shouldn't be crowded on a Sunday. I imagine we'll find each other easy enough."

"Very good then. Until Sunday. And thank you, Mrs. O'Connor. Thank you for taking care of Madeleine, and for agreeing to meet with me."

Don't be thanking me yet. "Maddy's never been any trouble to us, Mrs. Mason. Her father left plenty of money for her keep, and she helps out besides. She's like one of me own."

"I cannot tell you how good it is to know that. I look forward to seeing you on Sunday."

"Until Sunday, then."

Margaret didn't say anything to the girls until after breakfast the next morning, and they knew better than to ask. Margaret O'Connor would talk about a subject when she was ready to talk about it, and not a moment before.

She brought in the last pile of dirty dishes and stacked them next to the sink, where Katherine washed as Maddy dried. "I don't know how you could possibly in a million years think Cary Grant is better looking than Humphrey Bogart," Katherine was saying, elbow-deep in gray dishwater.

"Shake the plates off a bit more, will you please? I think it because it's true. Bogart isn't even handsome."

"It's not all about pretty boy faces. It's about impact. It's about a man who can look at you a certain way and—"

Margaret took a seat at the heavy oak table that served as work counter, desk, and dining table for the family, and bore the scars to prove it. "About that telegram."

The chatter stopped. Katherine pulled her hands out of the dishwater and grabbed Maddy's towel to dry them as she spit out questions. "Is Maddy going to meet her? Where's she from? How did she find Maddy? Does she know anything about Maddy's father?"

Margaret held up her hands. "Mary Katherine Anne O'Connor, calm yerself. This isn't some news interview. Sit down."

Katherine darted to a chair. Maddy froze for an instant, like a gazelle on alert for a predator, before cautiously taking a seat.

"I don't know anythin' yet," Margaret began, "but I did want to tell ya that I'll be meeting with this woman tomorrow, this Mrs. Mason. And to ask, Maddy, well, you were so very young when ya lost yer mum, but if there's anythin' ya can remember that might be helpful, ya know, in figurin' out what's what—"

Maddy shook her head. "Nothing I haven't told you before. I remember my mother sometimes talked about her sister, Bernice, and a little about Munich, where she grew up." "*Wait until we get to Germany, Maddy. There's so much I want to show you, like the streams that run so fresh and clear through the mountains. Not like the river here, all yellow and slow and stinky.*" *Her mother held her nose and Maddy laughed. The Whangpoo did smell bad.*

Her mother's voice retreated. "I never met anyone in my mother's family. Or my father's. It was just us."

Margaret nodded. "So we'll see who this lady is, and what she's up to." She reached across the table for Maddy's hand. "I'll not be lettin' anyone take ya away, Maddy, unless and until it's yer own heart and yer own two feet showin' me it's what ya want, and me own good sense tellin' me it's the best thing for ya."

Maddy gave her hand a squeeze. Katherine started to say something, and then, quite uncharacteristically, seemed to think better of it, and stayed quiet.

"Well then," Margaret said, "there's a load of dishes to be done yet. So you'd best be gettin' back to it."

There were three customers in the Brew Stop when Margaret entered, and only one was a woman. She sat in a booth in the far corner, facing the door. Margaret unconsciously patted the tight bun into which she'd pulled her once-red hair. She prided herself on being able to spot deceit in a person. In the many years she'd run her boardinghouse, she'd not once been cheated. And, more often than not, she caught on when one of her brood tried to pull any sort of trick. She had a sense for these things, she did, and she intended to use it now.

The woman was headed toward her, hand outstretched. "You must be Margaret O'Connor."

Margaret was not used to this new business of women shaking hands. She grasped Bernice Mason's for an instant and let it go.

"And you're Bernice Mason, then."

"Yes. Please, sit down. Shall I order some coffee?"

"I'd have a cup of tea, if you don't mind."

Bernice signaled to the waitress behind the counter. "Miss? We will take one coffee, black, and one tea, please." Except the "we will" came out as "vee vill," making Margaret wince. Bernice did not appear to notice.

"Well then," said Margaret stiffly, once the two were seated, "who are you, and what is all this about?"

"I'm Madeleine's mother's sister."

Margaret's raised eyebrows communicated her skepticism. "Is that right? Well, you'll pardon me for sayin' so, but ya don't look a bit like Maddy's mum. The child has a picture. Her parents' wedding picture."

"I should like to see that." The waitress brought their drinks. Margaret tended to her tea. Bernice pulled a small leather satchel up from the bench and put it flat on the table. As she talked she pulled out two official-looking documents and several photographs.

"I understand your concern. Martha inherited our mother's beauty, and her . . . what shall I say? Her restless nature. Here, you see? This is Martha and me, with our father. You can see who I resemble."

Margaret took the photograph. A young lady with a heart-shaped face, large almond-shaped eyes, and a petite build stood between a younger version of Bernice Mason and a stern-faced gentleman. "Merciful heavens. Maddy is the spittin' image of her mum."

"Is she really?"

"Like a twin, but with darker hair. How old was she in this picture?"

"Fourteen. I was seventeen."

"Well, you look like yer father, that's for certain."

Bernice smiled. It was a fact she'd long ceased to regret. "Yes."

Margaret put down the picture. It was pretty good proof that this woman was who she said she was, but that was just the beginning.

"And where have ya been all this time? Why is it that poor child was left alone for so long?"

"We did not know how to find her. Let me back up a bit. In the summer of 1926, Martha eloped to Shanghai to marry Leo Hoffman." She handed Margaret one of the documents she'd pulled from the leather case. It was a copy of a wedding certificate. Margaret barely glanced at it.

"And when Maddy was born, did yer sister tell ya she had a daughter?"

"Yes, we kept in touch, but—"

"Then if you knew where Maddy was, why didn't ya go and fetch her? Why did ya let her father send her off with that awful woman?"

"It took us a while to find out what had happened, and by then it was not easy for Jews to get out of Germany. By the time we tried to—"

"Did you say *Jews*?"

Bernice sat back in her booth. "Does that surprise you? Never mind, I can tell by the look on your face that it does. Yes, our family is Jewish."

Margaret read the marriage certificate she held in her hands. "Leopold Hoffman and Martha Levy," she whispered. *Levy.* She'd never met a person with that name who wasn't Jewish. That surname was as Jewish as O'Connor was Irish. But Maddy? She examined the document.

"But it says right here: 'Religion: Catholic.' And Maddy went to a Catholic school in Shanghai. She told us all about the French sisters, and how she learned all her prayers in French, and—"

"I am sure that everything you are saying is true. But none of that changes the fact that Martha came from a Jewish family. Not a religious family, but a Jewish one."

Margaret did not know how to react. Of all things, she had not expected this. Almost three years of loving the child like one of her own, only to discover that Maddy was, well, she was not an *us*. She was a *them*. How could that be?

"But I thought you were from Germany?"

Bernice's voice went cold. "I am. I also happen to have a Jewish heritage."

Margaret took a deep drink of her tea before she responded. "Mrs. Mason, I didn't mean to offend. But we are at war—"

"Germany and America are at war. But the Germany that Hitler controls is not the country in which I grew up." For the first time during their conversation, real emotion registered on her face. "You have no idea how intolerable our situation became. My father was no longer allowed to teach. The university was his life. And then there were restrictions on where we could go, on what we could own—"

"Beggin' yer pardon, Mrs. Mason, but I do know. I'm Irish. It wasn't so long ago the newspaper employment pages right here in New York were full of 'no Irish need apply,' and that after we'd come to America, willing to work and work hard, to get away from a place where we were starved and thrown off our own land by the English."

Bernice fell silent. At last she said, "Yes, perhaps you do know."

For a long time neither woman spoke. Margaret tried to sort out her thoughts. *Maddy was a Jew.* This woman was her blood relation. What should she do? What was the best thing for Maddy? How much more shock could the child stand?

With sudden shame, Margaret thought about the many times she'd complained about the Jews moving into their neighborhood, with their irritating mannerisms and their mysterious ways. But that wasn't the real problem. For the last ten years, with everyone she knew struggling to make ends meet, Jews were leapfrogging right over the Irish, taking away the very jobs that Margaret's people had fought for three generations to win and hold.

Most of the Irish blamed the new mayor. *We ran the city, and ran it well, until the Little Mongrel was elected, courting the Jews and Italians like a shameless rooster tempting chickens out of the henhouse.* Margaret shared many Irish New Yorkers' dislike of Mayor La Guardia. He was part Italian, part Jewish, and nothing but trouble for the Irish, whose fifty-year grip on power was slipping rapidly now that he governed the city.

She considered herself a fair-minded woman, and didn't like to see folks at odds with one another. It worried her that more and more out-of-work Irish boys joined that so-called Christian Front, fired up by the garbage that radio priest, Father Coughlin, spewed out about how all Jews were Communists, plotting to take over the world. Beating people up who couldn't defend themselves. Awful. The pope himself had declared that anti-Semitism was wrong. There was no excuse for what they were doing.

But there was always an *us* and a *them* in life, people whose aims and interests competed with your own and the interests of those like you, and the chasm between the Jews and the Irish in New York grew wider every day. She'd never expected to find Maddy on the other side of it. *Would I have taken her in if I'd known? Yes, of course I would've. Maddy is still Maddy, as lovely as she ever was. Calm yerself, Margaret. Go have a talk with Father Cassidy. He'll help you sort it all out.*

"And what about Maddy's father, then?" Margaret finally asked. "What do you know about him?"

Bernice shook her head. "Very little. He is Hungarian, and was in the hotel business in Budapest before moving to Shanghai."

Margaret did not want to seem ignorant, but she had to know. "Hungarian? And where would that make him from, exactly?"

"He is from the country Hungary, next to Austria. It was part of the Habsburg Empire until the last war."

"So he's not German either, then?"

"Unlike our family, if that is what you mean, he is not German."

"And Jewish? Is he Jewish as well?"

Bernice gave Margaret a look that communicated nothing. "Yes, Martha did tell us that much. Although if they enrolled Madeleine in Catholic school I think it is unlikely that he was very religious. Not a religious Jew, at any rate."

"And you've never met him?"

"No."

"I see. Well, I've met him. Once."

Bernice leaned forward. "When? What was he like? I did not know he was ever here. What is he doing? Why is Madeleine not with him?"

"Oh, he's a charmer, that one. But I'll tell ya this. He loved yer sister. He loved her so much it almost killed him to lose her."

"I cannot say that I feel much sympathy for him, Mrs. O'Connor. Loving him did kill my sister."

FIVE
TANGIER

"It's interesting, isn't it, how quickly the world changes. As of two years ago, only a handful of Europeans had ever sought out my company. Yet here you are, Mr. Hoffman, the third such visitor to my home this week."

"And I doubt I will be the last."

The two men sat in the formal reception room of Hamid Belafej's *riyad*, a traditional Moroccan town house built around a central interior garden. Blue and white tiles created intricate and colorful geometric patterns up the fourteen-foot walls. Soft carpets covered the stone floor. Mahogany shutters filtered out the late afternoon sun, creating a wall of ladderlike shadows across the far side of the room.

Belafej bit into the dark flesh of a fresh fig and talked while he chewed. "To everyone but the French, Morocco was no more than a flea on a camel's ass before Hitler's invasions. Now it seems my beautiful country has become the center of the universe."

"It's common sense. If the British and Americans don't attack Hitler directly through France, then they'll come this way. They'll have to. North Africa will be the footstool they use to reach the rest of Europe. And for men like you and me, that means opportunity."

"Men like you and me? Pray tell, what is it that you think we have in common?" Belafej leaned back against the pile of silk-covered pillows covering the low-slung divan he used as a chair. "I am a Muslim, and you are an infidel. I have pledged my life to winning freedom for my people, who have lived without freedom for over a hundred years, while you have no loyalty to your own country, and hunt for opportunities to capitalize on the weakness of others. The similarities between us escape me, Mr. Hoffman."

Leo took a sip of his honey-sweetened mint tea before answering. "We are both men driven to achieve our goals. Different goals, true— you want the French and Spanish out of Morocco. I want to earn enough money to live securely, no matter who wins this war. What we share is the ability to take advantage of the current political situation."

Belafej's wide brown eyes narrowed into slits, and his slight double chin became more pronounced. "Carleton Coon, the American vice-consul, comes here to pay his respects, although I am the leader of a recently outlawed political party. He asks if the Americans can rely on me to rally my people against the Germans should they attack through Spain. I ask him if the Americans will, in exchange for such a promise, ally themselves with us to fight for our freedom from the French, the people who swore allegiance to their German conquerors. And do you know what Carleton Coon says to me?"

"What does he say?"

"He says, in his pretty schoolboy Arabic, 'The United States government can make no promises that might destabilize the domestic political situation in North Africa.' We have a saying, Mr. Hoffman. 'The enemy of my enemy is my friend.' The Germans are enemies of the French, and enemies of the Jews. That would make them friends of the Berbers and Arabs in North Africa."

"If you could trust them."

"Just so. And we are better off trusting no one."

"Nonetheless you will fight, when it is advantageous for you to do so. And for that, you will need weapons."

Leo's comment was rewarded by a flicker of interest in the other man's eyes. "We do not need a war. What we need is the opportunity for education, and to be treated like human beings. And we must have an end to the repressive taxes. The French try to squeeze money from us like milk from a dry goat. Yet, I will ask. What do you have in mind?"

"Grenades."

"How many?"

"Six crates."

"Where are they? How are they guarded?"

"That is the information that I am willing to sell to you."

"For how much?"

"Five hundred U.S. dollars, and some information."

"What information?"

"The name of your undercover German contact in Tangier."

Belafej looked at Leo suspiciously. "And why should I tell you this?"

Leo smiled indulgently. "Because you will need weapons to fight the French, when the opportunity arises, and I can sell that man's identity to the British. Then the Germans will replace him, and you will have lost nothing."

Belafej brushed a few crumbs off the table in front of him. "You will rot in hell, Mr. Hoffman."

"No doubt. And when the time comes, you can send along some Frenchmen to keep me company."

Leo stood on the balcony of a spacious villa set high up on one of the cliffs overlooking the port of Tangier. The city spread out beneath him like a cubist painting, its low-slung buildings reduced to basic shapes and monochromatic tones: squares, spires, semicircles, and rectangles, rendered in white, off-white, and beige, all hugging the flanks of the hills that separated the sea from the sandy plains to the south. From here one could not see the city's riotous colors: not the fabrics ablaze in red, yellow, and green; not the exotic rugs woven from silk and wool; nor the walls, floors, and fountains covered with tiles of blue, white, green, and rose. One could not see the details in the lattice-work as intricate as Belgian lace, nor the mother-of-pearl inlay gleaming in deeply polished wood. Bougainvillea plants added the only splashes of color, their fragile magenta and orange blossoms hiding the talonlike thorns that enabled the plants to grip and grow along doorways and fences. From this vantage point Tangier looked deceptively simple and peaceful.

A man walked toward him carrying two short crystal glasses. "Single malt," he said, handing one glass to Leo, "with a treat: an ice cube."

"Thank you." Leo tasted the scotch. "Excellent."

The other man turned to admire the view. The criers of the Muslim evening call to prayer had just begun their chants. The disembodied voices blended into a complex harmony as they wafted up the hillside from the city's mosques.

"I was lucky to find this place," he said. "The city filled up like a barrel after Paris fell. The owner of this villa was able to get out about six months ago, to Argentina, I believe. Good fortune for both of us."

"Here's to good fortune," Leo repeated, lifting his glass before taking another sip.

They were speaking German, and the nuances of his accent revealed to those with an ear for such things that Leo's host was a German Swiss. His name was Rolph Schmidt. Leo had discovered that the man loved good food and expensive liquor. He also enjoyed other, less socially acceptable, sensuous pleasures. Schmidt was an architect, the Swiss representative of the Red Cross in Tangier, and a German spy.

"So you're from Austria, you said?" Schmidt asked Leo.

"A long time ago."

"And you've been where since then?"

"Shanghai, mostly."

"Were you there during the Japanese invasion? I heard that was an ugly business."

In his mind's eye Leo watched again as the Wing On department store shattered and disappeared from view behind a cloud of smoke and dust. Shards of glass, chunks of cement, and bloody bits of human flesh rained down upon and around their car. He heard his daughter's screams, felt his heart and lungs contract in terror. *Martha was in that building.*

He took a long pull on his drink. "Yes. I was there. It was an ugly business."

"So forgive my curiosity, but why didn't you go back to Austria? Why come to Tangier?"

"Opportunity."

"Of what sort?"

"Desperation and chaos always yield opportunity. I took advantage of this in Shanghai. When the Japanese took over, the opportunities diminished. I left and came here."

"Tangier certainly supplies plenty of chaos and desperation, if that is what you seek. But as an architect, my goal is to impose organization. What do you have in mind to build?"

"An empire."

"That's ambitious."

"Yes. But as with many things, we start with one small piece: one brick. That's what I do, Herr Schmidt. I take one small piece, one small piece of information, and I use that to connect people who have complementary needs. Weapons with warriors. People with hard currency with those who must travel. People with assets they must sell with people who have money."

Schmidt pondered this information before he responded. "You're not here to give me an architectural commission, are you?"

"I confess I am not. I want to help you."

"How?"

"I want to help you help the Führer."

Schmidt put his glass down on the top of the balcony rail. "Switzerland is a neutral country. What makes you think that I have any interest in helping Germany?"

Leo looked him in the eye. "A mutual acquaintance, someone who is in the position to know."

"This is preposterous. How can you stand there, in my home, and accuse me—"

"I did not make an accusation. I made an observation, and offered to assist you."

"The only assistance you can give me is to leave my house at once."

"No, I don't think that's accurate. I can tell you some things that the Germans would very much like to know, like when and where the Allies plan to attack."

"You're bluffing."

"And that is an admission of interest."

Schmidt went to pick up his drink, knocking it over in the process. The two men listened to the muffled sound of breaking glass as it struck the rocks fifty feet below.

"Damn," Schmidt muttered. His face was red, and Leo could see beads of sweat popping up along his brow. *He's close.*

"I'm sure this must be very disconcerting, Herr Schmidt, but I assure you that an alliance will prove advantageous for both of us. And while I would much prefer to work *with* you, now that I know the true nature of your activities here, that information also has its price, a price others would be very willing to pay."

"And no doubt the services that you're proposing also have a price."

"Yes. And as part of that payment, I expect to receive permission to reside permanently in Switzerland, along with my daughter."

"I can't arrange for that."

"But you know others who can. You're not the only man in Switzerland hoping that the Reich will succeed."

"Very well, Mr. Hoffman. I will communicate with my associates regarding your offer. They'll want to know how you're getting your information, of course."

"I'll be happy to let the right people know, when the time comes. Thank you for your cooperation, and for the scotch."

"Forgive me if I don't see you out," Schmidt replied, his voice brittle. "Leave the glass on the table."

Leo started to leave, and then turned back around to face his host. "We all have our weaknesses, and Tangier has many temptations."

Schmidt's face broke out in a full sweat. "You really are a bastard, aren't you?" he stammered, pulling out his handkerchief.

"I'm sure there are many who think so. But when I get you the in-formation you want, you'll find that I am, at least, a very useful bastard. And I believe the German High Command will think so as well."

William Eddy sat in the office of Carleton Coon, former professor of anthropology at Harvard University and Arabian specialist, now sta-tioned in Tangier as a vice-consul under J. Rives Childs. He was also a spy.

They'd met only a few weeks earlier, but the two men got along ex-traordinarily well. Both had spent years living and working in North Africa; they respected the history and culture of its people. Both came to Tangier from academia, though Coon looked more professorial. Eddy entered a room with the broad-shouldered confidence of a ma-rine; Coon was denied a naval commission for being overweight, and one of his legs was a full inch longer than the other. Ungainly, with prominent ears and a large nose, Coon's intellect was his salvation, and he knew it.

They got along well for another reason: both men believed that it was necessary, in their current line of work, to bend the rules. Or, if need be, break them.

Eddy was shaking his head. "What is it that Childs said, exactly?"

"That his wife has been complaining about the 'clicking' noises up on the roof of the consulate at night. We'll have to move the trans-mitter."

"Because the missus can't sleep? He expects us to give up the most secure transmission site we've got?"

"You know how concerned he is about keeping the Snake Pit out of our 'clandestine' operations. He won't even let me use diplomatic li-cense plates on my car, even though I'm a vice-consul."

Eddy smiled at Coon's use of the derogatory term the espionage team used for the State Department. "Well, he's been pretty good at turning a blind eye. We'll move the set to my place for the time being. Rives should leave us alone for a while. He'll have his hands full with that Hollywood guy in town. What's his name?"

"Zanuck. Darryl Zanuck. Director. Or producer. Or both."

"Right. Zanuck will prove a useful distraction." He skipped to the next subject. "The weapon transfers are going well?"

"Exceedingly well. I just hope you're right that the tribes will use them against the Germans and French when the time comes. If the time comes."

"Oh, it's coming, all right. North Africa is the only realistic avenue we have. Roosevelt will come around soon enough."

"And you're convinced the French will resist an invasion?"

Eddy shook his head. "What I think doesn't matter. We have to prepare for a fight. Vichy has eight divisions in North Africa. The leadership vowed to resist an attack, and the Nazis are holding a million French POWs hostage to seal the deal. If the French fight back, we'll need native support."

"And then hope the natives don't use those same guns against us later, when they don't get the freedom they want."

"One war at a time, Carleton. Now tell me, what do you know about a Leo Hoffman?"

"Not much. I've seen him around. He doesn't exactly melt into a crowd. I hear he's quite the operator."

"Meaning?"

"You know, always able to put 'interested parties' together. A broker of sorts. Makes money coming and going matching up something someone has with someone else who wants it. Why do you ask?"

"He's one of us."

"You're joking."

"It's no joke. I inherited him from the Brits. Actually, being a wheeler-dealer is a pretty good cover, if everyone assumes he's out for himself."

"He's a Brit? Funny, I thought he was . . . well, I'm not sure what I thought. French, maybe."

"Hungarian. And he's done some good work. Those grenades we wanted to get to Belafej's group? He arranged for them to be 'kidnapped.' Got half the money from Belafej in advance, then paid off the depot guards."

"That was clever. The French can't be pissed off at us when Arabs succeed in stealing their grenades."

"Exactly. He's come up with something that could prove very useful, and we're going to have to be very careful how we work it."

"I'm listening."

"He's uncovered a high-level German undercover operative here, in Tangier. Hoffman has the man thinking he can be a conduit."

"Hoffman can pass on false information? That's great."

"In theory, yes. But the problem is we have to make sure that Hoffman won't put his personal interests ahead of ours. He's a man without a country. No loyalties. Doesn't care much about anything, other than his daughter."

"He has a daughter? Here?"

"No. She's back in the States."

"How did that happen?"

"American wife, or ex-wife. Anyway, to make this work, we'll have to pass along tidbits that are true but not really damaging, and false information that is truly misleading. Hoffman has to believe that most of it's true, and we have to make sure he doesn't find out anything that we don't want him to know. A delicate mix."

"I'd say so."

"I'm counting on you to come up with enough harmless stuff to keep the Germans interested. Travel plans for major diplomats, names of cooperators we've already exposed, that sort of thing. I want you to be the point person."

"With pleasure. And do we have an ultimate goal of some kind?"

"Yes. We want to mislead the Germans as to the time and place for the invasion of North Africa, once the date's been set."

"Oh. Is that all?"

Eddy grinned. "Yes, Carleton, that's all."

SIX
NEW YORK

The three of them had tea in the parlor. Bernice sat in one of two wing chairs near the fireplace. Margaret kept acting like the nervous mother hen she was: straightening a picture, grabbing a runaway napkin, adjusting the curtains so the afternoon sun didn't shine in their eyes. So far they'd spent ten uncomfortable minutes making conversation about Maddy's school and the weather. *Surely the woman would soon turn to the subject at hand.*

To Margaret's considerable surprise Maddy introduced the topic. It wasn't like her to charge ahead in a conversation, but the child was always one to surprise you.

Maddy laid her cup and saucer back down on the small oval table beside her, sat up a bit straighter, and began speaking with exaggerated formality. "Mrs. Mason, I've seen the photograph you gave to Mrs. O'Connor. It's very convincing."

"Please, Madeleine, call me Aunt Bernice."

"No, no, thank you. Not yet."

"As you wish."

"Well, as I was saying, after examining the birth certificates for you and my mother, and my parents' marriage license, as well as the other family photographs, it does seem that we might be related."

"Indeed. I am glad that you have come to that conclusion."

"I do have some questions."

"I am sure you must. I have some of my own to ask. But, by all means, you go first."

Maddy hesitated, and when she spoke again her voice was infused with five years' worth of loneliness and longing. "What was she like? My mother? When she was young?"

"Ah. As you might imagine, she was always beautiful, even as a child. And she was full of energy and enthusiasm. Martha could always see a bright side to things, although she was a bit reckless."

Maddy took a minute to soak this in before continuing. "And do you know why they—my parents—moved away to Shanghai?"

"I know a little. You see, our mother died during the influenza epidemic, in 1919. Martha was about your age at the time. I was older by three years, and I am afraid it went easier for me than for Martha. My father and I were very much alike. We didn't need great gulps of life the way Martha did.

"I left home in 1925, to study in Austria. At the time I thought it a fait accompli that your mother would marry a fellow by the name of Harry Jacobson, whom she was seeing at the time. Instead, during the summer of 1926, she disappeared, leaving a note for my father, explaining that during a brief trip to Paris she had met a man with whom she had fallen in love, and that she was going to Shanghai to marry him."

"My parents eloped?"

"Yes, and from her letters, she sounded happy enough. For reasons that were never really well explained, they told us they could not come to Germany, but invited us several times to visit them in Shanghai. My father hated to travel, and I was busy with my studies, then my work. We never went."

Maddy took a deep breath, summoning her courage. "And then why did it take so long for you to find me?"

Bernice glanced over at Margaret before answering. Margaret looked down, suddenly absorbed with her tea. *So she has decided to let me tell the whole story,* thought Bernice. *Very well. At least the child will get only one version.*

"I did not know what happened until months after your mother died, and by that time our lives were very unstable."

"What do you mean?"

"Well, Madeleine, our family is Jewish, and by 1937, it was becoming more and more difficult for Jews in Germany—"

"Our family is Jewish?" Maddy interrupted, bewildered. "But we're Catholic. We've always been Catholic." She looked to Mrs. O'Connor for support.

"Now Maddy," Margaret said soothingly, "you were confirmed with Mary Kate. You're certainly Catholic now, and we Catholics aren't as particular as some about what came before. It's yer history she's speakin' of, isn't that right, Mrs. Mason?"

Bernice tempered her response in light of the troubled expression Maddy wore. "I suppose. We cannot sort everything in one conversation. We were Jews according to Hitler, and that meant our lives were becoming very difficult. By then I was married myself. You will soon meet my husband, I hope. We decided to leave Germany, but my father was ill, too ill to travel. So I stayed in Munich until he died. Archie, my husband, made it to France.

"About this time we heard about the war in Shanghai. We tried to communicate with your mother, but never received a reply. After almost a year Archie was able to confirm through the French embassy that your mother died during the first bombing of Shanghai, but at that point we did not know how to look for you.

"I will not go into the details, but because of some patents we hold we were allowed to immigrate to the United States before the war broke out in Europe. With some money in my pocket, I was able to hire a private detective." She reached over and touched Maddy on one knee. "You see, I never gave up. I knew that if you were alive, I would find you."

Maddy hopped out of her chair, her eyes fixed on Bernice. "I'll be right back," she announced, and then raced out of the room.

Margaret called after her, "Maddy, where—"

"I'll be right back!" they heard her answer from down the hallway.

Margaret addressed her guest. "I don't know what to say, Mrs. Mason. It's all so—"

"Melodramatic?"

"Yes, I suppose it is that."

In a moment Maddy was back, carrying a long gray velvet jewelry box. She reclaimed her seat, opened the box slightly, then snapped it shut again.

"This necklace belonged to my mother," she said in a small but firm voice. "If you can tell me what this is, I will know you are my aunt."

Bernice shook her head. "This is not realistic, Madeleine. The last time I saw your mother she was eighteen years old. The only piece of jewelry she owned then was a gold medallion that Harry had given her. There was a bird, I think. It was a sort of nightingale—"

"Mr. Songbird. She would take it out, and let me play with it, and she would sing to me." Maddy opened the box, took her mother's golden medallion in her hand, and clutched it to her breast. Then came the tears.

The decision to allow Maddy to move in with the Masons did not take long. To Margaret family was family, and as much as she cared about Maddy, she thought the girl had a right to be with her own people, if that's what she wanted. Bernice Mason made it clear that Maddy would want for nothing, and that weighed on Margaret's conscience, too; how could she insist that Maddy stay with them, when a life of luxury awaited her?

For Maddy, the knowledge that a place existed where she truly belonged was enough. She loved Mrs. O'Connor, and Katherine was her dearest friend, but her aunt brought with her a fragment of the family that had been ripped away from her. As different as she was from Maddy's memories of her mother, her aunt was the closest thing she'd ever have to getting her mother back.

The Masons lived in Englewood Cliffs, a posh and verdant New Jersey suburb twenty minutes outside Manhattan. Their house was immense: bigger, even than the respectably huge Georgian estate Maddy had lived in as a little girl in Shanghai. But this house was unlike anything Maddy had ever seen, or even imagined. She did not know that windows could line up side by side and form a wall, or that lights could shine straight down like eyeballs from the ceiling, or that stairs could float like airy sculptures while connecting one floor to the next. She'd become used to modest rooms where faded curtains hovered protectively over small windows, and overstuffed, squeaky chairs greeted you upon arrival like endearingly cranky old relatives. But the Masons' home, as unfamiliar as it was, was also intriguing. It was intimidating but fascinating, just like her aunt Bernice.

Maddy had only a vague idea of what Mason Industries manufactured, that it had something to do with supplying the U.S. military with some of the electronic and chemical staples of modern warfare. She knew that her aunt and uncle were doing well. They were rich enough to live in Englewood Cliffs, rich enough to own a brand-new Cadillac, and rich enough to buy her new clothes at Saks Fifth Avenue.

Bernice was as involved in Mason Industries as her husband was, if not more so; she was a chemical engineer, with a Ph.D., no less, and knew more about the science of what Mason Industries manufactured than anyone else there. Archie handled the business end of things; he met with their clients and negotiated contracts. He traveled frequently and worked late. Maddy was usually left to herself from the time school was out until it was time for dinner.

After a few weeks a nagging loneliness began to tug at the edges of the happiness she'd felt upon being found. She saw Katherine at school, but her friend was busily involved with the school paper, her studies, and her chores. She lacked the abundance of free time that Maddy now enjoyed. After school Maddy did her homework and then listened to the radio, or prowled around the house, restless and bored, trying to stay away from the one room that drew her like a magnet.

The library contained two chairs: large, elongated leather recliners that reminded Maddy of enormous caterpillars. Built-in bookcases lined three of the walls; the fourth consisted of floor-to-ceiling windows. And tucked into the corner sat a baby grand piano.

The first time she walked into the room Maddy jumped as if she'd seen a gremlin. Her aunt completely misinterpreted her reaction.

"Oh, do you play?"

"No" was the curt reply.

"Neither do we. We bought the house partially furnished, and the piano stayed. It's handsome, and I thought it would be useful for entertaining. You may take lessons if you wish."

"No, thank you. I can't play."

Bernice gave her an odd look, but said nothing more.

Now, once again alone in the house, Maddy gravitated to the library. She could feel her heart pounding. "Stop being a baby," she chided herself aloud. "You'd think there was a ghost in there. Don't be so stupid."

But there was a ghost in there. Her mother's ghost.

Bernice had waited several days after Maddy had settled in to her new home before asking about Martha's death. "Madeleine, I know this will be difficult for you, but I would like to know—for you to share with me—how your mother died."

"I don't know very much. I wasn't there." *Liar! You were there. And your mother was there, in that store, only because you'd begged her for that doll.*

"I see. I realize that you were only seven, and might not remember much about it, but is there any information that you can give me? We have been in the dark for so long."

The parlor was my favorite room in the house. The walls were made of golden wood, and when the sun shone on it in the afternoon it glowed like Maman's amber necklace. One day Papa opened the parlor door, and there it was: my piano. As soon as I saw it I could already hear the music it was going to make.

Then the first bombs fell, and after that Shanghai was horrible. Everyone was so afraid that another bomb would fall, afraid that the Japanese would come. Maman and Papa tried to pretend that they weren't afraid, but I knew. There were too many whispers, too many times when Maman and Papa spoke German to each other, because they knew that I couldn't understand.

But I had my piano. Gaston, who played the piano at the country club, showed me the sound that each key made on his piano, and after that it was all so easy. I was a prodigy, Gaston said. I'd never heard that word before. He said it meant that I had a special talent, that I could do something almost no one else could do, not even grown-ups. He wanted to tell my parents, but I made him promise not to. I wanted to surprise them. I wanted to show off.

And they were surprised, and for a little while it was wonderful. Papa was so proud of me. He asked me if there was anything I wanted. A new doll, maybe. And there was a doll, a ballerina, dressed in red velvet and lace. Maman knew exactly which one I meant. So we went right away to the department store to buy it, but because the street was so crowded the driver couldn't find a place to park the car. Maman got out, kissed Papa, and went into the store to get my doll.

Papa told the chauffeur to circle the block, but we couldn't go in a circle. There were too many people, all the Chinese who'd come into the city to escape the Japanese soldiers. So we had to go down a street that led away from the store. And then there was the noise, that awful thundering noise, and the building disappeared. A hand fell onto the hood of our car. A woman's hand, with pink painted fingernails. I was screaming and screaming. And my father left me there, with the driver. He yelled at the driver to take me home, and he left me there.

And then he sent me away. Of course he did. How could he stand to be around me after I'd killed her?

"No, I'm sorry, Aunt Bernice. All I know is that a bomb fell on a department store where she was shopping. My mother and a lot of other people were killed."

And she wouldn't have been there if it hadn't been for me.

Maddy walked into the room and sat down on the piano bench. She'd taken lessons during her two years as a boarding student at the convent, coerced by the threat of being locked in a dark closet if she refused. Almost despite herself, she'd learned something about major and minor keys, chords and fingering, but she'd not played since.

As if by instinct she laid her fingers out in middle C position and practiced a few scales. Excited and more curious by the second, she got up, lifted the lid on the bench, and uncovered several books of sheet music. She flipped through a couple of them, looking for something easy and familiar. *Christmas carols. That should do.*

"'O Holy Night,'" she murmured, and began to play. By the time she reached the second verse she'd stopped looking at the music. Some part of her brain, long dormant, came to life. Her ears and fingers were connected in some mysterious way. What she'd told her astounded parents five years ago was still true: *I know where the music lives. I just play.* Playing for herself, by herself, she felt a rush of energy like nothing she'd ever felt before. Within an hour she had played every simple Christmas carol in the thin volume.

By the time her aunt came home, Maddy was exhausted but exhilarated. She did not say a word about the piano. Bernice, assuming that her happy mood was the result of a pleasant day at school, asked her niece a few questions about her day, pleased that her choices for Madeleine were working out so well.

That night Maddy lay awake, savoring her accomplishment. But her joy was laced with guilt, as if she had done something both delightful and deplorable. *I won't tell anyone. It will be my secret. My home. My piano.* And with a thousand sweet notes playing in her ears, she fell asleep.

SEVEN

The following Saturday Maddy went downstairs promptly at eight to breakfast with her aunt. Bernice had already made coffee and toast, which along with an occasional piece of fruit was all she ever ate for breakfast.

"Good morning." Bernice greeted Maddy as she took her place at the table, and then proceeded with same inquiry she made every morning, "Did you sleep well?"

"Yes, thank you. And you?"

"As well as I ever do. Were you warm enough? I could give you another blanket. I dislike turning up the heat. It seems a silly waste of money to heat a whole room when a good blanket is sufficient."

To Maddy, the simple act of climbing into her own bed in her own room was such a long-lost luxury, it never occurred to her that the room itself could be warmer.

"No, thank you. I'm quite comfortable."

"Very good." And then, changing the subject in her usual abrupt way, Bernice announced, "Madeleine, there is someone I would like for you to meet. An old friend of mine, and of your mother's: Harry Jacobson, the man who gave your mother that necklace."

"Here?" Maddy looked around as if she expected him to pop out from behind a door.

"He lives in Chicago, but he is in New York for a few days. He is an architectural engineer and has a commission here. Because he has achieved some renown in his field, it was not difficult to find him once we arrived in the States. Archie and I visited once when we were in Chicago, and Harry has been here several times, working on various projects." Bernice put down her toast and looked directly at Maddy. "It was a very long time ago, but he and your mother were once very close. He would love to meet you."

Maddy felt as if a treasure trove had been laid at her feet. After so many years of knowing nothing, she was to be given another piece of the past: someone else to whom she was connected.

"That would be wonderful."

"Very good. I was thinking he could come for dinner this evening, if you like."

"I would like that very much."

"Then I will call and invite him. I believe I will make an apple strudel. I seem to remember that Harry loves strudel."

By the time six o'clock rolled around Maddy had tried on every outfit she owned. She finally settled on a plain blue skirt and white blouse; she thought the simple combination made her appear older. Before leaving the room she took her mother's necklace, put it around her neck, touched the medallion, and then briefly closed her eyes. *I am so sorry, Maman. So very sorry.* Then she went downstairs to await the arrival of Harry Jacobson.

The doorbell rang at exactly seven o'clock. "Well," said her aunt, confirming the time, "I see that Harry is as punctual as ever. I will put the strudel in the oven. Would you please answer the door, Maddy?"

She'd practiced her greeting in the mirror all afternoon. *What a pleasure to meet you, I'm Madeleine Hoffman. Please, come in.* But when the time came to deliver it she did so with such alacrity that she'd finished her welcome before the door was fully open.

The man at the door stared at her. Maddy saw his eyes fill with tears. "Mein Gott," he stammered, "you're as beautiful as your mother."

Maddy blushed. She didn't know what she'd expected him to say, but that was certainly not it. "Please, come in," she repeated, embarrassed, and backed up enough to allow Harry through the door.

Once inside, he pulled out a handkerchief and wiped his eyes. "I'm sorry. I've embarrassed you. It was just such a shock, seeing you there, looking so much like your mother."

Bernice's arrival immediately changed the course of the conversation. "How good to see you again, Harry, though there's more of you to see this time; my friend, you are getting fat."

He smiled ruefully. "Yes, Bernice. How very kind of you to notice. And despite your candor, it's nice to see you again, too. Thank you for the invitation."

"The pleasure is mine. Madeleine was very excited to meet you."

"And I her," Harry replied, not looking in Maddy's direction.

"So am I correct in remembering that you are very fond of apple strudel?"

Harry patted his portly midsection. "Too fond, I'm afraid."

The trio moved into the living room. Bernice rang a bell, signaling the housekeeper to bring in the appetizers.

"Would you care for something to drink? As you know I do not drink alcohol, but I am sure that Archie—he is in Washington, by the way, working on another contract—that Archie has a bottle or two of something stashed in the cabinet."

"How about a Manhattan?"

"Nothing that complicated, I am afraid. Would a glass of bourbon be sufficient?"

"That will do nicely, thank you."

"Very good." She called the housekeeper. "Eileen? Please get Mr. Jacobson a glass of bourbon. Ice?"

As the housekeeper fixed his drink, Harry found it hard to take his eyes off Madeleine. It was as if Martha had greeted him at the door: the same eyes, the same room-brightening smile. She was even wearing Martha's necklace, the one he'd given her the day he left for America.

So many years ago. Martha had never really been his; she'd never given him anything other than a mercurial glimmer of hope, no sturdier than a dragonfly resting on water. But he'd captured it, and then relied upon that hope as if it had been a promise.

Was it possible to hate a man you'd never met? He hated Hitler. He hated Mussolini. But these were abstract, intellectual animosities. Harry was an engineer. He was devoted to disciplines grounded in physics, dependent upon forces one could measure. He made sense of things. It made sense for him to hate Hitler.

It had never made sense for him to hate Leo Hoffman.

Harry believed what his rabbi taught: hatred was an acid, corrupting every vessel that tried to contain it. Harry made an effort to set aside his hatred, to move his life away from it. He'd finally succeeded in getting to the point where the hatred no longer burned its way through his sleep, but he still thought about her—no, he thought about both of them, for they were inseparable, the yin and the yang of his pain. He thought about both of them nearly every day.

He'd learned that the opposite of love was not hate. The opposite of love was indifference. For the past sixteen years he'd craved it, and for sixteen years the peace that indifference brings had eluded him.

Bernice was asking him a question. "What project brings you into town?"

Harry pulled himself back into the present. "An office tower on Park Avenue. Interesting project on an L-shaped lot. Took a while to get started because there was such a ruckus about tearing down the old hotel that was there."

Maddy tried to look interested, but she was studying Harry more than she was following the conversation. His hair was curly and brown with bits of gray. His eyes were brown, too: big, brown, and friendly. He was altogether soft looking, and so very normal. He was the sort of person, thought Maddy, who would blend in on the subway platform with all the other businessmen going to work, wearing a suit and a hat and carrying a briefcase. Not at all like her father.

"Dinner is ready," her aunt was saying. "Let us go to the table."

"Bernice," Harry responded, "you live in America now, and American is a delightfully informal language. You must start using more contractions. *Let's* go to the table. Dinner smells wonderful!"

"Contractions I can probably adapt to. But I won't—you see?—I won't use my fork in my right hand. Switching one's fork from one hand to another? What a ridiculous convention."

"Indeed."

All through the soup course, while Harry and Bernice talked about boring subjects like discount rates and labor shortages, Maddy tried to think of a way to bring up the subject of her mother. Maybe Mr. Jacobson didn't like to talk about her because he was still in love with her. Maybe . . .

At last an opening presented itself and Maddy leapt in. "Mr. Jacobson, are you married?"

Harry scraped the last drop of soup from his bowl and set his spoon down before answering. "Yes, I am."

Married? To someone else? This answer did not fit into the romantic drama unfolding in Maddy's imagination. "Oh. Do you have children?"

Harry looked at Bernice. "The child converses like an adult."

"Yes, and in two languages." For the first time Maddy had the sense that Bernice was proud of her. She felt a tingle of pleasure, but it was coupled with annoyance; she hated it when adults talked about her like she was not in the room.

"Well, then don't I deserve an answer to my question?" she asked, sounding a bit more peevish than polite.

Harry wiped his mouth to hide his amusement. "I don't have any children."

"How long have you been married?"

"Three years."

"What's your wife's name?"

"Ruth."

"And Mrs. Jacobson, is she Jewish, too?"

"This is not an inquisition, Maddy," her aunt admonished.

"But I don't mind, Bernice. I'm sure the child's had to answer many questions herself over the past few weeks." He turned back to Maddy. "Yes, dear. My wife is Jewish."

"But is she *really* Jewish? Does she go to synagogue and everything?"

"Madeleine!"

Maddy started. "I'm sorry, Mr. Jacobson. I didn't mean to offend you."

"No offense taken."

"Harry, there is no need—"

"It's really fine. I know this is a sensitive topic for you, Bernice, but she's not being overly personal. Yes, Madeleine. I wasn't raised in a religious household, but my wife was, and she reintroduced me to my faith. So what about you?"

"What about me?"

"Tell me a little about yourself."

Maddy felt nervous again. "Um . . . well, I just found out that I'm Jewish. We always, I mean, I always *thought* we were Catholic. But now it's like the more I find out, the more I don't know."

"So you're on a journey of self-discovery. That's—"

"Not a topic designed to aid one's digestion," Bernice declared. "Eileen? We're ready for the next course."

For the rest of the dinner Maddy gave brief answers to the adults' questions about school, how she liked living in New Jersey, and Bernice's plan to send Katherine and Maddy to summer camp in Maine. It wasn't until they'd made their way through generous portions of Bernice's perfect apple strudel that the conversation again returned to the past.

"Madeleine, you look so much like your mother," Harry began. "Would you happen to have any pictures of her?"

"Yes, I do." Maddy hopped up from her chair. "Aunt Bernice, may I be excused?"

"Certainly."

Harry switched to German once Maddy left the room. "How's she doing? Adjusting, I mean."

"Very well, I believe. She appears to be happy. She does not neglect her studies. I try to give her plenty of privacy. I do not want her to feel forced into any uncomfortable intimacy."

"And has she heard from her father?"

Bernice shook her head. "She received one letter, posted from London not long after he waltzed into New York, announced that he'd annulled his marriage to that tramp of a second wife, and agreed to let Madeleine stay with the O'Connors. That letter was very chatty, but did not contain any real information about what he was doing. About ten months later, Madeleine received the oddest message from the U.S. Navy, explaining that Leo was 'in fine shape,' but that he was being released from the service. Neither Margaret—Mrs. O'Connor, the woman I told you about—neither Margaret nor Madeleine even knew that he'd been in the navy. All he told them when he left was that he had to do some sort of military service for two years, to earn his citizenship. Well, he's been gone well over two years, and but for those two communications, they have not heard a word."

"And no ideas?"

"None. All evidence indicates that he has abandoned the poor child. Again."

Maddy burst back in, holding a framed picture. "Here," she panted as she put the photograph in Harry's outstretched hand. "My mother, and my father."

Early in his career, while inspecting the construction site of the first skyscraper he'd helped design, Harry had seen a worker fall from the scaffolding. He'd watched as the man lost his balance, watched as another crewman grabbed at him in vain, and then watched as the man plummeted seven hundred feet to the ground. It had taken a million years for him to fall. Time stopped, and Harry felt his heart stop along with it. It wasn't until the man hit the ground, generating an eruption of blood, shouts, and sirens, that the world, and Harry's heart, began to move again.

Harry looked at Leo and Martha's wedding picture and felt time stop for a second time. Martha looked radiant. What Harry would have given for her to ever, even once, have looked at him with that light in her eyes! And standing next to her was Leo Hoffman, gazing at his new bride with complete adoration. Harry felt a burst of pure envy sweep through him. *Of course you lost her to this man. He looks like a movie star.*

"Harry? Are you all right? You've gone pale." Bernice's voice broke through the haze. Harry felt his heart starting to beat again.

"Yes, fine, sorry. Could I have a little more water, please? I do tend to sleep too little and work too hard on these trips."

"I'll get it myself."

Maddy was eyeing him cautiously, as if she'd seen what had been going through his mind. He groped for a new topic of conversation.

"Have you ever been to the top of the Empire State Building?" he asked her.

"No."

"Now that's a situation we must correct. Bernice, may I take Maddy on an outing the next time that I'm in New York?" he asked as Bernice came back into the room with his water.

"I don't see why not."

"Very good. Maddy, I'll be coming back to New York very soon, and then we will make a day of it, ja?"

EIGHT

Lorraine Callaghan had never been to New York. She was more than a bit intimidated by the thought of going there on her own, but nothing could keep her away from her sister in her time of need. Not the train fare or the petrol shortage; not her husband's rheumatism or her own bad back; not the Nazis, or the bloody Japanese emperor himself. Margaret had lost her youngest son, and although she and her sister didn't keep up with each other day by day, Lorraine would see to it that she did not have to mourn her child without a sibling by her side. Minutes after she got the phone call, she packed her suitcase and caught the first train south.

She'd lived in a small town in Canada since she came over, married to a young Canadian soldier who'd been lucky enough to finish up the last war all in one piece. Lorraine hadn't worked in the grand houses like Margaret had. She'd never been to a place where they had skyscrapers, subway trains, or hot dog stands. It would have been nice if she could've spent a day or so seeing the sights, but this was not a tourist trip.

A polite, very young police officer picked her up the next morning at the Grand Central Station, introduced himself, and somberly offered to take her one small suitcase.

"How do you do, Mrs. Callaghan. I'm Ryan Sullivan. I worked on the force with Jamie. He was a good officer. We all feel terribly sorry about your family's loss."

Lorraine felt a bit uncomfortable riding to the house in his blue-and-white car, even distracted as she was by the size of the buildings and the sheer number of people on the streets. But then Margaret's house looked like a regular police station when she arrived; there were at least a dozen police cars parked along the curb, stretching down the full length of the block.

Lorraine let herself in, the nice young man who'd brought her trailing behind. It was as if every member of New York's finest was crammed into the place, paying their respects, honoring young Jamie. She knew what they'd be saying. *Terribly sorry for your loss, Mrs. O'Connor. He was a fine man, your son. A brave man, who could handle his liquor and knew how to fight fair. You should be proud of him.* In addition to sending a police car to pick up Lorraine, Police Chief Valentine himself sent a telegram expressing his condolences. The officers were passing it around as if it were a picture postcard.

She knew how hollow all the words would sound to her sister, if she could hear them at all. There was nothing in the world worse than outliving your child. Nothing. Lorraine's only daughter died when she was barely fifteen, as fair and full of promise as a spring crocus breaking through the snow. Until the polio got her, and there was nothing anyone could do.

She found Margaret exactly where she thought she'd be: in the kitchen. She was sitting in a chair at the head of the large oak table, her strong features crumpled into a mass of doughy wrinkles. Shoulders bent, she stared with swollen eyes at a plate of eggs and toast as if she didn't remember what she was supposed to do with it. Four women, dressed in black, fluttered around her like magpies, chirping useless condolences.

"Margaret?" A hush fell over the room. Her sister looked up. The instant their eyes met Margaret's filled with tears.

"He volunteered. Ya know that, don't ya, Lorraine? He didn't wait to be drafted. He upped and volunteered."

Lorraine walked over and laid a calloused hand on her sister's cheek. "I do know that, Margaret. I know."

Margaret placed her own hand over her sister's. "Thanks for comin'," she managed to say before the fragile threads holding together the pieces of her heart disintegrated, and it broke apart completely.

It took a long time to clear out a houseful of Irish in mourning. No one who showed up at the door could be sent away without a bite to eat and a small glass of hospitality, and after the last of them had taken their leave, there was the business of putting all the food that had been brought 'round into the icebox, the gathering up of all the empty whiskey glasses, the dumping out of too-full ashtrays, the washing of dishes, and the general sweeping up. By late afternoon Lorraine was the last one standing. Margaret and her two girls were off to the church. There was no body to be buried; no part of Jamie would ever make it home. But arrangements had to be made nonetheless.

She answered the knock on the door quickly, expecting to find another friend or relation coming by to express condolences over a glass of whiskey. Instead she was greeted by the postman.

"Good afternoon, ma'am. Is Mrs. O'Connor in?" the young man asked, full of timid courtesy.

"No, she's gone off to church. Can I be of help to ya?"

"Well, I heard about her son. I'm new on the route, but I went to grade school with Jamie. I wanted to tell her how sorry I am." He handed over a small stack of letters.

Lorraine flipped through them. "That's very kind. And who shall I say called?"

"Kevin. Kevin Wilson."

"Well, thank you, Kevin. Hold on—you've got one that's been mis-delivered. I met the three boarders today. They've all been here a don-key's age, and there's no one here by this name." She handed him back a fat white envelope.

He glanced at it. "No return address. One more for the dead letter off—oh, I'm so sorry. I didn't mean—"

She smiled to put him at ease. "Can't be helped. I'll tell Margaret you stopped by."

Later that day she had second thoughts about that letter. Madeleine Huffman. Or had it been Marilyn Hoffman? Wasn't there something familiar about that name? No matter. She could only stay for a few days, and there were more important things to worry about.

NINE
TANGIER

The Medina, the oldest section of Tangier, was an architectural maze of small, square, flat-roofed, and whitewashed buildings, all piled across, alongside, under, and on top of one another, as if some child of the gods had used gigantic sugar cubes for building blocks. Its passageways were as narrow and crooked as a ferret's tunnel, winding up, down, around (and occasionally under) the congested array of homes and shops.

Navigating the Medina required a good sense of direction, decent powers of observation, and some physical stamina, for little of the ancient walled city rested on level ground. Good reflexes helped, too. Leo had already dodged one resentful overladen donkey, two burly Bedouin men who had no intention of moving out of anyone's way, a woman carrying several dozen loaves of bread stacked on a board atop her well-covered head, several stray dogs, their droppings, and the spittle of a beggar whose aim may or may not have been intentional.

Warily making his way up and down stone staircases worn concave by centuries of sandal-clad pedestrian traffic, Leo was once again struck by the similarities between Shanghai, his home for fifteen years, and Tangier, his home for hopefully not much longer. Like the ancient walled heart of Shanghai, the Medina was surrounded by solid ramparts originally designed to keep invaders out while keeping slaves, concubines, and prisoners in. During the day both places echoed with the raucous noise of merchants hawking their wares, the gossip of matrons, and the grunts of men carrying twice their own weight. Conversations in a dozen different dialects blended into an indecipherable sea of sound.

Like the native Chinese residents of Shanghai, the people of the Medina moved quickly, at a pace set by the speed of commerce or the timing of an opportunity. Both places were saturated with the pungent odors produced by too many people living too close together; although, unlike Shanghai, the residents of the Medina masked some of the more unpleasant smells with fragrant ones, like orange, jasmine, sage, and clove, their efforts aided by an occasional breeze from the ocean.

But of all the similarities between the two cities, what hit Leo hardest was the look he saw in the eyes of the children, the ones who had not yet learned to keep their eyes lowered in order to hide their hatred or feign submission. In Tangier, as in Shanghai, suspicion and desperation haunted the eyes of the very young.

He checked his watch. Normally he met Carleton Coon at night, at Colonel Eddy's villa. Coon and Gordon Browne, Coon's longtime friend and fellow spy, stayed at the hillside mansion whenever Eddy was out of town. Leo would meet Coon or Browne in some remote rendezvous location, then climb into the backseat of their consulate car, crawl underneath a blanket or carpet, and wait, cramped and sweaty, until they arrived at the villa and he was given the "all clear."

On one such trip Leo had nearly suffocated from the smell of something foul in the trunk. "What the hell have you got in the boot?" he demanded as he crawled out of hiding, gasping for fresh air. Coon and Browne looked at each other and grinned before Browne answered.

"Just what it smells like," he said. "The toymakers at SOE wanted us to send them samples of local rocks so they can make harmless-looking roadside bombs disguised as, well, rocks. But we—"

"We discovered there really aren't a lot of rocks on the roads around here," Coon interrupted. "There is, however, a copious supply of mule turds, because there are so many damn donkeys everywhere. But they don't look like good, healthy British mule turds. They're more sepia-colored, with a bit of green. So today we had to collect samples to ship off to London."

"Mule turds? They're going to make *mule turd bombs*?"

Coon nodded, the grin still fixed on his face. "And the little buggers will blow a jeep's tires to smithereens, or slow down the pace of an entire division while the advance guys flip and poke thousands of mule turds, trying to check for explosive ones."

"Shit, it might just work."

"Exactly."

It was all ridiculously cloak-and-dagger, but so far their stereotypical espionage tactics appeared to be working.

Today was different. Today's meeting was designed to be overheard, but it could not seem that way. They had to make the person listening in feel that he'd scored a major coup. Leo was prepared. He knew his lines. He could only hope that everything else went according to plan.

He found the key-shaped entryway for which he'd been searching. Verses from the Koran decorated the top of the archway. The opening led into a tiny courtyard, where four brightly painted doors opened into four different establishments: red, blue, yellow, green. He knocked on the blue one.

A skinny Arab man opened the door seconds after Leo knocked. His sun-ravaged skin made him look at least fifty, but Leo knew that underneath the deep wrinkles and his heavy beard he could have been twenty years younger. The man grinned at Leo with the insincere manner of a servant willing to pretend that he knows his place as long as the pretense remained lucrative, or at least entertaining.

"Ah, welcome, welcome, good sir," he proclaimed in French, gesturing for Leo to come inside.

It took a minute for Leo's vision to make the transition from the bright sunlight to the darker interior of the small room. While his eyes adjusted he focused on the smells wafting from beyond where he stood: the burnt-sugar odor of *kif*, a tobacco-like, mildly narcotic substance concocted from hemp leaves; cooking oil; and human perspiration.

"Please, come this way." His host gestured toward a doorway covered by a drape of thin cotton. Leo followed him into the next room.

Beyond the curtain Carleton Coon sat cross-legged on a large cushion, on the floor beside a long, low wooden table. A half-finished bottle of wine sat on the table in front of him. He did not stand as Leo approached.

"Mr. Hoffman, we meet at last."

Leo sat across from him and glanced around. "Are you sure this place is secure?"

"Positive. The proprietor, Ahmed, is one of our native operatives. It's one of the few places in Tangier where I feel comfortable discussing sensitive issues."

How long would it have taken you to discover Ahmed was working both sides, if I hadn't come across that helpful detail? "Privacy is certainly a rare commodity here. Tell me, are you inclined to share that wine?"

Coon signaled the man who'd answered the door. "Ahmed, my friend, bring us another glass, and some food."

As soon as Ahmed left the room Coon leaned forward. "I understand that you're in touch with men who have large stores of weapons at their disposal."

Leo almost laughed. "Is that your way of making polite conversation?"

Coon lifted his wineglass. "Despite the fact that I trust the owner of this establishment, it's a good idea to talk about important issues while he remains out of earshot."

Leo knew full well that the absent owner was listening to everything being said. "Well, I have no reason to trust the owner of this 'establishment,' as you rather generously describe it, so I'll be brief. You've heard correctly. There are certain parties with whom I'm in touch, who have held on to substantial munitions since Franco put an end to the 'unrest' in Spain. I believe they could be persuaded to part with their inventory for the right price."

"I assure you we will be generous, if the goods can be transported to where they will be needed."

"What sort of distance are we talking about?"

Carleton lowered his voice and managed a fair imitation of a stage whisper. "Dakar. We will need whatever armaments you can muster to arrive in Dakar no later than the middle of November."

Leo pretended to consider this information. "Well," he said after a brief pause, "I think that can be arranged, but that delivery requirement will require a substantial increase in the price."

"Freedom has no price," Coon declared melodramatically. "Name yours."

"I'll have to consult with the concerned parties first," Leo replied, "but here comes our proprietor. I suggest we change the subject."

Three weeks later a beaming William Eddy welcomed Coon and Browne into his paneled study, where a bottle of Kentucky bourbon awaited them. "I don't want to celebrate prematurely," he said as he opened it, "but I've received word that the Dakar cover story is taking hold. Our code breakers have intercepted some German ciphers indicating that the Reich is becoming concerned about an Allied landing in Dakar sometime this fall. Excellent work, gentlemen."

Coon and Browne exchanged worried glances. "We've got some bad news to report on that, sir," Coon said. "Hoffman may have been compromised."

Eddy's smile faded. "Compromised? How do you mean?"

"One of our sources in Algiers, a cleaning woman, overheard Schmidt—the Swiss architect—telling a German member of the Armistice Commission that he thinks Hoffman has been feeding him false information."

"When was this?"

"About a week ago, as far as we can tell. Now Hoffman's after us to give him something significant they can verify. No more license plate numbers. Something serious."

Eddy rubbed his chin, not saying a word. Then he poured three glasses of bourbon. He handed one to Coon, one to Browne, and then picked up his own. "Well, gentlemen, I hate to say this, but I think it might be time for Leo Hoffman to die."

Leo knew that meeting Schmidt in the middle of the day, in a place as public as the bar across the street from the Continental Hotel, was a risky business. There were many reasons for the two men to meet over a sandwich and a glass of beer, but anyone who knew that Schmidt was a German agent would dismiss all innocent justifications, and in Leo's opinion that group of people was growing distressingly larger by the day. Still, this was not the first time that Leo had gambled with the devil. He woke up each morning hoping that his luck would hold. It had to; given all that he was involved in, talent not laced with luck would lead straight to an unmarked grave.

Schmidt wasted no time in bringing up the real reason for their meeting. Evidently subtlety was not a Swiss trait. "My associates don't feel that you've been earning your money," he announced after washing down a large bite of rye bread and cheese with a quantity of warm beer. "You agreed to communicate certain information that you've not yet provided."

Leo looked around before answering. *Who was listening?* "I didn't want to convey any information I couldn't verify."

Schmidt snorted impatiently. "If you stacked up everything you've told me so far, it wouldn't amount to a pile of shit. What makes you think that you could deceive us so easily?"

Leo blanched. "Quieter, please. I'm sure there are other people here who speak German."

Schmidt seemed to enjoy Leo's anxiety. "Isn't that the goal? To create a world where everyone with power over other human beings speaks German? What information have you supplied that would enable that to happen?"

"These things take time."

"If you don't have the information we want by now, then you're of no further use to us."

There, at the next table: a face Leo recognized, a local who'd worked on some of Coon's archaeological digs long before the war began, who was well-known as a friend to the Americans. *Had he overheard their conversation?*

He focused again on Schmidt. "And you? Have you arranged what I asked of you?"

Schmidt looked quizzical. "What are you talking about?"

"Citizenship," Leo hissed, keeping an eye on the man at the table next to them, who was shoveling his lamb stew into his mouth with astounding rapidity. "Swiss citizenship for me and my daughter."

"What have you done to deserve it?"

Leo exhaled. At least Schmidt was speaking more quietly. "Very well. I'd hoped to have more corroboration, but I'm nearly positive it's to be Dakar, late in the fall."

"And how do you know this?"

"Eddy's been spotted there twice. Coon's negotiated a gun shipment, presumably to arm some anti-Nazi native force. And the woman I have working for me in the consulate says there's been a dramatic increase in the number of transmissions received. Something's up, and everything points to Dakar."

Schmidt considered this as he took another swig of his beer. "Well, that little morsel might save your double-crossing neck, if we can substantiate it."

Leo's eyes grew icy with anger. "I work for no one but myself. I'm not betraying anyone."

"A figure of speech. Nothing more."

Leo pushed back his chair and stood up. "I've given you what you wanted. See that you do the same for me."

Schmidt smirked up at him. "You've shown your cards too early, Hoffman. We'll see how the hand plays out before you're paid." Leo glared back at Schmidt, then left without another word. The man at the adjoining table hastily choked down one last bite of lamb, and walked out right behind him.

Schmidt returned to his food as Leo stalked out. He didn't even mind being stuck with the measly check; he'd gotten what he wanted. And it would be a cold day in hell before Leo Hoffman was welcome in Switzerland. Dakar. That made some sense. He did not look up from his fried potatoes until he heard the gunshots and the screams.

Murder was common in Tangier. But to see a man shot in the back, in broad daylight as he was crossing the street in front of the Continental Hotel, now that was noteworthy. And to see a Ford coupe arrive at precisely the right moment, and watch the driver and the front-seat passenger leap out and fling the bloodstained corpse into the trunk— that was interesting. That was a bit of gossip worth bringing home.

And who would investigate such a murder? The Spanish police, who were allegedly in charge of the city? They had no interest in who'd killed Leo Hoffman. The American consul, because the Arab who fired the shot and then disappeared into the Medina had once worked as a ditch digger for one of his vice-consuls? Not likely. The dead man was a man without a country and a known racketeer. His luck had run out, that was all. The denizens of Tangier dismissed his fate with a collective shrug.

Rolph Schmidt celebrated that evening. It seemed clear to him that the Americans were behind Hoffman's death. He must have posed a real danger to their operations. And, despite the scarves covering their faces and their Berber clothing, there was something familiar in the movements of the two men who'd grabbed the body. Café gossip even hinted that the two men in the Ford were none other than the American vice-consul, Carleton Coon, and his cohort, Gordon Browne.

Good thing I found out what we needed to know before they did the bastard in. Though he had to admit, he wouldn't have thought that Eddy and his group of amateurs had the skill to uncover someone as clever as Hoffman, or the balls to do what was necessary. Killing Hoffman gangster-style, in broad daylight, sent a clear message to others: do not betray us. He'd make sure to communicate that bit to his superiors. One should never underestimate the enemy.

PART TWO

TEN
CHICAGO

Harry first saw Ruth at the Art Institute of Chicago, in front of Georges Seurat's *A Sunday Afternoon on the Island of La Grande Jatte*, at two o'clock in the afternoon on an April day that threatened rain.

She was standing in front of the painting when Harry entered the room, a look of total concentration etched across her face. She stared at it so intently for such a long time that Harry's attention shifted from the monumental work, one of his current favorites, to the little brunette in front of him, still and quiet as a statue herself.

"Well, do you like it?" he asked, as if he'd been awaiting her judgment.

"That's what I'm trying to decide," she responded, without taking her eyes off the painting.

"Come closer." Harry walked within a foot of the large canvas and gestured for her come closer. "You have to appreciate the technique to appreciate the painting."

She did as he asked. "You see?" he said, pointing to the long skirt of the most dominant figure, a well-to-do matron holding an umbrella.

"It's nothing but dots. Tiny, disconnected points of color. Now close your eyes. Don't worry—start walking backward—no; don't open your eyes yet." He waited as she stepped backward, one uncertain baby step at a time, until she was in the center of the large room, a good twelve feet from the wall. "Now open your eyes. You see?"

"All the dots come together to form the figures."

"Yes. Can you imagine the time this took? First, to determine all the colors one must use for everything to blend together in such a way that a real-life scene is created, and then to apply them all, one by one, with the very tip of the brush."

"Yes, but one can admire the technique without liking the painting. I don't like it."

Harry was not prepared for this response after his clever demonstration. "Why not?"

"They aren't happy. It's a beautiful day, they're all outside, surrounded by trees and sun and the river, and not one person looks happy. There are brilliant colors there, but no joy."

Harry looked back at the painting. "I'd never considered that. I guess you're right."

She rewarded his admission with a tentative smile. "There's no right or wrong to liking art."

"What a very sophisticated point of view." He wanted to keep talking to her, but did not know how to continue the conversation without sounding too forward. "Well, enjoy the rest of the museum."

"And you do the same. Thank you."

She lowered her eyes as she finished her sentence, as if she'd just realized how inappropriate it was for her to be speaking to a strange man, and an older man at that. Harry was in his late thirties; she looked as if she were barely past twenty.

As Harry walked out of the room a large group from a girls' school swarmed in, vibrating with barely contained energy, and it struck him again how tranquil that young woman was—peaceful, in a way that reflected some inner serenity. And she was pretty, too.

So Harry was delighted to see her in the museum courtyard an hour later, sitting at a table near the center fountain. He started to approach her several times, and then stopped. What would he say?

Suddenly, to his surprise, she twisted around and smiled broadly at him, as if she'd known all along that he was standing there and needed a bit of encouragement. He walked over to her table. "I think I forgot to introduce myself. Harry Jacobson."

"Ruth Goldman," she responded, offering him her hand. "Would you care to join me for a cup of coffee?"

They were married seven months later, in the synagogue containing the Torah that Ruth's great-grandfather had brought with him from Russia. Ruth's family welcomed Harry with open arms. He was successful in his own right, so there was little chance he was marrying into the family to take advantage of their wealth. He didn't drink to excess, and he treated Ruth with respect. He even played the violin. He didn't know much about the faith of his own people, but this was a problem that could be corrected, and Harry was perfectly willing to cooperate.

Ruth wanted to have children right away, but Mother Nature did not seem inclined to cooperate with those plans. Harry told her not to worry. She was young, and he was not in a hurry. Being childless did not bother Harry. He loved his work, music, art, and Ruth. He loved her, he suspected, the way Martha had loved him; her calmness and her confidence provided a shelter for his soul. And he tried very hard in his marriage, as he did with his work, not to make mistakes.

But after two years he made one, and like a crack in the keystone of a bridge, that mistake created a flaw that kept growing, until the integrity of the entire structure was compromised.

Honesty should not be considered a mistake, but it could be, when the truth caused so much pain. He should have been able to predict it. He should have lied.

They were having a snowball fight, of all things. Ruth was better at it than he was; he could throw farther, but she could rebuild her arsenal much more quickly, and before he knew it, she'd pelted him three times, leaving him unable to aim for the snow covering his face. Once he surrendered she'd come up to him and brushed off the snow, laughing and even kissing him on his cold cheeks, right there in public. But Ruth was like that, Harry knew, after two years of marriage; she liked winning.

And then it came, as she wrapped her arms around his shoulders and looked up at him with her golden brown eyes, her little nose pointed up at him like a bunny's: the question he should have answered differently.

"Have you ever been in love with anyone else? Before me, I mean?"

"Only once, a very long time ago. A girl in Germany."

"Oh." She studied his face, as carefully as she had scrutinized Seurat's painting on the day they met. Then she dropped her arms and turned away from him. "Let's go. I'm cold."

How could she have known? What was there in his voice, on his face, that had given so much away? It wasn't true that he had once loved Martha. He still loved her. Even now, even though he knew she was dead. Martha was the crack in the keystone.

"I'll be going to New York again next week."

"So soon? You were just there. Usually at this stage you work from the plans. It's all physics, you've always said. As long as you have the right information, the actual location doesn't change anything."

They sat at the table in the formal dining room. Ruth liked to eat there. She liked the fact that the furniture had belonged to her grandmother. She liked the smooth sheen of the linen tablecloth, and the glow of candles reflected against the wood-paneled walls. She liked the elegance of her wedding china. She enjoyed the comfort of her things.

"Yes, well, this trip is more for the clients," Harry explained. "It's a novel design. They like having the engineers around."

"But there's nothing for you to inspect yet, Harry. It's just a hole in the ground. You told me so yourself."

Harry put down his fork. "Why don't you come with me? You love going to New York. You can do some shopping."

"There's nothing to shop for. My cousin told me you can't even buy a pair of stockings on the East Coast."

"Is it stockings you'll be shopping for?"

"Is it your business you'll be going for?"

There was no point in answering that question. "What is it, Ruth? Why don't you come out and tell me what's wrong?"

Harry had never seen a dam break, but he knew how to calculate the forces behind such a calamitous event, and could describe in detail how they worked. And that's what he thought about, right at that moment, when he saw the tears in Ruth's eyes. *The dam is about to break.*

"I wonder, sometimes, if I would have married you, had I known."

"Known what?" He had to at least pretend not to know what she was talking about.

"That I would share my husband with a ghost."

"Don't be ridiculous."

"At first I thought I could do it. I thought, 'He only thinks that he loves her because he doesn't know what it's like to be loved.' But I don't know if I was right about that. Not since her daughter came back to haunt us."

"Do you know how foolish you sound?" He wanted to get up and go to her, to comfort her somehow, but he could not. He was pinned to his chair by the force of her emotion, a tree limb pushed up against the rocks by rushing water.

"I can feel it, Harry. The distance between us, growing like a shadow. It's as if she knows she made a mistake, losing you when she was alive, so she's sent her daughter here to take you away from me."

"Ruth, this is nonsense. You know I love you. I married you. This is not fair—"

"Oh, I agree with that. It's certainly not fair."

It's not fair, he'd thought as he read Bernice's letter telling him that Martha had eloped with a man they'd never met. *I've loved her for years. I've been good to her. It's just not fair.*

He said nothing.

"So I've been thinking." Harry saw her fork tremble in her hand. "I'm not going to New York with you. I'm going to Switzerland."

"What on earth are you talking about?"

"I'm going to Switzerland, Harry. There are children, Jewish children, who may or may not have parents once this is all over. Children who need a home."

She looked right at him then, piercing the dark place where he licked his wounds and tended the flame of his hatred. He came roaring out of the shadows.

"You can't go. It's too dangerous—bombs—submarines—you'll be killed! Your family will never let you go." He'd never raised his voice to her, but as he grew louder, he felt her defiance grow stronger. So much strength in such a small person. Where did it come from?

"You're wrong about that, Harry. My parents are coming with me."

"What are you saying?"

"There's a whole group of us going, people with means. We're volunteering with the Red Cross, and when we come home, we're coming home with the children, as many as we can bring with us. And then, Harry, you'll have to choose. You'll have to choose between loving your family, and loving a ghost."

"*If* you come home," Harry whispered, and felt tears rise in his own eyes.

Ruth's calm demeanor had returned. "I suppose that's right," she said, and took another bite of her dinner.

ELEVEN
CAIRO

"Leopold Hoffman. Looks like the kind of guy who'd end up shot in the back." Coon took another look at the passport he held in his hands and then tossed it on the ground, laughing. Gordon Browne laughed along with him.

Leo was not amused. His back hurt from where the two rubber bullets bruised his flesh after breaking the bags of stage blood taped to his skin, and his knee and shoulder hurt from the way Coon and Browne wrenched them as they'd picked him up.

"Very funny." He stretched forward to retrieve the passport from the sand at his feet, trying to find a way to move that did not cause more pain in his back, shoulder, or knee.

"C'mon. Zanuck thinks he deserves a medal for teaching us how to kill someone Hollywood-style. I think we deserve an Oscar. We pulled it off beautifully," Coon chided him.

"I'll give you this: you died very nicely. Fell the right way and everything," Browne added, taking a swig from a hip flask and then passing it over to Coon.

"Very nicely indeed," agreed Coon, who took a drink, and then handed the flask on to Leo.

"What's in it?"

"No idea. Burns, though. Brandy, maybe. Really shitty brandy."

"Thanks." He'd trade tomorrow's headache for some pain relief tonight. Given the way he felt, he did not relish the idea of sleeping in a tent.

"So what do we do with a dead spy?" asked Coon, aiming the question at Browne.

"Send him to Cairo, that's what I hear," Browne answered.

"Cairo?" echoed Leo. "What the hell am I supposed to do in Cairo?"

"Wait," said Coon, suddenly businesslike. "Keep your mouth shut, and your ass out of trouble, and wait."

"And if I run into someone I know who thinks that I died in Tangier?"

"Well then, tell him that the reports of your death have been greatly exaggerated." Coon started laughing again. Browne also found this comment very amusing. He was very good at laughing at Coon's jokes.

"Hoffman," Coon continued when he caught his breath, "the truth is that at this point it wouldn't matter much; you're not a big enough fish. But you should try to lay a little low, just in case. You'll have to use your old passport, so you can't change your name, but you can cut your hair short, grow a mustache, and act French. And wait."

"Wait for how long?" Leo winced again as a shot of pain reverberated through his shoulder.

"Wait for as long as you're told, until something shakes loose around here."

"Such as?"

"Well, I suppose we'll know it when we see it, won't we?"

The first time Leo saw Christine Granville she was laying on a chaise lounge by the pool at the Gezira Sporting Club in Cairo. She wore a modern bathing costume, one that exposed the full length of her slim legs, her tanned arms, and an alluring patch of shoulder. Dark brown hair, pulled away from her face by a headband, formed a crown of curls around her wide forehead; her mouth, resting slightly open, would have been too large for her face, had it not been shaped so perfectly. One hand lay upon the ground, two fingers tucked into a book, as though she'd fallen asleep reading yet managed to keep her place before dozing off.

Leo located an empty lounge chair and pulled it into the small puddle of shade created by a palm tree. He also had a book to read, a well-worn copy of *Gulliver's Travels* left in his hotel's lending library by a previous guest, but his attention kept straying from the page in front of him back to the woman by the pool.

"Aha," a man's voice said. "I see you've discovered our Cleopatra."

Shielding his eyes from the sun with one hand, Leo looked up to see an English officer, Roger Mayes, standing next to his chair.

"What was it that you said?"

Mayes squatted down and spoke directly into Leo's ear as he gestured toward the sleeping woman. "I said I see you've found our Cleopatra, Christine Granville."

"Cleopatra? That skinny brunette with the long nose?"

"Oh, yes. To quote an ancient Roman who'd fallen under the spell of the legendary queen, 'It was not the comeliness of her face or the fineness of her figure that created her allure, but the combination of merely sufficient beauty with extraordinary intelligence, wit, and cunning.

Enthralled, men came away from her presence with an impression of great beauty, when in truth, beauty was the least of her attributes.' "

"You sound pretty enthralled yourself."

"Hopelessly. But alas, she has a husband in England and a lover here. And, if one listens to the rumors, there are other men as well. I only pass along that last bit of gossip because I'm insanely jealous that I've never been one of them."

"Well, I suppose that's honest," Leo said in French-accented English, punctuating his response with a typical Gallic shrug.

Mayes stood up with a sigh. "Yes, though it's not likely to get me anywhere with the countess."

"Countess?"

"Oh, did I neglect to mention that? Yes. She's the daughter of a Polish count. Have no idea what Polish titles mount up to, but unlike most of the czarists around here, they're legit. What is it? What's so funny?"

"Oh, I've had a few dealings of my own with a countess. Of course, that was a very long time ago."

"Already had your own countess, have you? Bloody hell. You Frenchmen. Well, good luck with this one. You don't choose her. She chooses you."

"Thank you for the warning, but I have no intention of getting in line."

Leo watched as Mayes strolled off, stopping to take a long look at the sleeping countess before ducking back into the main clubhouse. Was it true, Leo wondered, that Mayes was with the British spy network in Cairo? He and Peter Wilkinson were often together, and Wilkinson was reputed to be the new SOE head. Whenever Leo saw the lanky Englishman he was tempted to disobey Coon's orders, tell Wilkinson exactly why he was in Cairo, and ask the man to verify that he was, in fact, on the British undercover asset list. He wanted to ask Wilkinson if someone was reassuring his daughter that he would come back to her.

He'd taken Eddy up on his offer to send one letter home via the diplomatic pouch, but then the State Department cut him off. Too complicated, the consul said, to use the diplomatic pouch for personal business. *Too much ass-covering involved if something should go wrong, that's what he meant.* No wonder Eddy, Coon, and Browne called the State Department the Snake Pit.

No, as much as he itched to ask Wilkinson for some enlightenment, he couldn't do anything that might jeopardize his good standing. As he'd told Eddy, for once in his life, he was going to play by the rules. He'd done decent work. The ONI and the OSS and the SOE and whatever other alphabet-soup operations he'd been spying for had better let him go soon. Until then, he would obey his orders and sit tight, pretending to be a French businessman waiting to see which way the winds of war would blow.

The heat sent a drop of sweat trickling into his mustache. It took some getting used to, having facial hair after a lifetime of being clean-shaven. His new addition was thin and close trimmed, unlike the huge, curling mustaches worn by the men of Budapest in his youth: mustaches that were groomed, pampered, and fussed over like expensive pets. He'd also cut his hair short, as Coon had suggested. Not much of a disguise, but, he hoped, enough of a change to keep him from being recognized immediately.

Upon his arrival Leo learned that Cairo was full of people waiting. At the exclusive Gezira Sporting Club, British residents organized polo tournaments, amateur plays, and ladies' teas. At Shepheard's Hotel, British officers drank gin, played cards, and waited for orders from the desert front. Polish military men drank vodka, ran their own spy network, and waited for the chance to fight the Germans again. Everyone waited to see what the Allies would do next. Russia couldn't hold off the Nazis for much longer, and England couldn't defend itself forever without help. The Americans had to force Hitler to divide his resources. They would have to strike somewhere in Europe, and soon.

Leo tossed his book aside. He'd lost his enthusiasm for plowing through English. He'd go swimming. No, he'd go for a walk in the marketplace. No, he'd go over to the stables and see if anyone's horse needed a bit of exercise.

As he walked by her chaise lounge on his way back into the changing rooms, a cloud passed over the sun, and Cleopatra stirred.

TWELVE
NEW YORK

"Five years you've lived in New York, and no one has taken you up to the top of the Empire State Building?"

Maddy started rolling forward and back on the balls of her feet, an unconscious habit both Mrs. O'Connor and her aunt Bernice had tried to break. "Yer makin' me dizzy, Maddy. For goodness' sake, keep yer feet still, darlin'," Mrs. O'Connor would say.

"Madeleine, it's very disconcerting to watch you bob around that way. It's quite childish. Please stop," Bernice would chastise.

She stopped herself, not wanting to earn a reprimand from Mr. Jacobson, although he didn't look like he was about to say something critical. She smiled up at him, ignorant of the effect her smile had on him. It was her mother's smile.

Into the grand lobby, up eighty floors in one elevator, cross over the hallway, up the next elevator bank to the eighty-sixth floor, then into a third to take them to the observation deck, 1,250 feet high. As they got off the last elevator Harry reached out and took her hand. Maddy felt a tingle of elation having nothing to do with where she was. No man had ever held her hand except for her father. Her uncle occasionally administered a clumsy nighttime hug topped off by a quick kiss on the top of her head, but that was all the paternal affection she received.

"Don't be scared," Harry said, jiggling her hand slightly. "Just close your eyes if you feel dizzy. The building is very stable."

They stepped out onto the platform. Maddy looked gratifyingly awestruck.

"It's *amazing*. You can see the other side of the world."

"Not quite. Five states I think, and eighty miles out to sea. But it is impressive. Do you know that Henry Ford, the man who makes the cars, was so concerned about this building that he didn't want it built? He said digging a hole that big and filling it with steel and cement would create an imbalance that could knock the world right off its rotational axis. Well, he was wrong, of course. You know what the earth's axis is, don't you, Maddy?"

She nodded, her eyes filled with wonder. "How can you do it, Mr. Jacobson? How can you build something that stands up so high in the air like this?"

Harry smiled at her. "With lots and lots of stable little pieces, Maddy. Everything you see—buildings, boats, bridges, even people— are held together by stable little pieces, all linked together. The important thing is to understand the forces that connect them, in order to guarantee that stability. Now let's look at some of the other buildings. Okay, that one over there, the Chrysler Building, you know it, yes? You see how it's cut in right there, and again there? Can you think of why that was done?"

"Because it's pretty?"

"That's a good reason, but there's another one. It cuts down the size of the shadow the building creates. You see, people figured out right away that the skyscrapers would block out the light, so there's a law requiring them to get skinnier as they get taller."

"Really? And you design them?"

"I don't come up with the idea for the building. Architects come to me with preliminary plans, and I come up with a way to do it: a way to accomplish their vision while making sure it's safe."

They walked around the entire platform. New York's capricious September weather had produced a clear, sunny afternoon, yielding a splendid view in all directions. Facing the Hudson they could see the piers where the big ocean liners came to dock. Four of them were anchored there, side by side, like neatly lined up toys. There were no cheerful bon voyage parties at the gangplanks, or pursers sorting trunks full of fancy dresses. All the big liners now served as troop transport ships.

Maddy closed her eyes, trying to blot out the painful memories of her own sea voyage. Harry could tell something was wrong.

"Do you feel all right, Maddy? Do you feel dizzy?"

"No, I was thinking about a trip I took once, on a ship."

"Did you get seasick?"

"A little." *I was so frightened. I wanted my mother, but she was dead. I wanted my father, but he didn't want me. He put me on the ship with Amelia, who told me I'd regret it if I didn't stay out of her hair. The waves were so huge. I kept throwing up and throwing up. The steward brought me buckets to throw up into, then he'd rinse them in the sink so the room didn't smell so bad.*

When I was feeling better, I went up to the ship's dining room. There was Amelia, laughing and smoking, with her face too close to this other man's face. Then she saw me, and I knew then that she hated me as much as I hated her. "Well if it isn't the little albatross," she said. "What do you want?"

I didn't even want to be there, but I was so hungry. I asked her if I could have some dinner. She laughed at me. "Do I look like the cook? Go ask the steward for some food. The less I see of you, the better." I stayed in the cabin after that. The steward brought me clear chicken broth and crackers. All I saw was a view of the ocean from my cabin. The ocean was gray and empty. Like me.

"My father sent me away on a ship like one of those."

"You poor little thing." Harry wrapped his arms around her, enveloping her little body in a big warm hug, and she buried her face in his shoulder. "You're safe now, Martha. You're with people who love you."

"I know," came the muffled reply. Then she looked up at him. "You called me Martha."

He heard Ruth's words in his head. *She sent her daughter to haunt us.* "I did? How foolish of me. I'm sorry, it's all those M's."

"It doesn't matter."

Maddy said very little as they made their way to the O'Connors' house, where she was going to spend the night. She dashed inside as soon as the door opened, leaving Harry on the doorstep. Mrs. O'Connor invited him in for a cup of tea, but Harry declined. He wanted to walk, and think.

Everything is held together by stable little pieces, all linked together. Even people. Harry Jacobson was not impetuous. He was not an artist; he was an engineer. He never did anything without thinking first and planning ahead.

Until that moment.

He did not need to be in New York to finish his current project. Ruth was right; it was nothing more than a hole in the ground, and would likely remain that way until the war was over. He was an American citizen. He could travel. There were a dozen European consulates in New

York. He would start at the Swiss consulate, and if he was unsuccessful there, he would go to all of the others, one by one, until he got a visa that would allow him to board a boat bound for Europe, and from there he would find a way to get to Switzerland. The Red Cross would know exactly where to find his wife.

THIRTEEN
CAIRO

By noon the word was all over Cairo; they'd done it. The Brits and the Americans had invaded North Africa. A hundred ships brought thousands of men. They'd landed troops on the beach in Algeria and French Morocco, catching the French completely by surprise.

But the French under Vichy were making good on their promise to Hitler; they were fighting back. For the first time in their long history as allies, American and French soldiers were deliberately killing each other.

Rumors flooded the city. Algiers was taken. Algiers was lost. German planes were slaughtering American soldiers; no German planes had been sighted. No one in Cairo wanted to be more than a few feet from the nearest radio.

Leo spent most of the day at Shepheard's Hotel with a horde of other expatriates from fifteen different countries, analyzing each fresh piece of information, obsessing over and reworking all the possibilities. How long would the French fight? How would Hitler react? It was late in the evening when he excused himself from the bar and wandered out to the terrace, to escape the cigarette smoke and nurse his after-dinner drink.

"Would you like to go to a party?"

Christine Granville stood a few feet away. Leo looked behind him, assuming the question had been addressed to someone else. She laughed with a deep, throaty chuckle, as if he'd performed an engaging little trick for her private amusement.

"Yes, it's you I'm talking to. Would you like to go to a party? An invasion celebration?"

Her French was near perfect, betraying hardly a trace of her Polish origins. She could have been French, thought Leo, with those wide brown eyes. What did he see in them? Warmth, certainly. Laughter. But what else? Frustration? Restlessness?

No, thank you, he was about to say. *I'm not really the sort who likes parties.*

"Why would you invite me to a party?" is what came out.

Everything about her suddenly softened. "Because you're bored, and lonely, and tired of waiting. We're all so tired of waiting." Before he could reply her gentleness disappeared, replaced by a buoyant frivolity. "So come on. It will be fun."

"That's very kind of you, Miss—"

"Christine."

"Well, Christine, I do appreciate the courtesy, but I'm tired, and I'm sure I'd be boring company at a soiree. I think I've celebrated sufficiently for today."

She responded with a smile that gave him the odd impression she understood the one thing about him that he would never comprehend himself: an elusive piece of self-knowledge, perpetually dangling out of reach. Then her dark eyes flickered with mischief. "It's not because you're pretty, you know, that I invite you. Not that you aren't," she added, with a coy glance that took in his whole body, "but that's not the reason."

Leo was smiling now. He couldn't help it. "What sort of party is it?"

She tossed her head and shrugged, as if the whole subject had just lost all significance. "An American party. And I don't speak very much English. So you can come and interpret for me. And don't go saying that you don't speak English. I've heard you."

"Surely someone else—"

Good Lord, how the expression in those eyes could change! Before she even spoke, they communicated a kaleidoscope of emotion: amusement, anticipation, irritation.

"Yes, yes. Surely someone else. But you see, I have not invited *someone else*." Her eyes locked on to his.

Cleopatra, he thought, as he flagged down a cab.

The taxi pulled up in front of the colonial-style villa overlooking the Nile. Dozens of people moved about on the wide terrace, like bees clinging to a swollen hive, buzzing through a fog of river mist and cigarette smoke.

"I can see why you said one more person wouldn't be noticed," Leo remarked as they made their way up the front staircase. They had to walk sideways through the overcrowded main hallway to get to the dining room. Luxuries rapidly growing scarce in other parts of the world were still plentiful in Cairo. Champagne bottles sat in silver ice buckets. Platters of savory pastries filled with lamb, fresh cheese, tiny shrimp, deviled eggs topped with caviar, chocolate tarts, figs, and honey-drenched baklava covered the tables in the banquet room. A trio of musicians played lively jazz that was roundly ignored, even by those who could hear it.

Christine did not seem interested in the food; she was nervously fidgeting with a button on her sweater. Concerned, Leo reached for her hand. "Are you okay? Do you want to leave?"

She shook her head as she clutched his hand, and he did not know which question the gesture was meant to answer. "I have to find someone who is supposed to be here."

"Good luck. What does he look like?"

"He's Polish."

"That narrows it down. Could you be more specific?"

"He's shorter than you, with a round face. His hair is light brown, and he does that thing where you part it on one side to cover up the baldness. So silly."

"Does he have a name?"

"Truszkowski. And he's in the army."

"One balding Polish military man coming right up, madam."

A loud cheer from another room caused a general movement in that direction, pushing people even closer together. Leo fell in behind Christine, clasped her shoulders, and used his outstretched elbows to negotiate their breathing space.

"Whose house is this?"

"He was a movie star in America. He likes living here, in Cairo, because he likes men."

"I didn't realize that Cairo was known for that sort of thing."

"It's known as a place where you can buy what you want, including silence, if you're rich enough."

Leo eyed the marble and silk surrounding them. "I'd say he's rich enough."

"There he is!" With a burst of energy Christine broke away from him and headed toward the other side of the room. Leo trailed behind her. At once he saw the man Christine was headed for—and the look of dismay on his face when he saw her.

She got right up to him and started speaking in rapid Polish, loudly, to be heard above the din of the crowd. Leo saw the man's expression change from discomfort to annoyance. He gave a long reply. Leo moved closer. He could not hear well over the noise, and he did not speak Polish, although he could make out a few words based on its similarities to Russian and German, both of which he spoke fluently. Leo thought he overheard what could have been "Wilkinson."

Wilkinson. Could that be Peter Wilkinson? Why would he be a topic of their conversation?

Christine made a dismissive gesture and kept on talking. Leo caught another word, something like "assignments." Whatever the response this time, Christine was not pleased to hear it. She whipped around and shouldered her way back across the room like a slender battering ram. Leo watched her go. She did not appear to notice that he was no longer behind her.

The man, whom Leo assumed was Truszkowski, looked very agitated. "Is everything all right?" Leo asked him in French, then wondered what he'd do if his simple query provoked a confrontation.

Truszkowski answered his question with a question. "Have you known Mrs. Granville long?" He also spoke French. Not a surprise. Most Polish noblemen did.

"Not really."

"I would advise you to be careful. A very dangerous woman. She has a lover, you know. Andrew Kennedy. Man with a wooden leg. Also quite charismatic in his own way. They live together openly, although she's married to someone else. Amazing what we put up with in wartime that we'd never tolerate otherwise."

"My sentiments exactly." Leo turned his back on the man and went to find Christine.

He found her out on the terrace, staring up into the moonless night, watching the shadow of a small plane traverse the sky.

"Do you know how planes fly?" she asked as he approached.

"Vaguely. The engine produces a force that provides lift—"

"No. It's magic. That's all. Just magic."

She sounded so convinced, he almost believed her. "Do you want to stay?" he asked at last, not anxious to disturb her reverie.

She shifted her gaze away from the sky and focused on Leo. "No, and I'm sorry I dragged you here. It's not really my kind of party. Too many loud, stupid people doing nothing useful. I can't tolerate sitting around doing nothing when there's so much to be done."

"What assignments were you talking about? Are you a journalist?"

She looked at him as if she thought he might be joking but wasn't quite sure. "I was under the impression, Mr. Hoffman, that we are engaged in the same line of work, and that we are both currently unemployed."

Then she brushed past him, back into the crowd, a slight figure soon swallowed up by the crush of overheated, inebriated bodies. He heard someone call out her name. *Who is this woman? What does she know about me? And how?*

To hell with all of them. Tomorrow morning he was going to see Wilkinson.

"I'm not sure what it is you want from me, Hoffman." Major Peter Wilkinson had a pinched look on his narrow face. This was not unusual.

"I want to know if I can leave. I want to know if you're going to live up to your side of our bargain."

"And the 'you' to whom you're referring would be?"

Leo put his head in his hands. "I'm not sure I know anymore."

Wilkinson tapped a pencil on his desk, thinking. "Mr. Hoffman," he finally said, "this is a volunteer business. No one can make you do this sort of work. Leave whenever you like."

"And go where?" Leo was on his feet now. He walked around his chair and grabbed the back of it, his knuckles white with frustration. "Eddy told you I'd be in Cairo, didn't he?"

"I did receive word that you were a valuable asset, that you'd been operating successfully in Tangier, and that you were being sent to Cairo for an indefinite period, awaiting further orders. That's as much as I know about you."

"Am I on your list of spies? The payroll? Whatever it is I need to get credit for what I've been doing?"

"I'm not sure what you're driving at. You're Eddy's asset. You're not on my list."

"Eddy was supposed to work this out for me."

"Colonel Eddy is otherwise occupied at the moment. We've just begun a major offensive. I'm sure you can understand why your personal bureaucratic problems did not rise to the top of his agenda."

"What am I supposed to do? Sit here and wait? I have to get to New York!"

"Then go see the American consul. Try explaining your problem to him. Of course, that may take some time. From what I understand, there's quite a long line outside the consulate."

"You know that would be useless. They're not letting anyone into the States. I need your help."

"I'm sorry. I don't have any authority to negotiate your passage to anywhere."

"You mean I'm stranded here?"

"I don't mean to be insensitive, but the soldiers in Algeria and Morocco are doing a bit more than passing their afternoons drinking lemonade and sunning themselves at the Gezira Club. There are worse things than being 'stranded here,' as you put it."

Leo slumped back down into the chair in front of Wilkinson's desk. "So I do nothing."

"Do what you like. You're not under my jurisdiction."

"And what about Christine Granville? Does she work for you?"

Wilkinson's already pale face went a shade whiter. "What are you talking about?"

"She must. How else would she know that I've been doing 'this type of work,' as you so eloquently put it?"

"Christine Granville does not work for me and never has. What is it you've heard?"

Leo told Wilkinson about the comment Christine had made the night before. He could see the man was shaken.

"All I can tell you is this," Wilkinson said after a long silence. "Christine Granville volunteered to do some work for our office at the beginning of the war. She was dropped because certain sources maintained that she was working both sides. I have no idea how she found out about you. Perhaps it would be in your own best interest to discover that for yourself. And I'd appreciate your sharing what you find out."

"I'll think about it."

Leo took his leave and went straight back to Shepheard's. *Do what you like*, Wilkinson had said. *You're not under my jurisdiction.* Before going to his room, Leo stopped by the concierge's desk.

"I'd like to send a telegram to the U.S.," he said. "To an address in New York."

He caught up with Christine the next day at the Gezira Club. She was again near the pool, sitting atop a towel on a sunny section of the wide, well-watered lawn, chatting with an English officer whom Leo frequently saw at Shepheard's. The man looked hypnotized.

Christine saw Leo watching them and beckoned him over. "Mr. Hoffman, how nice to see you again. Do you know Major Hawthorne?"

"Only by sight. Good afternoon, Major."

The man got up and offered Leo his hand. "Pleasure's mine."

"I find that the major speaks French very well for an Englishman." Christine delivered this compliment in a manner that made the major blush. "He's going to help me with my English, which is very poor. Would you like to join us for a lemonade? The major is about to find someone to bring us some."

The man hid his surprise with gentlemanly courtesy. "I'm sure I can arrange that. Won't be a minute."

Leo sat down next to Christine. She pulled at a small weed poking up through the blades of grass next to her pretty bare feet. "You do like lemonade, don't you?" she asked without looking up.

He ignored this. "How is it that you know so much about me, when I know nothing about you?"

"I think we should talk about this later."

"I'm not going anywhere until you answer my question."

"Sit here and rot if you like." She said this without spite, almost without emotion, as she extracted the weed from the manicured lawn and tossed it away.

Leo grabbed her hand. "Why do you think that we are, to use your words, 'in the same line of business'?"

"Only two types of people come back from the dead, Mr. Hoffman.

Saints and spies. Are you a saint? Ah, you'll have some time to think about your answer—here comes our lemonade. Now, please, let go of my hand."

Bernice read the telegram a second time:

> Maddy, I am okay. I will come home as soon as I can.
> I think about you every day and hope you are well.
> I love you. Papa

It was a shame, really, that Leo had chosen that form of communication, thought Bernice. Poor Margaret was still white and shaking three hours later when Bernice came by to pick up the message. For Margaret, a telegram would always be an omen of evil. Bernice respected Margaret O'Connor, despite their many differences. She was a strong woman, or had been. One could never tell what loss, what hardship, would be the one burden too difficult for a specific individual to bear. There were so many unknown variables when it came to predicting human behavior.

Cairo. What on earth would he be doing there? More important, how would Madeleine react? Her marks in school were satisfactory. She was well behaved. Was it fair to disrupt her life with this message? To raise her hopes, only to have them dashed again? No, the child needed stability.

Margaret knew that a telegram had come for Madeleine, but that's all she knew. Bernice could easily make something up: a message from Harry, now that he and his wife were in Switzerland. That would do.

She tossed the telegram into the fire that was blazing away in her modern, double-sided fireplace. *He's only seen her once in the past five years. It's very unlikely he'll ever come back. And if he does, I won't let him take her. He took my sister away from us. I won't let him take her daughter as well.*

He'd agreed to meet Christine the next evening, at a small bar close to where she lived, away from the expatriates' center of gravity. The room had a comfortable neighborhood pub atmosphere, with dark wood floors and a mirrored bar, behind which a grizzled old Dutchman with little hair and few teeth poured drinks with a heavy hand. He kept a radio going in the corner. Every once in a while he would shuffle over to it, cup a hand to his right ear, and bellow, "Pipe down! There's news!" Then he'd shake his head and grumble something unintelligible. No news worth repeating, it seemed.

Leo sat in a booth in the back of the room, his eye on the door. No one paid the slightest bit of attention to him, which was a good sign. Christine was already thirty minutes late. *She's the type who'd keep men waiting.*

The door opened, letting in a shaft of evening light and a gust of fresh air. A man entered. Large round face, decent height. *He looks Irish*, thought Leo. *Maybe Slavic.* The man's fine brown hair had receded almost all the way to the top of his head. He wore a thick, broad mustache. And he had a wooden leg.

He headed straight over to Leo's table. "Christine sends her apologies," he said in French as he slid into the booth. "She'll be along in a while. Ready for another beer? Sorry, I'm Andrew Kennedy. But I presume you already know that."

"I don't know much about anything at this point. That's why I wanted to speak to Christine."

"Well, there are no secrets between Christine and me. You can ask me whatever you like."

"I think I'll wait."

"As you wish." The man did not act defensive or jealous. *Perhaps the rumors of Mrs. Granville's infidelity have been greatly exaggerated.* He decided to ask Kennedy a few questions after all.

"I find it very disturbing that you know things about me that only a very short list of people should know."

"We've been at this game for nearly three years, Mr. Hoffman. It's not that complicated. Christine has many contacts within the Red Cross. We recently learned that the main Red Cross representative in Tangier, an architect by the name of Schmidt, was sent packing under allegations that he was spying for the Germans. This was coupled with rumors that the Americans had very boldly assassinated one of the men from whom Schmidt had been getting information. Soon afterward, Christine learned from another acquaintance that this dead man from Tangier was observed among the living in Cairo."

"Was that acquaintance German? Or Swiss, by any chance?"

Andrew gave him a steely look. "People of many nationalities travel from Tangier to Cairo, if they aren't stuck without a visa in that bit of hell on earth, and most foreigners with financial means end up at Shepheard's. Don't believe everything you hear, Mr. Hoffman."

"I'm having a hard time believing anything."

The door opened again and Christine walked in. Everyone in the bar looked up. A few men looked a good long time before turning back to their drinks and newspapers.

"Sorry I'm late." She slid in beside Andrew. "What have I missed?"

"Mr. Hoffman was just accusing us of working for the Germans."

Christine made a noise communicating irritated contempt. "That again."

"Why would the Brits have cut you off if it wasn't true?"

"Politics," Christine snapped. "The Poles didn't like the fact that we were working for the British instead of their operation. Stupid jealousies."

"That's all? That doesn't sound quite credible."

"Stick around Cairo for a few weeks more. The politics of the espionage community have the makings of a great comic opera," Andrew countered. "When we arrived in Cairo, I had microfilms showing that the Germans were amassing artillery on the Russian border. Two rolls of solid evidence tucked into my hollow leg. But by that time we were 'under suspicion' and no one took the information seriously. The Germans attacked Russia two weeks later."

Christine jumped in. "Find a Polish aristocrat, here, in Cairo. There are plenty of us here. Ask about my family. Ask about my Jewish mother, who was dragged out of her house screaming. Ask any one of them if they think it's plausible I'd work for the Nazis." Christine spoke with such intensity her dark eyes looked as if they might actually catch fire. It was hard not to believe her.

"So why contact me? What makes me so interesting?"

Andrew answered. "The real work is being done out of Tangier, Algiers, Holland, and France. Cairo is where spies are sent to cool their heels."

"There are worse places."

"I'm sure. But what's worse than being forced to do nothing while the world is being destroyed? Inactivity is the real torture. That's why we contact people like you. Good operatives, who for whatever reason have been shoved to the side. To see if we can get something accomplished, with your help."

"You'll have to find someone else. I'm out of the business. I'm leaving as soon as I get permission to go to New York."

"Why New York?"

"I have family there."

"And you'll be leaving soon?"

"I think so."

The Dutchman let out a roar. "The French have surrendered! It's ours! North Africa is ours!"

They could hear noise growing in the street. Cheers broke out everywhere, punctuated by car horns, the banging of pots, and a few gunshots. The door to the bar swung open, and a young boy stuck his head in. "The French have surrendered!" he shouted, elated. The patrons raised their glasses and joined in the revelry.

Leo raised his glass along with them. *Maybe now I can get Eddy's attention and get out of here.*

Neither Christine nor Andrew joined in. On the contrary, her expressive eyes grew wide with apprehension. "The first thing they'll do is close the French borders. We have to move quickly."

"Move quickly with what?"

Christine leaned forward and squeezed Leo's hand, hard, as if she didn't already have his complete attention. "The Jews in France are disappearing."

He remained silent while Christine continued, her words laced with earnestness and horror. "Last July, they had a roundup in Paris. The police—the French police, not the Germans—went from house to house, and they rounded up refugee Jews. Thousands of people. They brought them by bus to a place outside Paris, and piled them onto trains headed east. Sealed boxcars. Cattle cars. There are witnesses—we have seen letters—but no one will listen.

"People are trying to pretend that all the Jews are being sent to work in factories, or to do some kind of forced labor. But I know differently. I've seen it, in Poland, what the Nazis will do. First, they will make them dig their own graves. Then they will line them up, rows and rows of them, and shoot them down with machine guns: men, women, and children. Slaughtered.

"For the past two years all the Jews who'd managed to escape to Vichy France from Germany, Austria, Poland—all the conquered countries—if they couldn't find a place to stay, the French put them in prison camps, where they live like rats. There's not enough food, no decent shelter, no proper hygiene. But at least there they had a *chance* to survive.

"In August, a month after the Paris roundup, the French started emptying out the camps. They sent thousands more Jewish refugees to Germany. And since the Allied invasion the Germans have been moving into southern France, and we've heard terrible things."

"What are you going to do?"

"We're going to go to France and help some of them, as many as we can, get out."

FOURTEEN

"No, I can't help. I can't jeopardize my own chance to get out of here."

He'd believed those words when he'd uttered them. Nothing was more important than getting back to his daughter. And if that meant waiting in Cairo until Eddy or someone else in authority could give him permission to go to New York, then he would just wait.

You'll hide, is what you meant. You've always been very good at hiding.

He was warned not to go home the night his foster mother was murdered. He'd never had a chance to say good-bye, had never even seen her body. She'd disappeared in the raging sea of vengeance that flooded Hungary after the last war. Most of those killed were Jews, slaughtered by their own countrymen for no better reason than the Nazis had now.

But he'd escaped, by hiding the truth about his past, his Jewish heritage, and his connection with all the people who had ever loved him. By hiding he'd been able to get away. And he'd been hiding ever since.

The only person to whom he'd revealed himself was Martha, and he'd told her the truth too late to save her. Now he was a spy, still hiding.

Christine's face haunted him. Why had the condemnation he'd seen in her eyes affected him so? She had no idea who he was, or why it was so important for him to wait here, in Cairo, and play by the rules. *They live like rats.*

What if it were Maddy there, in one of those camps? Who would save her?

I just have to wait.

He saw Christine two days later, in her favorite spot by the pool at the Gezira Club. She looked like a cat, the Egyptian goddess Bastet perhaps, stretched out in the sun, surrounded by her worshippers. He walked over and stood in front of her, blocking the sunlight. She opened her eyes.

"How long would I be gone?"

Christine gave him a smile that would cause any man to sprint joyfully to his doom. "Three weeks at most," she said. "How soon can you leave?"

They would first fly to Algiers, she said, in the private plane of a friend, then take a boat to Marseille; that port was open. Andrew would go with them only as far as Algiers. He would help by leaning on Allied ears, Christina explained.

"How long will we be in Algiers?" Leo asked.

"Only long enough to get married."

"What?"

"Not really married, you goose. A marriage license is the easiest document to forge. Granville is my English name, the one I have on my temporary British passport, but I also have my Polish passport, under my maiden name, Skarbek. I assume you have a French passport, as you are in Cairo as a visiting Frenchman?"

"Yes."

"A good one?"

"Authentic, yes."

"Perfect. With that, my old passport, and a marriage certificate we should be able to get into France without a problem. What nasty bureaucrat would refuse permission for a loyal Frenchman to bring his new bride home to meet his mother? People are desperate to get out of France. They'll be delighted to let one loyal Frenchman back in with his new wife."

"And how will we get back to Cairo?"

"Once we've accomplished our mission, you'll get papers authorizing you to enter Spain. From there, it will be easy to get to Tangier, and then back to Cairo. If the border guards give you any trouble, bribe them with cigarettes. A pack of Camels works better than gold."

"We won't come back together?"

She shook her head. "I may be gone longer than you need to be."

"How long have you been planning this?"

"We began receiving information about the deportations late in the summer."

"Who is this 'we'?"

"Friends from before the war. People with whom we used to going skiing in France. A man who once sold me a beautiful piece of jewelry. A friend whose horse I used to ride when we lived in Kenya."

"And that 'we' would be you and your husband?"

"Do you always ask questions to which you already know the answer?"

This response startled him. What had he been expecting? A denial? An explanation?

She did not wait for him to reply. "There is very little we need to know about each other, Leo. You're doing this because you've found some reason to trust me. Let that be enough."

He felt it again, that sense that she understood something about him that he did not, rendering his defenses worthless. He changed the subject.

"Isn't it possible that someone in Algiers will recognize you?"

"Oh, no." She executed a melodramatic pantomime as she spoke. "I'll wear dark glasses, a big hat, and a scarf. It's a busy place, and we won't be there long."

"Let's hope not."

Leo checked out of Shepheard's and asked the concierge to hold any messages he might receive. "Time to go see the wonders of Luxor," he explained, "before I have to leave this fair land for good. I'll be back in a couple of weeks."

Marseille was a fishermen's town of no particular refinement. On the night he and Christine arrived a cold November mist clung with bone-chilling damp to every nook and cranny of the narrow streets. The fog suited the dark mood of the city. German soldiers were already arriving, setting up checkpoints, and the French police stopped people everywhere, demanding identification, looking, everyone knew, for Jews.

Leo stretched out on one of the two twin beds, listening to the horns and bells on the boats as they moved cautiously through the fog. So far everything had run remarkably smoothly. The only tense moment came when the immigration official at the port in Marseille started asking Leo questions about how long he'd been away from France. But Christine, with her magnetic smile, immediately began to ask *him* questions: about his wife, and if she could cook, and if French cooking was hard to learn, because she wanted to cook well for her new husband. The man was under her spell within seconds. He handed Leo's passport back to him, and told Leo that he was a very lucky man, to have a woman like that. A very lucky man.

The pretense made Leo uncomfortable. Martha was the only woman he'd ever loved; he'd never wanted to marry anyone else. But he'd entered into one fake marriage to get Maddy out of Shanghai, so why not another? Why did pretending to be married to Christine, whom he actually admired, make him uneasy? Since they arrived in Algiers, she'd not displayed any embarrassment at sharing quarters, or shown any interest in exploring the physical implications of their charade. She was totally professional, and completely unfathomable.

Christine returned from the communal bathroom down the hallway. She wore a silk housecoat, and had wrapped her hair up in a towel turban. Despite his determination to remain aloof from her charms, the sight of her bare neck made Leo's pulse skip a beat.

"There are already more Germans here than I'd thought there would be," she said, pulling the towel off her head and then using it to dry the ends of her damp hair. "You're sure your German is excellent?"

"Ja."

"Good. One never knows, and I don't speak it at all."

"Hopefully I won't have to talk long."

"True." She dropped her towel on the floor and sat down on the opposite bed, chin propped in her hands, elbows on her knees. "Where are you from, really? Not from France. Not from Vienna. Not from Shanghai. Where?"

"Why does it matter?"

"I would like to know."

There it was again. That look. *I know who you are. I know you've suffered. I've suffered, too.*

"Hungary."

"Really?" She sounded genuinely surprised. "When were you there last?"

"A long time ago. I left in 1925."

"I was there two years ago. In Budapest. It's a beautiful place."

Budapest. A wave of homesickness swept over him with a severity he hadn't felt in years. The Danube. The bridges. The music, the parties, his foster mother's laugh . . .

"Leo, what is it?"

"Nothing. It's been a long time, that's all."

"Poles and Hungarians have that in common: we never get our country out of our soul."

He did not reply.

"Why did you leave?"

"It's complicated."

"I have time."

"Well, perhaps there are some things I don't want to talk about."

She got up off her bed and moved closer to him. She put her hand on his shoulder. Her hand was so warm, her touch so comforting. *Leave it alone. Leave her alone. Don't do this—*

He looked up at her, his eyes asking just one question, and he saw his answer in hers. Her lips parted slightly. He reached up, grasped her with both hands, pulled her down to him, and kissed her with more hunger than tenderness. Her body cried out to him: *lose yourself in me.* There were no boundaries, no uncertainties. He was on top of her; he was inside her. She was so wet, so yielding and demanding all at once.

Too fast, *too fast*; everything was beyond his control. He came with his eyes wide open, groaning aloud as she reached around and pulled him in deeper, and she was watching, watching, connected to him with every breath, a shared existence that left everything else behind.

He could not move. She shifted slightly, and he drifted off to sleep, resting inside her. He did not wake up, not even when she moved away to the other bed. Leo slept soundly through the night, undisturbed by his dreams for the first time in years.

Their destination was the Gurs prison camp, located fifty miles from the Spanish border in the heart of the French Pays Basque, the home of a fiercely independent people who traced their mountainous kingdom in the Pyrenees back a thousand years, and their unique language back to the beginning of time. The French built Gurs in 1939 to detain refugees fleeing from Franco's wrath at the end of the Spanish civil war. Later it was used as a prison for Frenchmen who fought or plotted against the Vichy regime. Finally, it had become a dumping ground for thousands of Jewish refugees, rounded up by the French police, obeying Hitler's command that France rid itself of all "stateless" Jews.

They could see the barracks stretched out below them: long, even rows of single-story buildings, hundreds of them, on an empty plateau as barren as an abandoned chicken yard. The camp was surrounded by two rows of barbed wire set fifteen feet apart and pierced by a dozen weather-beaten watchtowers. The guards seldom had to shoot. The real deterrent to escape was the viscous mud that surrounded Gurs like a septic sea.

Leo checked his image in their van's rearview mirror. What German soldier had worn this hat, this warm wool coat? Had he been an enthusiastic Nazi, or a reluctant conscript, like Leo himself, back when he was drafted in 1917? Was he dead? Or sitting in an army camp somewhere, wanting desperately to go home?

Their driver, Daniel, was a short, brave son of a bitch: a German Jew who'd fled first to Belgium, then to Paris, then to Lyon, then said "enough" and turned to fight. He worked for a network that spirited Jewish children out of French internment camps to safe houses in the countryside. Those who had no hope of passing as French Christians were smuggled into Switzerland, where they were placed in convents or found homes with families willing to keep them until their parents—if their parents—could come for them. Daniel had been across the Swiss border half a dozen times himself, and had always come back into France, leaving safety behind.

"Are you ready?" he asked Leo.

"Ja." Leo was no longer Hungarian, no longer French, no longer a spy. He was a German officer, with orders to pick up as many Jews as they could squeeze into the back of their van for deportation east.

"Let's go." The three other men with him—Daniel, Val, and Charles—were all dressed in Vichy French uniforms. Christine was already there, inside the camp, with a group from the Red Cross. He hadn't seen her in three days. They'd spent their last night together in the leaky basement of a farmhouse close to the camp, and made love in the darkness, muted but frantic, sensing, without confirming, that it would be the last time.

The morning they left Marseille was the only time they'd talked about what was happening between them. They made love as the sun rose, and before leaving her bed, Leo asked, "Why me?"

She put her finger on his lips. "Because we are so much alike, Leo. And you needed me." After that, he'd never asked her about Andrew, or her husband, or what would happen when they both made it back to

Cairo, and she never offered any explanation. They'd found each other. It would have to end. That was all.

But he ached for her. Since the day that Martha died, Christine's embrace was the only place he'd found peace.

The van pulled up in front of the main gates. Leo stepped out, followed by the two Vichy imposters, Val and Charles. Daniel beeped on the horn, loudly, as if their arrival had gone unnoticed. Of course, it hadn't.

Two guards appeared. "Open up, you idiots, I have orders here," Leo barked at them in German. They gazed back insolently. Good. They didn't speak German. That was safer.

Leo gestured to one of his men, who dashed up to the gate. "Tell them to let us in," he ordered, again in German. The fraudulent Vichy said in French, "Open up the gates. We're here to collect some Jews."

The two guards looked at each other. "Go get the boss," said one with a sneer. A small crowd of women had gathered up against the wall of the building closest to the gates. Leo glanced at them and then spat on the ground, using this gesture of contempt to cover his shock. The women watched him with hollowed-out eyes, and clutched at their mud-stained, ragged clothes with raw hands. Only a few had coats. He could smell their unwashed bodies, and see the fleshless elbows of their undernourished arms. *Rats live better than this.*

A rotund Vichy officer strolled up to the gate. "Here again?" he asked in barely comprehensible German. "We just marched over a thousand of them out of here a few months back. They had to walk to the train station. What do you have there, a Jewish limousine service? Why spoil them? It's only a few miles!" He laughed, and the two guards laughed with him, despite the fact they had no idea what he'd said.

"It'll be your hearse if you keep me here another goddamn minute. Open the gate and let's get on with it," Leo growled.

The camp administrator contemplated this command. "Let them in," he finally said.

Leo entered on foot. The truck drove in behind him. "Your name is Gruel, yes?" he asked, shoving his orders into the man's hands.

"That's right."

"So tell me, what did you do to deserve this pleasant duty?"

"Could be worse. These types don't fight back."

Leo snorted. "We'll have German officers in here to replace trash like you soon enough."

The man bristled, but Leo's words hit their mark. Unoccupied France was unoccupied no longer. Gruel handed the papers back to Leo. "Do you have names?"

"Doesn't matter. We'll take as many as we can stuff into the truck, including women and children. No more exemptions. I have a quota to fill."

"Come to my office."

Where was Christine?

Gruel led him down a muddy path cut between flat buildings with sealed windows and sagging roofs. From somewhere he heard the sound of children singing, their lilting voices so out of keeping with the vile surroundings that Leo felt a lump rise in his throat. He coughed.

"What kind of diseases are you breeding here?"

Gruel laughed. "Dysentery, mostly."

There she is. She was bundled into a threadbare woolen coat; she must have given hers to someone at the camp. Her Red Cross armband was already covered in grime. The woman approaching them had no sparkle, no warmth; evidently Christine could turn her sexuality on and off like a light switch. *A complete chameleon.*

She thrust a paper toward Gruel. "Monsieur, I have a list of some of the women who are sick. I'm afraid it might be typhoid."

She spoke in rapid French. Leo looked at her blankly, feigning incomprehension. Gruel looked from Christine to Leo, and then back to the list she held in her hand.

"Are they all Jewish?" he asked her in French.

"Juden?" Leo repeated, as if he'd caught only the one word.

Christine looked alarmed. "I don't know. I suppose so."

Gruel snatched the paper out of Christine's hand and gave it to Leo. "Here's your list."

Leo glanced at it. Fifteen names. "Round these women up, their children, too. I want to leave as quickly as possible. I can't stand the stench."

Gruel executed an exaggerated salute. "At your service. Heil Hitler!"

Christine did not give up. "But Monsieur, the deportation orders exclude women with young children, and these women need medical attention. Most of them have children they're too sick to care for; they won't survive a journey—"

"That's not my problem," Gruel snapped. "And if the Red Cross doesn't stop meddling in the camp's administrative affairs, you'll be much less welcome to try and accomplish whatever good you think you're doing here. Do you understand me?"

Christine did not answer. Head bowed, shoulders sagging, she trudged away.

An hour later fifteen women and twelve children piled into the van, clinging to their small, dirty bundles, cowering and crying under the rough hands of the Vichy guards herding them in. There was not enough room for anyone to sit down.

Leo climbed back into the cab and ordered his driver to leave. They needed to make it five miles without running into any patrols, and then he would hand his cargo over to someone else who would give them food and fresh clothes, and help them find hiding places or an escape route. If Christine had done her job these women were strong enough to travel. For the mothers, their next home might well be an internment camp in Switzerland—the Swiss would not issue any more entrance visas—but their children would find safety with a willing family, or in a convent run by sympathetic nuns.

The van was barely ten minutes away from the camp when Leo felt the truck sag on one side, then come to a stop.

"Shit!" Daniel banged the steering wheel. They both got out and walked around to the back of the vehicle. A length of barbed wire had wrapped around the right rear tire, tearing it in several places. The two other men, Val and Charles, who'd been riding outside on the rear running board, were already inspecting the damage and adding their own expletives.

"We'll have to walk," Daniel declared.

Leo surveyed the dense growth of trees that surrounded them, his senses alert. "I've got to get out of this uniform."

"Soon. Aren isn't far. We'll find help there. Germany bombed the hell out of a couple of Spanish Basque towns as a favor to Franco during the civil war, so the Basque hate the Germans even more than they hate the French."

"That's my concern."

Daniel moved to the back of the van and pulled back the bolt to the lock. He'd opened the door less than six inches when a hand holding one end of a cloth-wrapped bundle swung out of the small opening and smacked him soundly on the head. Daniel's knees buckled, and he fell to the damp ground with a thud.

The doors flew open and women and children poured out, breaking into a run the instant they emerged, urged on by panicked shouts in several languages.

"Stop! We're here to help you!" Leo called out in German, trying to get to Daniel before he was trampled to death. Val and Charles cried out in French while making wild attempts to grab the women and children as they raced by.

"Don't run! You'll get lost! Stop!"

The crack of gunfire broke through the chaos. Those closest to the van froze.

"I won't shoot you, but you have to listen," Val shouted. "We want to help you."

"We'll get you and your children safely out of the country. You have to trust us," Leo added loudly in German.

A few of the women walked slowly back to the van. Leo could hear the others thrashing through the trees and shrubs, some coming closer, others moving farther and farther away.

Val looked worried. "We have to get going. That gunshot will have been heard for miles. But I didn't have much choice, did I?"

By now more than half of the women and children hovered within twenty feet of the van, their eyes wide with a terrible combination of fear and hope. One of the women called out something in Polish. Two more women crept out of the woods, their toddlers in their arms.

"What a mess. How's Daniel?" Charles asked.

"Alive," Leo answered. "He's not losing much blood, but he got quite a wallop on the head, and that trampling didn't help."

"We'll have to split up or we'll attract too much attention. The ones who speak French can travel with me," Val ordered. "Everyone else should go with you and Charles."

"And Daniel?"

"You're both sturdy. Take turns carrying him. It's only two miles to Aren. We have a friend there who can at least get us some food, and may even let us stay in his barn. I'll get in touch with someone who can contact the leader of the next leg of this operation, and they'll figure out how to get the group out. We have to be careful, though. Not all the Basque are sympathetic."

"Very well," Leo responded. "Charles? Do you know the way?"

"I'm traveling in my own backyard. How many have we lost?"

Leo did a quick count. "All but three of the women are back."

"They won't last long out here. Once the sun goes, they'll freeze." He hefted Daniel across his broad shoulders like a sack of grain. "Call 'em. Let's get going."

The women soon sorted themselves out. Leo and Charles led away their group of seven women and six children. Given the number of children they had with them, it was a fairly orderly procession.

Leo was starting to feel optimistic about making it to the safe house when one of the women moaned and fell over. Her daughter, a small child with long curly hair and enormous dark eyes, screamed and pointed.

"Christ, what now?" Charles grumbled, setting Daniel down as carefully as possible while Leo made his way through the circle of women surrounding the one who'd collapsed. He knelt down and put a hand to the woman's head. No fever. What then? Exhaustion? Starvation?

He took her hand and spoke to her gently. "Madam, what's wrong? Are you ill?"

The woman's free hand went to her stomach. "I'm losing my baby."

"Don't worry, we'll take care of you." Leo looked around at the circle of women. "Does anyone have anything we can use to absorb the blood?"

"Ja," one woman volunteered without hesitation. She unknotted her dirty bundle and pulled out a blue cotton dress. "Take this. Poor girl. No one even knew she was expecting."

Leo took the dress, then paused, embarrassed. "Could one of you ladies please tuck this up where it will soak up the discharge?"

Another woman nodded and took the dress. Leo politely turned his back. "It's done," he heard, and then squatted down next to the bleeding woman.

"What's your name?" he asked the little girl, who was holding her mother's head in her own tiny lap. A stream of tears flowed down her chapped and dirty cheeks.

"Gabriella," she answered between sniffles.

"What a beautiful name. How old are you, Gabriella?"

She held up three grubby little fingers. "Three."

"What a lovely grown-up girl you are. So I'm going to carry your mommy, but we have to walk more before we lose the light. We don't want to get lost in the dark, do we?"

"I'm scared of the dark."

Leo pulled out his handkerchief, wiped Gabriella's face, and helped her blow her nose. "You'll be fine. Walk right next to me." He picked up Gabriella's mother. "Charles, can you handle Daniel? I've got to carry this one."

"Leo, we can't take anyone who can't travel. It's too risky."

"I'm not leaving her."

"As far as Aren, then. We'll have to leave her there, whether or not we can find someone to take her in, you understand?"

"Let's just get there."

After struggling through another mile of dense forest the group came to the edge of the Basque village of Aren. A few hundred feet away they could see a small farmhouse, corral, and barn.

Charles laid Daniel down. The unconscious man groaned. "Well, that's a relief," Charles observed. "He must be coming out of it. I'll go see what the welcome is like. You wait here. Keep everyone quiet and out of sight."

He was back in twenty minutes, a good deal more cheerful than he'd been when he left. "Val's already been there. We're good for tonight, anyway. We'll split into two smaller groups and move into the barn after dark."

Gabriella lay fast asleep at Leo's feet, wrapped in the German officer's coat that was now heavily stained with blood. Her mother's lifeless body lay beside her.

"We lost her," Leo said, exhaustion punctuating every syllable.

"Probably for the best, hard as it sounds."

"Get me a shovel when you come back for the second group. I want to bury her, at least."

"I'll see what I can do."

Charles came back with a shovel and Leo's coat. "Never mind the blood. You'll freeze out here without it," he warned. Leo found a place barely inside the tree line where the ground was relatively soft and dug a shallow grave for the woman he knew only as the mother of little Gabriella. Charles would have to tell the girl when she woke up. Leo couldn't, not after he'd had to tell his own daughter that she would never see her mother again.

His fingers were stiff. Digging had helped keep him warm, but the temperature had dropped significantly. Leo tossed one last pile of dirt on the shallow grave. "If God's listening, if he ever listens to any of us, may he give you peace," he murmured. Then he leaned his shovel against a nearby tree and stretched his aching back muscles.

A noise in the underbrush ignited his senses. He reached for the shovel. *Who was out there?* He stayed motionless, concentrating on every sound. Nothing. Shovel held high, he backed slowly toward the field.

Two noises pierced the silence, so close together it was hard to tell them apart: the crack of a shotgun, and the ring of metal ricocheting off metal.

Two Basque villagers sprinted out of the woods toward Leo's fallen body.

"Great shot!" said one, setting down his trace of rabbits as he leaned over the body. "Well, he's not dead yet, but you hit him somewhere lethal. Look at all that blood." He gave Leo's chest a quick poke with the barrel of his own rifle and grinned.

"Now that makes for a good day's hunting," said his companion. "Half a dozen rabbits and a fuckin' German!"

"Too bad we can't eat this bastard."

"You could tempt me to cut off a few pieces."

"Enough fun. We better get him out of here. One of his friends finds him in this field, and they'll be shooting everyone in the village."

"Tell you what; let's go dump him in the middle of the camp road. Maybe one of his Kraut buddies will run over him in the dark and finish him off."

He was in the countess's car, the Rolls-Royce, and the chauffeur was driving too fast, way too fast. The car would crash, and he would never get there. He started to sweat. "Slow down," he shouted. The man would not listen. He shouted again, in Russian this time. Then French. Then Chinese. The refu-

gees crowded around the car. Hands were touching him, hands covered in blood. He saw Martha in the distance, walking into the store. He had to stop her! He struggled to get away, but the hands held him too tightly—

"Sleep, now. Hush."

He saw a woman's face. It wasn't Martha. He lost consciousness again.

He heard the dim hubbub of nearby voices and tried to open his eyes. He had never exerted so much effort to move any part of his body. *If he could only open his eyes.*

The voices drifted away.

She smelled like honey and vanilla. He felt silk and rippling warmth. Then she was gone and he saw Amelia looking down at him. She was talking to him, telling him something in German. He needed to ask her what she'd done with Maddy. Why couldn't he speak? He had to get the words out! Where is my daughter? Where is my daughter?

"Wo ist meine Tochter?"

The blond nurse who'd been updating Leo's chart gaped at him, then called out, "He's talking." Two more nurses ran into the room. One of them grabbed Leo's wrist.

"Wo ist meine Tochter?" he said again, directly to the nurse who was taking his pulse. She put a finger to her lips and gave him a small, flirtatious smile. The two other nurses giggled and she shot them a menacing scowl before speaking.

"You're in a field hospital, mein Herr," the nurse answered in German that was heavily decorated with a French accent. "You had no identification with you. What's your name? Maybe then we can find your daughter for you."

"Hoffman. My name is Leopold Hoffman. Where am I?"

Another presence filled the doorway. "Hoffman?"

Somber looks replaced the playful smiles on the nurses' faces as a German officer moved into the room. A blast of adrenaline instantly cleared the lingering fog in Leo's head. He started to execute a salute, but stopped himself. A German junior officer would not speak to his superior until addressed.

The man shrugged. "Unusual, but not unheard of, for a Jew to have such a name." He meandered over and took Leo's medical chart from the nurse. Still, Leo said nothing. *Where are the others? How long have I been here?*

The officer spoke again. "You were found wearing a German uniform, a very bloody German uniform, despite the fact that your injuries were limited to exposure and a concussion. You had no identification. However, you are circumcised and therefore a Jew, yes?"

"No, sir, Herr Colonel. I'm sure whoever wounded me stole my identification for nefarious purposes, sir. And my family had that," he explained, gesturing toward his lower body, "done because of an infection I had when I was a child."

"Better that than to cut if off altogether, ja?" the officer remarked, without a trace of amusement. "And the explanation for the uniform—?"

"I was honored, sir, that despite my age I was permitted to join the Führer's army, as a reward for my loyal service as a soldier under the Kaiser. No one asked about—the issue you have just addressed—when I enlisted."

The officer sighed and handed the chart back to the nurse, who kept her eyes lowered. "It's a very intriguing lie, I'll give you that. Who could imagine a Jew joining the Führer's army? Come to think of it, that's not a bad way to hide, for a short while. A little less cowardly. At the moment I don't have time to investigate this small matter. I could have you shot, but you seem fit enough. You'd prove more useful in a work camp. I understand we're sending prisoners from this area to Meyreuil."

"Katherine?"

"Hmm?"

"Are you asleep?"

"Yes."

Ignoring this, Maddy sat up in her bed. Katherine lay curled up in the twin bed near her own. But for a swath of red hair, her friend was buried under a down comforter.

"Do you think I would know if my father were dead?"

Katherine rolled over to face Maddy. "The War Office would send you a telegram, or the Red Cross. Somebody would tell you."

Maddy shook her head. "No, I mean, do you think that I would just *know*?"

"I don't believe in that stuff, Maddy. If anyone could know that, Ma would have known that Jamie was dead. An angel would have come and told her in a dream, or some crazy Catholic nonsense like that."

"What do you mean? What's nonsense?"

Katherine paused, as if she needed to ruminate a bit before she committed blasphemy, but then gave a forceful answer. "I think a lot of all the religion stuff is nonsense. Look at your aunt and uncle. They don't go to church, do they?"

"They're Jewish, dumbo."

"Temple, then. What I mean is they're decent people. I don't think you have to be Catholic to be a good person."

"But what about what the nuns told us? About going to hell if you're not baptized?"

"What about it?"

"Do you think that means Jews, too?"

"Geez! How am I supposed to know?"

"But what about me? What if I wasn't baptized?"

"Don't be stupid."

"What about original sin?" Maddy laid back down, her heart thumping in her chest. "What if I'm going to hell, and there's nothing I can do about it?"

"You're gonna get there quicker if you don't go to sleep, 'cause I'm gonna kill you."

"Please don't joke about this. We're talking about my *immortal soul*."

"Are you really scared?"

"Wouldn't you be? Aren't you afraid of hell?"

Katherine didn't answer this. "C'mon. Look at the facts. You went to Catholic school in Shanghai, right?"

"So?"

"They wouldn't have enrolled you without a baptismal certificate. They wouldn't take a chance on letting any little heathens in by mistake."

"But what if baptism doesn't help . . . Christ killers?"

Now Katherine sat up. "Maddy, what's gotten into you? All of the original Christians were Jews, right? The Apostles? If you're baptized, then the pope has your name on a list somewhere, and you're covered."

This made some sense, and Maddy let out a small sigh of relief. "I sort of wish I could see that list."

"So write to the Vatican. Now go to sleep. I'm bushed." Katherine laid back down and curled up into a ball under her covers.

"Okay. G'night."

The silence lasted only a minute. "Katherine?"

"What is it now?"

"I'm really sorry I wasn't there when you found out about Jamie."

"You've told me that a million times. It's not like you could've done anything."

"But I'm sorry I wasn't there."

"All you missed was a bunch of Irish cops getting drunk and watching Ma fall to pieces. I don't think it would've hit her so hard if it had been me lost at sea."

"Now *you're* being an idiot."

"Can we please go to sleep?"

"Okay. Sorry. Good night."

"Good night, already."

Maddy pulled her own covers up under her chin. Just as sleep overcame her Katherine's muffled sobs edged into her consciousness, and Maddy carried them with her into her dreams.

PART THREE

FIFTEEN
WASHINGTON, D.C., 1945

Lieutenant Colonel Gregory Sharpton and Major Douglas Hagman walked briskly down an empty, windowless corridor deep in the bowels of the Pentagon. They returned the salute executed by the soldier stationed at the end of the hall, then each displayed a special pass that the young man inspected carefully before stepping aside.

Hagman opened the steel door that led into a small office furnished with two plain desks and one filing cabinet. The cabinet was bolted to the floor and protected by two separate combination locks. Sharpton knew one code, Hagman the other. There was no way one single human being, operating alone, could invade the contents.

Each man removed a stack of files from the top drawer and retreated to his respective desk. Sharpton, a career military man in his late fifties, pulled a pair of reading glasses from his pocket. Hagman, younger by almost fifteen years, removed his cap, put his feet up on his desk, leaned back in his chair, and began to read.

All was quiet for a few moments. Then Hagman broke the silence.

"Greg?"

"Hmm?"

"Do you think ol' Harry really knew what those atom bombs could do?"

"I assume so."

"I saw pictures today. Have you seen pictures yet?"

"Yes, I have. Very effective."

"Effective? Guess that's one way to put it. Who would've thought we could make something that could do all that? The whole place disintegrated."

Sharpton put down the file he'd been reading and looked over his bifocals at the younger officer. "Would you rather have been on the beach yourself, attempting to take the Japanese homeland? The war could have dragged on for years. The president did the right thing."

"I suppose so."

"Douglas, Truman is shutting down the Office of Strategic Services in a month. Debate nuclear ethics on your own time. Right now, read."

There was silence for a few more minutes. Then Hagman emitted a long, low whistle, swung his feet to the ground, and leaned forward in his chair.

"Now this is some hotshot spy. Hungarian national, recruited out of Shanghai in 1939. Loaned to the Brits and worked in North Africa under Colonel Eddy, where he was instrumental in effectuating the Dakar decoy plan. Then, get this—he's in France, wearing a German uniform—"

"Why?"

"Hmm . . . doesn't really say. Anyhow, he gets some kind of head wound and wakes up in a Vichy hospital. Someone there figures out that he's not really a German soldier, so he's sent to Meyreuil, a work camp outside Marseille, where he spent two years digging coal and

then escaped, bringing fifteen other prisoners with him by masquer-
ading as a German guard in charge of a work detail. Hooked up with the
Penny Farthing network in Avignon in time to assist with Operation
Dragoon—geez, the guy is a regular Scarlet Pimpernel."

"A what?"

"You know, *The Scarlet Pimpernel*, that movie with Leslie Howard,
where he saves all his friends from the guillotine during the French Revo-
lution by adopting different disguises. Don't you ever go to the movies?"

"Not lately."

"This movie is at least ten years old."

Sharpton ignored this. "Where's the man now?"

"Ah, let me see. Released to Naval Intelligence, then given a special assignment in Berlin for postwar debriefings. Handy guy to have
around, I guess, since he speaks fluent English, German, French, Russian, Hungarian, and Chinese, and excellent Arabic. Discharged with
permission to immigrate, destination New York, less than a month
ago. I think they made this guy up, Greg."

"It's not our job to decide that. But I'd say his file should make the
cut, don't you? We only have a few weeks before they dismantle the
whole OSS, and if Donovan convinces Truman to go ahead with a
peacetime agency—"

"We'll need some good spies. I know." Major Hagman tucked the
dossier back into its manila folder and tossed it into a box marked SPE-
CIAL CLEARANCE: DONOVAN that sat on the floor between their two desks.
He then leaned back in his chair, put his feet back up on his desk, picked
up the next file from his stack, and began, again, to read.

He had to knock twice before someone came to the door. It was answered by a young woman who looked to be about Maddy's age. Her

face was pleasant but not beautiful, and surrounded by a wild mass of curly red hair, most of which was captured in a haphazard ponytail. Leo was pretty sure he knew who she was.

"Hello, Katherine."

She must have recognized him as well, for the expression on her face shifted from anticipation to surprise to contempt in a matter of seconds; then she slammed the door shut.

"Ma! Ma! You won't believe who's here!" he heard her yell. He banged on the door again, this time not politely.

Margaret O'Connor opened the door. She looked so thin, and so fragile. Not at all the person to whom he'd said farewell when he was last in New York, almost six years ago.

"Mrs. O'Connor, may I please come in?"

She seemed uncertain. Katherine stepped in front of her. "You've got some nerve, showing up here—"

Her outburst brought Margaret to life. "Mary Kate, mind your manners. Haven't I raised ya better than that? It's me he means to talk to, not your uppity self. Go on now. Come in, Mr. Hoffman."

Katherine didn't move.

"Off you go. There's laundry to be folded upstairs."

"Ah, Ma—"

"Am I talkin' to meself, Miss Mary Katherine Anne O'Connor?"

Katherine knew that an order issued using her full Christian name left no room for argument. With a loud "humph," she clomped up the stairs, each step signaling her protest. Leo waited until he heard a door slam before talking again.

"Where's Maddy?"

Margaret shook her head. "She's not here. And she hasn't been, hasn't lived here that is, for quite some time."

"She doesn't live here? But why—where—?"

"I'll be the one asking questions, if you don't mind."

They faced each other, both sensing that they were about to become allies or enemies. Leo blinked first. "I'll answer any questions you have. But first, please tell me that she's all right."

"Right enough. We'll have some tea. This way to the kitchen."

He followed her down the narrow hallway to the room he'd been in only once before, the day he decided to let Maddy stay with this family rather than deposit her in a Swiss boarding school. Had that been one more of his many mistakes?

Leo took a seat at the table while Margaret put the kettle on. She continued to talk as she lit the stove. "She's living in New Jersey, your daughter is. With her aunt and uncle. Her mother's sister and her husband."

"Who?"

Margaret took the cups and saucers out of a cupboard and set them down on the table. "Martha's sister, Bernice Mason. Showed up here three years ago, sayin' how she'd been searchin' for Maddy ever since she heard of her sister's death. She had an old photograph of a man and two girls, one that was surely herself, the other a spittin' image of Maddy, but with lighter hair, who I figured had to be Maddy's mum."

Leo did not respond. His eyes were closed, and he was barely breathing. Margaret poured the tea.

"You can't blame Maddy for wantin' to go with her aunt. The woman was offerin' Maddy somethin' she didn't have: a piece of herself. Mrs. Mason seems like a decent woman. Not a warm person, but decent, and determined to do the best by Maddy. And the fact that the Masons are quite well-off didn't hurt; we've done well by Maddy, thanks to the money you left, but we are who we are. Maddy came from somethin' different, and she had a right to go back to it."

Leo overcame the lump in his throat. "I understand why you made the decision you did. And I appreciate everything you've done for my daughter, more than you will ever know. But I am her father."

"No one's arguing that point."

"Have you talked to her? Did you tell her that I was coming?"

Margaret shook her head. "No. I called Mrs. Mason, and she asked me to let her tell Maddy if you actually showed up, in case you didn't. No reason to disappoint her, you see."

"I understand."

"Do ya now? That's the trouble I'm havin'. I lost two boys in this war, Mr. Hoffman, our youngest son and our firstborn. There's nothin' that prepares ya for losin' a child. It opens a hole in your heart so wide and so deep there's no way to ever fill it back up. The best ya can do is learn to walk around it, for the sake of those left behind. So I can't imagine, havin' yer own child, how ya let her sit here thinkin' you were never comin' back, with no hope—"

"I tried—"

"We never got a word. Not one word, after the letter from the navy tellin' us you'd been discharged. Nothing until your telegram two weeks ago."

"But I did write! And then I couldn't—" Leo saw the full measure of Margaret's judgment in her gaze, and knew there was no point in arguing.

He stared down into his cup. "I know I've hurt Maddy terribly. But maybe there's a reason that I'm not dead like so many others. Maybe it's so that I could have this chance to try to convince Maddy that I do love her, and that it wasn't her fault that I left. I don't know if it's too late for her to believe anything I say. But I have to try."

When he finally looked up, Margaret had tears in her eyes. She coughed and dried her eyes on her apron. "Mr. Hoffman," she said, "you're either a decent man or a damn fine liar. Maybe only the good Lord himself knows the truth of that. But I'm afraid that for you and your Maddy both, it might be too late."

"Madeleine, your father is in New York and wants to see you."

Maddy thought the egg she'd just eaten was going to bounce out of her stomach and onto the tablecloth. *My father.* She'd wanted to see her father for so long that the desire had gone stale inside her, atrophying into something closer to dread. It hadn't been difficult to explain her father's absence during the war. So many fathers, brothers, uncles, and cousins had been away from home for so long that the details of Maddy's unusual circumstances blended into the background. Deprivation was the normal course of things, during the war; but the war was over.

Katherine had warned her. *Facts, facts, facts. Don't draw any conclusions until you have the facts.* She kept insisting that the government, or the Red Cross, or someone, somewhere, would have found a way to tell Maddy if her father was dead.

"He's in New York, at the O'Connors'. He rang last night. I told him I'd ask you if you wished to see him, and that under no circumstances was he to come here without your express permission."

Maddy sat up in her chair, eyes wide. She felt the power her aunt was giving her as palpably as if she were holding a weight in her hand, and the responsibility for making the decision terrified her.

"How long . . . how long will he be here?"

"That's not clear."

"Oh."

"Madeleine, I will follow your wishes in this matter. It's entirely up to you whether you want to see your father. I have no objection, provided he is willing to be reasonable."

Maddy was not entirely sure what Bernice meant by "reasonable," but she didn't have the courage to ask. She tried to decipher what Bernice wanted from her. If she didn't want her father to come, wouldn't she have said so? Didn't that mean it was all right? What was her aunt waiting to hear?

"Of course I'll see him," Maddy finally said, and then waited anxiously for Bernice's reaction.

Her aunt rewarded her with a self-satisfied smile. "That's what I was hoping you would say, my dear. It's better to get this settled once and for all. For that reason, before you talk to him, I think there are some things that you should know."

At four o'clock a taxi deposited Leo at the Masons' doorstep. He spent a couple of minutes outside the house, taking in the cold, geometrically striking exterior before he rang the bell.

Bernice came to the door. Leo tried to discern in that first instant whether there was any room for friendship between them. He was not encouraged.

"Leo Hoffman. We meet at last. I'm Bernice Mason. Come in."

"Thank you," he said, stepping inside. "Is Maddy—"

"Hello, Father. How kind of you to come visit."

There she was, framed like a photograph by the entrance to the living room. The dark green suit she wore set off the color of her eyes and made her hair look as shiny as polished onyx. Leo sucked in his breath when he saw her. She was Martha, except she wasn't.

"Maddy." He wanted to reach for her, but could feel her willing him away. He kept his distance.

"Well," said Bernice crisply, "shall we sit down?"

She led them into the living room. A low camel-hair couch formed a semicircle around a glass-topped coffee table. On it sat a contemporary silver coffee service, the pot as sleek as a missile.

"Coffee?"

"Please."

Leo watched Maddy while Bernice poured. She was trying so hard to emulate Bernice. Her rigid posture. The cool reserve. The little girl he'd known should never have turned out like this. She'd been too much like her mother.

But what choice had he given her?

"You look lovely, Maddy. That green is beautiful on you."

"Thank you, Papa."

So much time lost. *Start with something simple.*

"You sound so very American. Is English all you speak? Have you kept up with your French?"

To his consternation, Maddy glanced at Bernice before responding. "Somewhat. I take classes."

"If you keep up with it in school, it will come back when you need it."

"I can't imagine when I'll ever need to speak French again."

He took a sip of his coffee. "Well, one never knows. What an interesting home you have, Bernice. Very modern. The landscaping is lovely. Maddy, would you care to show me the garden?"

Again, Maddy looked to Bernice. "It's entirely up to you, Madeleine," her aunt replied.

"Very well." Maddy set her coffee cup back onto its saucer. "Aunt Bernice, would you like to join us?"

For an instant Leo was afraid the woman would say yes. To his relief, she shook her head. "No, it would be fine for your father to have you to himself for a few minutes, if you're comfortable."

"I'll be fine." Leo hoped the disdain in Maddy's voice was not aimed at him. But of course, it was. He felt his resentment of Bernice growing by the second.

They did not speak again until they were outside. Leo ran his hand across the top of his head and down the back of his neck. "I don't know where to start," he said, hoping that Maddy would feel comfortable asking him a question that could begin their conversation.

Maddy was not at a loss for words. She'd rehearsed this scene in her head for years. "Well, Father, what *have* you been doing with yourself?"

"I've been in the military."

"That's a lie. You weren't in the military. We got a letter. You quit the navy."

"Not exactly. They transferred me to a different division. I became a spy."

Surprise interrupted her internal script. "A spy?"

"Yes. I'm not supposed to tell you that, but I'm not going to let any more secrets get between us. That's why I couldn't write to you, or give you an address to write to. I was supposed to be gone for two years. But then the U.S. entered the war and I was stranded. Then I was captured."

"Captured? By the Germans?"

"Yes."

He could sense her wall of hostility wavering; then it snapped back into place. "Show me your number."

"My number?"

She pointed at his arm. "On your wrist. Show me the number."

"You mean a tattoo? I don't have one. Not everyone—"

"You're Jewish, aren't you? And you were captured? And put in a camp? Then why don't you have a number? You're lying to me again. You lied about where you were from, about being Jewish, and about Amelia. You stuck me with her because you'd had an affair with her while you were married to my mother."

"Maddy, it wasn't like that—"

"Oh, no? My aunt told me the truth about you. *She* doesn't lie to me."

It would have been easy to leave at that moment. Easy to run away from her anger, easy to let Bernice win. But what had he fought for, if not this? If not for her?

"Please. Let's sit and talk. Surely there's somewhere?"

His daughter glared at him, suspicious of even this simple request. She pointed behind him to a stone bench. He walked over and sat down. She perched on the other side of the bench—as far away from him as possible—but she was listening.

"I was captured in France when most of the French were still doing whatever they were told to do by the Germans. I was lucky. The Germans needed workers, and I was capable of working. As a prisoner of war I was not tattooed, or sent east to the death camps. I worked in a coal mine near Marseille."

She said nothing. He kept talking.

"As for the rest, I stopped acknowledging my Jewish background long before I went to Shanghai. After the first Great War in Europe, people in Hungary were being killed just because they were Jewish. My faith meant very little to me. It was more important to stay alive."

Something in his statement served as a tripwire for Maddy's anger. *Aunt Bernice was right. He betrayed my mother, and I'm not the first person he's abandoned. I'm not the only person he's run away from.*

"You were a coward," she lashed out. "Think of all the people Hitler killed, people who were willing to die rather than disclaim their heritage. You're a liar and a coward!"

"I suppose it's true that I am a liar and a coward," he said, remaining calm in the face of her onslaught. "I could have told the truth and been killed for it. But I was never a religious man, Maddy. Being labeled Jewish was a dangerous inconvenience. That's all I gave up."

"Just like you gave me up, when I became inconvenient," she spat out.

He sighed heavily, a long sound, full of patience and regret. "I know why you feel that way. All I can say is that I did what I did for your protection, because I love you—"

She leapt up before he could finish, rearing away from him like a wild horse. The depth of the hatred in her eyes stunned him.

"To *protect me*? Sending me off with Amelia? Do you have any *idea* what it was like? Living with strangers, knowing that you weren't wanted, hoping and waiting for someone who never comes? And do you know what happens then? *You give up.*

"I thought you were dead. It would've been *easier* if you'd been dead. Then there would've been a reason for you to leave me alone the way you did."

Maddy was shaking with rage. She'd never felt such anger before, had never let it emerge from her soul. She could feel the power of it, power she wanted to use.

"You were a prisoner of war, you said. What kind of prisoner did you make me? *What kind of prisoner was I?*"

"Please, listen to me—"

"Listen? *You* listen to *me*. I never want to see you again. Never, do you understand? Go back to your spy job or whatever you do. I do *not* want you back in my life. I found someone who wants me. And she's wanted me all this time, and would have found me, too, if it weren't for your sending me away and hiding me behind all of your lies. You stopped being my father eight years ago. It's too late to start again now."

Without another word, she turned on her heel and marched back into the house.

Bernice refused to meet with Leo anywhere other than her lawyer's office. *Behind enemy lines*, he thought as walked into the somber suite occupied by the Wall Street firm that Mason Industries kept on a generous retainer. A prim secretary ushered him into a small conference room where Bernice sat, flanked by two of her mercenaries. Only one of them got up to shake his hand when he entered the room.

"It would have been easier to meet me for a cup of coffee somewhere, Bernice. And a lot less expensive, I'll bet," Leo said as he took a seat.

"I think there are some details of this situation that require some technical elaboration," she responded, with a nod at one of her attorneys. "I don't want there to be room for any misunderstanding."

"What is there to understand? I have a right to see my daughter."

"No, you don't, actually," the lawyer interjected. "She's fifteen. She can live where she likes, as long as she's in no physical or moral danger."

"But I just want to talk to her."

"She doesn't want to talk to you. I think she's made that abundantly clear," Bernice replied. "And you can add these to your collection." She handed him two letters addressed to Maddy, marked with the word REFUSED.

The older of the two lawyers spoke up. "Mrs. Mason wishes us to inform you that if you show up at her home again, you will be arrested for trespass."

"I spent two years as a prisoner of war. Do really you think a few days in the county jail will keep me away from my child?"

"Miss Hoffman is no longer a child. She's a responsible young woman who wants nothing to do with the man who seduced her mother away from her own loving family, then carried on numerous adulterous relationships—"

"What the hell are you talking about?"

"We have an affidavit from your ex-wife, Mr. Hoffman, explaining the intricacies of your relationship with her, and with other women, prior to your first wife's death."

"You mean you talked to Amelia? And believed anything she said?"

"She swore out an affidavit under oath. It was enough to convince your daughter." The attorney held a paper out to Leo. He swatted it away and addressed his words directly to Bernice.

"You showed that spiteful, obscene garbage to Maddy? You don't even know me. Why are you doing this? Why won't you give me a chance to try to make amends with my child?"

"It's not my decision. It's Madeleine's. What chance did you give her? What chance did you give her mother?"

Her words, cold and sharp as a razor, found their target. The blood drained out of his face as Bernice continued her calculated assault. "What right do you have, after all this time, to disrupt Madeleine's life? Just how selfish are you?"

He couldn't listen to any more.

Leo called Bernice's house late in the afternoon the next day. Maddy answered the phone. Even her voice sounded like Martha's.

"Maddy, it's your father."

The next thing he heard was the dial tone in his ear. He held the receiver in his hand for several minutes before placing his next call. It took some time before the connection went through.

"Sharpton here."

"This is Leo Hoffman. I would like to reconsider the position we discussed."

SIXTEEN
NEW YORK, 1948

Maddy knocked on the familiar door.

"Here it is!" squealed Katherine, flinging it open in response to Maddy's knock. She wiggled a single page of paper inches from her friend's nose. "The ticket to my future: my acceptance to Barnard!" Holding the sacred letter close to her breast with a touch of melodramatic reverence, she added, "And after Barnard, wait and see: the Columbia School of Journalism!"

Bernice, right behind Maddy, added her congratulations. "That's wonderful, Katherine. And as you have lived up to your end of our bargain, I'm prepared to live up to mine. I shall pay your tuition at Barnard, as long as you maintain a B average or better."

"Thank you, Mrs. Mason, but that's really far, far too generous," Margaret announced from the doorway before Katherine could utter another word.

"Nonsense, Margaret. As I said when I made the offer, in light of everything you and your family have done for Madeleine, it's the least I can do. I only hope that Katherine's drive and ambition will inspire my niece. And today, to celebrate your daughter's achievement, I'll take the girls to lunch at the Waldorf."

"Thank you, Mrs. Mason," Katherine responded. "I would go change, except I'm already wearing my best dress."

"You look lovely, dear. Would you care to join us, Margaret?" Bernice inquired, with a touch too much graciousness.

Margaret cast a sympathetic look in Maddy's direction, which Bernice mistook for reluctance. "Thank you for the invitation, but I have far too much to do today, though I'm mighty proud of Katherine. You all go, and have a fine time of it."

By the time they'd arrived at the Waldorf, Maddy's pride in Katherine's accomplishment had vanished under a pile of resentment. She wasn't jealous of Katherine's talent, just her ability to win Bernice's approval.

During the six years Maddy had lived with her aunt and uncle, they'd been generous but demanding guardians. They made clear to Maddy that performing well in school was essential, and Maddy, with a significant amount of effort, was able to do decently well in all her subjects, but she did not excel in any particular discipline. To her—and her aunt's—disappointment, she hadn't been accepted at any of the Seven Sisters, the colleges that offered the equivalent of an Ivy League education for young women. She would go, instead, to a small liberal arts college in Manhattan.

Maddy realized, even if Bernice did not, that hard work was not enough. Real achievement required passion, like Bernice's own passion for science, or Katherine's for journalism, or Uncle Archie's for making money. Maddy did not feel passionate about anything except her music.

And that was still her secret.

Maddy's misery increased during lunch, while she played with her shrimp salad and listened to Katherine and Bernice discuss Katherine's plans for the future. Her friend held up well under her aunt's interrogation better than many adults would have.

"But why psychology?" Bernice was asking Katherine. "I can understand why you would choose to study history, but why a soft discipline like psychology?"

"Because I want people to open up to me. When I'm interviewing them, I want to be able to get inside their heads."

"All you have to do is prove yourself trustworthy, and show interest."

"I don't think that's enough. There are all kinds of strange things that go into making people do what they do. The more I understand them, the better I will be at my job. And I need to improve my Spanish."

"Good heavens, why Spanish?"

"The war has already rewritten the map of the world, Mrs. Mason. All of the old empires have fallen apart, but nothing's settled in this hemisphere. You watch: Cuba, Argentina, Chile—that's where real political change will come."

"Why not study Russian? There, at least, you'll be prepared to deal with a significant country."

"The Soviet Union is a closed society. No free press there. No, this foreign correspondent is going where the action is, and the action will be in South America."

"Katherine, you are truly a remarkable young woman."

Maddy felt another prick of naked envy. Katherine always knew what her goals were, and had never been afraid to reach for them. She never felt guilty about what she wanted, or fretted about the price she might have to pay to get it. It wasn't fair.

"Madeleine? Are you listening?"

"Yes. Revolutions in South America."

"No, dear. We're beyond that. I was telling Katherine that I hope you'll discover something that interests you when you go to Hunter. I would love for Madeleine to go into medicine, Katherine. It's important that a woman have a profession, and not just for financial security. Women are as capable of finding professional satisfaction as men are. They're just seldom given the opportunity."

"But I know what I want to study. Music."

Katherine and Bernice both stared at her. She tried to think of a way to retract what she'd said, but Katherine was already off and running with it.

"Music? Why not? You know, Maddy used to take piano lessons at the convent. That's how we met."

Bernice's flagrant skepticism was plastered across her face. "Well, that's marvelous as a source of amusement, or relaxation. But as a profession, music isn't very practical, is it?"

"Journalism isn't very practical, either," Katherine countered.

Bernice considered this. "I suppose there's always a way to make ends meet at the top of one's profession; I have no doubt you have the drive and the ability to get to the top of yours, Katherine. But for Madeleine, this is something brand new."

The patronizing tone in her voice rekindled Maddy's resentment. "You said if Katherine got accepted at Barnard, you would pay for her tuition. If I can get accepted at a music school, would you pay for me to go there instead of Hunter?"

"You're not serious."

"But I am. I'm grateful for all you've done for me—"

"Now Madeleine, please—"

"And I've tried for all these years to please you in every way I could. But I want one chance to do something that I love."

"But Madeleine—"

"If I fail, I fail. Then I'll study whatever you want me to. But I want the chance."

A short, intense period of silence followed. Katherine was afraid to look at either of them, and more than a little concerned that her own scholarship could end up as part of the deal. Under the table, she crossed her fingers.

"All right," Bernice finally replied, with an exasperated sigh implying she knew she had nothing to lose. "But we must limit this experiment to serious institutions. No fly-by-night nonsense."

Maddy wanted to thank her aunt but could not, for she was completely overcome by a strange mixture of emotions: nervousness and elation, pride and embarrassment, excitement and fear.

Across the table Katherine was grinning from ear to ear. She did not know exactly what Maddy had up her sleeve, but her friend did not take any step lightly, and she wondered what Maddy had in store for them.

Saints preserve us, she said to herself, in silent homage to her mother. *Saints preserve us all.*

Maddy knew enough about music schools to know that she had to audition. Bernice did not offer to help; she had no idea what had put such a preposterous idea into Madeleine's head, and chalked it up to some sort of delayed teenage rebelliousness. She'd never caught her niece smoking, or kissing a boy, or staying out after curfew, or committing any of the other nuisance infractions that so many other children foisted upon their parents. But music? To Bernice's knowledge Madeleine had never done more than sing in the school glee club, hardly a noble start for a musical career. She had no doubt that Madeleine would be safely at Hunter College come September.

With no other guidance, Maddy made an appointment to see her music teacher, Mrs. Thomas, after school the next day.

"How nice to see you, Maddy dear. What can I do for you?" her teacher asked when she saw Maddy hovering near the door.

"I'd like to talk to you about a letter of recommendation."

"But I thought you'd already been accepted at Hunter. And really, I've only had you in glee club. I haven't been in a position to assess your academic ability."

"No, you see, I want to go to music school."

"Music school?" Mrs. Thomas repeated lamely. "What sort of music school?"

"Well, you know, like Juilliard, or somewhere like that."

"Juilliard?"

Maddy edged closer. Mrs. Thomas could see the plea in her eyes. "I know it sounds crazy, but I think I can play the piano, and if you were to work with me a little, I could audition, and then maybe I could really learn."

Mrs. Thomas knew that she couldn't refuse the girl a quick listen; they were so sensitive at this age. "Very well, Maddy. I'll pick out a piece for you. Let's go to a practice room."

Maddy practically fell over as she went to sit down on the piano bench. Mrs. Thomas placed the sheet music for Liszt's Liebestraum no. 3 in front of her. The notes swam like little black fish on the page.

"Begin anytime, Madeleine."

Although Maddy did not know the piece, it was not especially difficult, and she played it with no mistakes. When she was finished, she twisted around to face Mrs. Thomas.

"Why, that's not bad at all," Mrs. Thomas commented in an overly supportive tone of voice. Maddy could tell she was not really impressed.

"Mrs. Thomas, would you please play something?"

"I really don't see—"

"Please? Just play anything. It will help me relax."

With a sigh Mrs. Thomas resolved that she would not let this little interlude eat up her entire afternoon. The two traded places. Mrs. Thomas evaluated her choices. Her instrument was the violin, but she was quite competent on the piano. She played Beethoven's "Für Elise," a piece she knew by heart.

"How was that?"

"Perfect. Thank you," Maddy replied as they switched places. "Now I'll play it."

And she did.

"There," Maddy said, half to herself. "That was better." She turned to the astonished teacher. "Would you play another one?"

"Maddy, tell me you knew that piece when you came in here."

"No, ma'am. I mean, I've heard it before, but I've never played it. It's easier for me to play if I'm not reading. The sheet music kind of gets in the way, I guess."

"Gets in the way?" Mrs. Thomas plopped down on the bench next to Maddy. "Are you pulling some kind of trick on me? Is this the senior class prank or something?"

"Oh, no, nothing like that. I guess it must seem a little strange. I can see I made a mistake—"

"Sit back down, Maddy. How long have you been taking lessons?"

"I haven't, at least, not for a long time. But I've been playing by myself for a few years. It's sort of my hobby."

Mrs. Thomas blew out a gust of air. "Play this." She played a short Viennese waltz.

"Okay." Maddy's fingers danced along the keys, and Mrs. Thomas felt that she could have been listening to a recording of herself, except that Maddy's rendition was slightly livelier: a shade more like what a waltz should be.

Her teacher was still incredulous. "This is astounding."

"Does that mean you'll help me?"

Mrs. Thomas patted Maddy on the back. "Most definitely. It would be my great pleasure to help you. But we have very little time and even fewer choices; most schools have already held their auditions. I do know of three where you may have a chance: Northeastern, in Connecticut; Oberlin, in Ohio; and the New Music School, near Boston. Those three schools usually audition in May." She pulled a calendar out of her desk drawer and circled the three important dates. "Do you know what you must do until then?"

"Practice, practice, practice," Maddy said. "And then some more practice!"

Ten days later, Mrs. Thomas received a telephone call at her home from a rather perturbed Bernice Mason. "I'm sorry to disturb you," she said after identifying herself, "but I need to discuss something rather urgent."

"Of course, Mrs. Mason. I'm delighted to hear from you."

"Madeleine tells me that you plan to take her to an audition in Connecticut this weekend."

"Yes, that's right, at the Northeastern Academy of Music. We'd liked to have tried for Juilliard, but I'm afraid the deadline has passed."

"You must be joking."

"I beg your pardon?"

"Mrs. Thomas, you're a professional, are you not? What on earth gives you the idea that Madeleine should be embarrassing herself, and you, by showing up to audition for music school, when she has no musical training whatsoever?"

Mrs. Thomas took the receiver away from her ear and looked at it, as if that would help her make sense out of what she'd heard. "Well," she continued, "I know that Madeleine is a raw talent, but she's marvelously gifted, and has made remarkable progress given the self-taught nature of her studies."

"Self-taught? Mrs. Thomas, are we speaking about the same girl? Have you actually heard her play the piano?"

"Mrs. Mason, we've worked for hours every day for almost two weeks. As immodest as it may sound, it's a thrill to be the discoverer of such a talented prodigy. I only wish she'd have come to me years ago. She's unusually shy about her music."

"Shy? That's an understatement. She's lived with us for five years and I've never heard her play a single note on the piano we have in the library."

"Really? My goodness. You mean she's kept her ability a secret from everyone? Even you?"

"Me, her uncle, her best friend—I daresay no one knows about it, which is why I have such a difficult time taking this whole thing seriously. You don't truly think she has some sort of musical talent, do you?"

"I know she does. She has an emotional feel for music that is truly extraordinary, and the way she can play by ear, why, it's phenomenal."

"I find this quite hard to believe."

"I suppose I would, too, in your position. But you're to be commended for giving your niece this opportunity. I'm sure that she will not disappoint you."

"Do you suppose I ought to come with you to the audition?"

There was a pause on the other end of the line. "Please, don't be offended, but I don't think that would be a very good idea. Maddy is already so nervous. I'm sure you understand."

"I should have thought of that myself. You will keep me informed of her progress, yes?"

"Certainly."

Bernice hung up the phone and called Harry in Chicago. "Ruth? Hello? This is Bernice Mason. Yes, it's good to talk to you, too. No, nothing's wrong. I wonder if I might talk to Harry. Is he in?"

Bernice flipped through the mental filing cabinet in her brain while Ruth went to get her husband. Their child, the little girl they'd adopted in Switzerland during the war—what was her name? Gertrude? No, no. Gurs was the camp she'd escaped from. Gladys? Greer? Gabby? That was it. Gabriella.

"Bernice?"

"Harry, it's been so long. How are you? And how is little Gabriella?"

"Not so little; she's nearly ten already. Such a beauty, you should see her. How are you? And Archie? And Maddy?"

"We're all fine, but it's Maddy I wanted to talk to you about."

Harry listened to Bernice's entire story, glad the grin on his face was a thousand miles away. He didn't think he'd ever heard his old friend so completely flummoxed.

"You're the only person I know, personally, who's gifted musically, Harry. I remember how you used to talk about playing the violin instead of going into engineering—"

"A totally impractical choice, of course."

"Yes, but is it possible? Can one just be born with this—gift?"

"Mozart was. There have been others. You remember Martha was very musical." He caught sight of Ruth and Gabriella, heads close together as they giggled about something, and his voice caught in his throat. "There is no explaining the gifts that God brings to us, Bernice. Ruth and me, for example. We, that is, Ruth is going to have a baby."

"A baby? Now? Are you sure you want another child, at your age?"

Harry laughed. "Well, luckily for me Ruth is a good deal younger. But yes, Bernice. We do want this child. This baby is a gift."

Bernice said all the polite things required, but shook her head as she hung up the phone. Harry was well into his forties. A baby? She would never understand some people.

Maddy was not accepted at the Northeastern Academy. Mrs. Thomas assured her that she'd done quite well, but each school had a specific idea of what type of talent it wished to foster.

"You'll find your place, Madeleine," she said reassuringly as the train rumbled back into Grand Central Station.

But I never have, Mrs. Thomas. I never have.

The next week they went to Cambridge, outside Boston, for Maddy's audition at the New Music School. When her name was called she took a seat on the piano bench and closed her eyes. She could not bear failure again. A few seconds ticked by. She heard someone cough. She heard a rustle of papers. *Let it all go away. Just reach inside, and find the music.* Her fingers started to move.

There was silence when she finished. A man was coming toward her. "Miss Hoffman, do you know Mozart's Piano Concerto no. 12 in A? The finale?"

"No, sir."

"If I play it for you, would you try to play it by ear?"

"I could try."

"Here—no, don't get up, scoot over a bit—that will do." Maddy was completely unaware of the many eyes glued on them. As the man next to her played, she watched his fingers. Then she closed her eyes. She could see the keyboard in her mind, and hear where his fingers were landing. She could see them stretch and curl, feel the downward pressure of his foot as he reached for the pedals. The music wrote itself into her brain.

There was polite applause as he finished.

He moved off the bench and gestured to Maddy. "If you please."

Maddy positioned her fingers, then readjusted them. She felt completely confident. When she'd finished, the man's face told her all she needed to know.

"Welcome to the New Music School," he said. "I'm Ernest Auerbach, and I will be your piano instructor."

She gave him one of her mother's radiant smiles.

SEVENTEEN
LONDON, 1949

He never thought he would see her again, and, in the deepest depths of his imagination, he never dreamed it would be so easy. All he had to do was ask.

Word got around that there was a pub in London, not far from Westminster Abbey, that had become a haven for the veterans of the army of shadows. It was the place where an undercover operative who'd won the Victoria Cross could leave behind his job as a file clerk in the office where no one remembered his name, and chat for a while with the men who shared his memories; where the man who now sold cars for a living could down a pint with someone he'd lived with in a cave for three days, not to talk, just to sit, because the sound of the other man's breathing had been all he'd heard for those three days, all he'd had to let him know that he was still alive. There were those who told the same stories over and over, and those who never spoke. They'd fought the war using assumed identities, risking their lives to make one radio broadcast or deliver one case of dynamite to blow up a train. And they'd survived, only to drown in the boredom of postwar life in London.

Leo sat at the bar, nursing a beer. Someone in this group would know what happened to Christine. He started with the bartender.

"Christine Granville? Lord yes, she survived the war, with enough medals to anchor a bloody battleship. Do you know her?"

"We met briefly in Cairo. She was very competent."

"That's one word for it. Think they'd have kept her on, don't you? One like her? Saved the head of the whole French operation she did, right before the end. But no. They dumped her off with the same month's pay they handed the lot of us. As if there's no more work to do, with Stalin eyeing every choice piece of real estate we won back from the Krauts with our own blood and guts."

"Do you ever see her around here?"

"Not her. Runs with a fancier crowd, she does. She's in and out of London all the time, though. Just got back from Nairobi, last I heard. Been living with some rich duffer who's starting up a tourist business there. That'd be the life, eh? Hunting lions, coming back to camp to find a hot meal and a cool glass of whiskey ready in your tent?"

Leo imagined Christine stretched out on a thick rug on the floor of a safari tent, skin warm from the sun, her bright brown eyes alight with desire. *Enough of that.*

The bartender leaned forward. "You're not the first one to ask about her. She made her mark, didn't she?"

"I guess she did." He paid for his beer and left.

She was alive. Did she know he'd survived? Probably not. He lived a life so fine-tuned by fabrications, at this point he didn't think his own supervisor knew his real name or where he was from. Leo Hoffman was probably already dead on paper somewhere, if there was even a piece of paper still around with his name on it, and surely nothing would be left from his time as a British asset. The Brits started shredding their files right after the war, and an "accidental" office fire at SOE headquarters had expedited the process of reinventing the past. The army of shadows disintegrated in a cloud of smoke.

He had a week in London before he went back to Berlin. After that he'd start working his way east, digging farther and deeper, until he could attach himself to some vital organ of this new enemy and suck information out like a tick.

He had seven days. How hard could it be to find her? He was a spy, after all.

He watched her as she exited the apartment. The turn of her wrist as she locked the door, the way she glanced up at the sky before putting on her sunglasses, the half-knot she tied into the belt of her jacket, the shape of her slightly too-thin calves: all this registered in his brain like individual notes in a piece of music he'd memorized long ago. He half expected her to wave to him, for it did not seem possible that he could be so acutely aware of her without her knowing that he stood only a few feet away.

He spoke to her as she was about to get on a bus, patiently allowing a bent old woman to make her exit before boarding herself.

"Christine, wait."

He could not see her eyes behind her dark glasses, but every inch of her body suddenly grew still. Then she took a step back and waved the bus driver on.

"Is that really you?"

He took a step closer. "It's me."

She flew at him, throwing her arms around his neck with such force it put him off balance, and for a second he thought they were both going to end up in a pile on the pavement, but he steadied himself and held on to her, saying nothing, resting his face against her soft brown hair.

"You made it," she murmured into his ear.

"I did."

She slid out of his embrace, but did not let go of his hands. "And now?"

"Can we go somewhere and talk?"

She dropped his hands and lifted her glasses, revealing the familiar sparkle in her eyes: one of the lights he'd used to help him stay alive during two years of darkness.

"We can go to my apartment. I live close by."

"I know."

Christine rolled her eyes, he laughed, and she punched his shoulder.

"Enough spying. Come, have a drink with me."

But the apartment wasn't hers. It was Andrew's. He saw a picture on the mantel of the two of them, taken together somewhere in the Middle East, both looking into the camera with vibrant joy. And then the truth he'd being trying to ignore hit him full in the face; his fantasy that somehow he and Christine could be together was no more than a delusion. It would, of course, always be Andrew, just as for him it would always be Martha. The difference between them was that Martha was dead.

"Where's Andrew?"

She looked surprised. "In the hospital. You didn't know? He was in a terrible car accident. Unconscious for days. I was in Nairobi at the time."

"Nairobi?"

She nodded. "Sherry all right with you? So British, but I'm used to it by now."

"That's fine."

"Have a seat. It's all right here."

He sat on the couch in front of the fireplace, took off his hat, and put it down next to him. She crossed the room and began chatting with the same vivacious animation Leo remembered, while she pulled two glasses and a crystal decanter out of a cabinet.

"Have you ever been to East Africa? You know I was there with my husband, in Kenya, when the war broke out. I enjoyed being back. So warm, so beautiful. I've always loved the sun."

"But you weren't with your husband this time, were you?"

This seemed to catch her off guard. Leo had the feeling she'd read some unintended criticism into his question. He tried again.

"I mean, you're divorced now, aren't you?"

She handed him his drink. "I was there with a friend. He invited me to help him organize a tourist business. But I suppose you know that already, don't you?"

A friend. The chill in her tone informed Leo that he'd stepped out of bounds. He took the sherry she offered him, trying to figure out how to start the conversation over.

"I hope Andrew is recovering well. I didn't know that he was—"

"He's doing quite well. His doctor assured me that he'll be home in a few days."

"Well, here's to Andrew's health." He took a sip of his drink. She did the same, and then sat down across from Leo without taking her eyes off him.

"Tell me what happened, Leo. After you left the camp. I heard that Val and Charles made it across the border with most of the women and children. Daniel was hurt, and you disappeared."

"I was shot and captured. Not shot, really. I think I was hit in the head by a shovel I was carrying when a bullet ricocheted off it. At any rate I woke up in a Vichy hospital, where the nurses, at least, thought I was German. But the commanding officer figured me out. Luckily they needed a few warm bodies to dig for coal, so I was sent to a work camp instead of being shot right away. I escaped. I went to America for a brief time. Then I came back to Europe."

"And your daughter? Did you find her?"

"Yes, I did." That was all he was going to say about that.

She didn't inquire further. "I never got to thank you for agreeing to help us."

"We didn't, any of us, really do it to be thanked, did we?"

Something about this comment enraged her, but as her words exploded in the small room it became obvious that her rancor was not aimed at him.

"No, we didn't fight in the war to be thanked. But a little more gratitude would have been helpful. At first they didn't trust me; then, after I accomplished something, they said I was 'too hard to handle,' and cut me out the minute the war was over."

She got up and began to pace back and forth in the small room, arms crossed, not bothering to temper her bitterness.

"It took me three years to get a proper British passport, did you know that? I couldn't get any sort of decent job without credentials. I worked as a telephone operator. I sold clothes at Harrods. I worked in the linen room at a hotel. I'm not afraid of hard work; you know that. But to be so useless . . ."

Her anger dissipated as suddenly as it had arrived. She settled back into her chair with a loud sigh.

"I can't imagine that you'd ever be useless, Christine."

This made her smile. She picked up her drink but did not taste it. "I suppose some of us are just not suited to the rhythm of ordinary life. What about you? Your life has never been ordinary, either. Have you found a place for yourself?"

"I think so."

She did not ask him to elaborate. "Good. I'm happy for you."

I'm not so sure I'm all that happy for me. When was the last time he'd felt real happiness? Had it been in this woman's arms?

"So do you plan on going back to Africa?"

"No. Andrew needs me here. We're going to have to find some way to make a living."

What if I needed you, Christine? Would that matter to you? Would it make a difference? Would it change both of our lives, right now, at this moment?

If the Russians could read him as easily as she could, he'd soon be a dead man. He saw the compassion in her eyes and it made him concentrate on his drink, just to have somewhere else to look, other than into those eyes.

"Leo," she said softly, "I'm sorry."

There were suddenly no more words. He could speak seven languages, and there wasn't a single word in his head. He drained his glass, put it down, picked up his hat, and got up.

"Thanks for the drink."

She closed her eyes and winced, as if she'd felt a sharp pain run through her chest. Leo headed toward the hallway. He stopped when he got to the door, waiting, hoping, hearing nothing. As he reached for the handle he heard her say, "Good luck, my dear friend."

He turned and looked at her: so small, so fragile. Stronger than anyone he'd ever known.

"Thank you," he said, and left.

Three years later Leo learned that Christine Granville had been murdered, stabbed to death in the hallway of her apartment building by a man who had briefly been her lover, then decided he'd rather hang than lose her to another man.

EIGHTEEN
BOSTON, 1950

"Oh, c'mon, Maddy. It's New Year's Eve, for cryin' out loud. The beginning of a new decade! You can't just sit in the dorm and listen to the radio. What's the matter with a blind date?"

Maddy shook her head. "No, thanks, Vick."

"You'd really be helping us out. We need three girls, on account of a friend of theirs just got stood up, and Allen and Theo don't want to leave him alone crying into his petri dish on New Year's. The med school guys don't have a lot of time to socialize, you know. It's not like dating some jock from BU."

"You should know," Maddy commented, with a smile that took the sting out of her words.

"Geez, Maddy. This from Little Miss Stuck-in-the-Dorm. The only guy you ever went out with was that guy from MIT, and he didn't last long."

"I didn't know you kept such close tabs on my social life."

"It's not difficult. Please, for me, one night out. Otherwise, the next time you need help in Composition 110, I'll tell you to blow it out your tuba."

Maddy could not help but laugh. "Okay, Miss Vicki Violin. What's the dress code?"

"That's swell, Maddy! And we'll be going to a private club for sure. These guys are loaded. You want to borrow something? Something a little more festive? Who am I kidding, anything I own would fall right off you. But thanks. You really saved us."

"Don't mention it."

Maddy started to regret her decision less than an hour later, after she'd strewn every outfit she owned across the length and width of her small dorm room. Vicki was right. She dressed like an old woman. She bought her clothes on shopping junkets when she went home on vacation or when Bernice came to visit, and her choices were heavily influenced by her aunt's conservative taste. Going one more time to her closet, she spotted her recital dress from the previous year. It was an understated black silk, but fashionably cut, with a pinched-in waist and a full skirt that fell in supple pleats to midcalf. Three little pearl buttons on the bodice led the way to a demure, narrow collar of white satin.

Maddy tried on the dress. She unbuttoned the collar, exposing a small V of flesh, and put on the triple-strand pearl choker Bernice and Archie had given her for her eighteenth birthday. The result was not really festive, but it was sophisticated. Confident. Everything she felt sitting at a piano, and nowhere else.

As she consulted the mirror for a final inspection she noticed, not for the first time, how much she resembled her mother. But no amount of affirmation from the mirror could make her feel beautiful. The beauty belonged to her mother. Maddy could not claim it.

The young men picked up their dates at seven o'clock. The six of them piled into Theo's enormous gold Cadillac, made introductions all around, and then the boys began to debate the best way to make it to the restaurant, given the traffic and the icy weather. Maddy took advantage of their distraction to study her date, Brad Gordon. He looked nice enough. His face was square, his nose long and masculine. Dark lashes fringed his brown eyes. His hair was more of a golden brown, and might have been wavy, had he not worn it fashionably glued down and brushed straight back from his forehead.

He caught her gazing at him and smiled back at her with a teasing look in his eyes. She blushed and lowered her gaze to her hands, daintily folded in her lap.

"Cute little hands," he said, lightly tapping one of her gloved knuckles with his forefinger.

"They're too small," she said automatically, then wished she hadn't.

"Why?"

"They're too small to reach a tenth on the piano."

"A tenth?"

"Any key, and the key that's ten keys away from it. At first I could only reach one octave, an eighth. I play a ninth, but I'll never make a tenth."

"So are you doomed? No Brahms or something like that?"

"Well, some pieces I'll never be able to play, but most of the time, I can cheat. I alter the fingering."

"Aha! I've discovered your secret. And when you play in Carnegie Hall, I will rise up and shout, 'Cheater! Cheater!' in the middle of your performance, and let the music-going public know about your foul schemes."

Maddy laughed, and he laughed with her. Then he held his own right hand out in front of him. "A surgeon's hands don't have to be large. Just steady," he explained.

Maddy was beginning to be very glad that she had come along.

They had cocktails and dinner in a restaurant that overlooked Boston Harbor, where the boys amused their dates with entertaining, sometimes gory tales about what could go wrong when trying to remove internal organs, and macabre stories about the stupid things people had done to themselves to land in the emergency room. Theo was in the middle of a story about the time their landlady had gone onto his back porch and fainted when she found a brain he'd been keeping in a bucket for his biology lab when Anna pleaded enough.

"Oh, please. I've never seen a dead person, and I hope I never do."

"Oh, you sheltered little musicians. Have any of you ever seen a corpse?" Allen queried, doing a decent impression of Bela Lugosi.

"I have," Maddy said in a low voice.

"You're kidding."

"Oh, God, Maddy. Yuck."

"In a funeral parlor, right?"

"In Shanghai," she said, quelling the general clamor.

"That's my friend," Vicki quipped, "Madeleine, the Mysterious Lady from Shanghai."

Brad was looking directly at Maddy, and she was struck by the sympathy she saw in his eyes.

"Okay," he announced. "Enough of the gory stuff. Let's finish dinner and go dance."

When they pulled up to the dorm at the end of the evening, Brad bounded out and helped Maddy out of the car. The two other couples obviously had some extended happy New Year kissing to do, and Maddy was grateful that Brad did not expect her to participate.

They moved quickly as an icy blast of air whipped in from the river. "I had a good time tonight," Brad told her when they reached the dormitory door. "I hope I can see you again."

"I'd like that."

"Okay, good. Well, happy New Year." Tucking his hand under her chin, he lifted her face and kissed her quickly on the lips. Before she could object he was on his way back to the car.

"Hands in the air, gentlemen! I'm coming in!"

"So are you telling me you like him?"

"I don't know, Katherine. He seems nice."

"Maddy, give me the scoop. Where's he from? What does his family do? What kind of medicine does he want to practice?"

"Whoa, slow down. It was a date, not an interview. He's from Marblehead, north of Boston. His family is in the banking business. He's the fifth generation to go to Harvard College, but the first to go to medical school. He's an only child, like me. And he has a good sense of humor. He made me laugh."

"Is he going to call you?"

"I think so."

"Keep me posted?"

"Sure. No secrets from you, Queen Snoop."

"You mean Queen of the *Scoop*, don't you?"

Over the next few months Maddy had many dates with Brad to report. He took her to the Harvard hockey games. He took her to the movies. He took her out for dinner. Then, in May, he took her to the symphony.

As they entered the music hall he looked around, a sheepish expression on his face. "We may run into my parents at intermission," he said apologetically. "They have a box. They'll probably only stay to hear the guest soloist, but we might bump into them in the lobby."

"I'd love to meet them." At this, Brad grimaced, leaving Maddy to wonder why.

They did see his mother and father at intermission. Mrs. Gordon was tall, and had Brad's warm brown coloring. Mr. Gordon was both tall and broad, and his once-blond hair had faded to silver. He had a deep, mellifluous voice, but moved awkwardly, as if he'd never quite adjusted to his own size. They were cordial, but not friendly. Mr. Gordon asked Maddy a great many pointed questions about her family. She told him that her father had disappeared during the war and that her mother was dead. He did appear to be impressed when she told him that her guardians were the Masons, of Mason Industries. Brad's mother said little, but seemed to be examining Maddy closely. They made no plans to meet after the concert.

"Well, not exactly cozy, are they?" Brad muttered in Maddy's ear as they retook their seats.

"What makes you say that? They were very civil."

"What a diplomat. Yes, they were civil. But they won't be, once they smell the threat."

"What threat?"

He looked at her intently and squeezed her hand as the orchestra started to play. "That you might take me away from them," he said lightly.

She dared not ask him to explain what he meant, not that she really needed to ask. Although she had fond feelings for Brad, she hadn't thought about marriage. But maybe she should. She was nearly twenty-one. Many girls her age were already married. Her mother ran away to marry her father when she was eighteen. But her aunt had married late, and Katherine did not plan to get married at all. Maddy remembered their conversation the previous summer, when Katherine had astounded her with her unorthodox views on the subject of wedded bliss.

"Why get married if you don't want to have kids? I have enough nieces and nephews to keep me happy when I want to hug a baby or change a diaper. I don't want to live at anyone else's beck and call, trapped in the house by a bunch of screaming brats. I think I'll skip that particular adventure."

"But don't you want to fall in love?" Maddy had asked her, thinking of love as a sort of magic spell that happened to you all at once, like in the movies.

"Of course I'll fall in love. And I'll have lovers, and they'll leave me, and I'll leave them, and one day my love letters will be found in an attic somewhere and be worth a fortune. But marriage? I don't think so."

Maddy wondered how Katherine, with her solid Catholic upbringing, could comfortably plan her life in a way that would assure a direct descent straight into hell, if hell actually existed. During her years at Catholic school Maddy had absorbed the message preached by the nuns; nice girls keep their legs crossed. Sex meant children, and children were reserved for marriage. Despite the fact that over time Maddy's childhood Catholicism had gradually devolved into a sort of disorganized agnosticism, some of the admonitions planted in her psyche by the good sisters stayed put—this one, more than any other: fornication was a sin.

Not that they actually discussed the sexual act: that was the subject of intense speculation and whispered gossip. At least it had been until, much to Maddy's chagrin, her aunt took her to lunch before she left for Cambridge and bluntly explained to her the "facts of life."

"Ignorance is dangerous, Madeleine. I trust you to be sensible. But you must know enough to protect yourself."

Then, fully armed with what Bernice considered to be appropriate knowledge, Maddy never had anything to protect herself from. She did not know that her shyness was often mistaken for snobbery, that her beauty was as intimidating as it was attractive. But she saw what other girls went through while chasing boys, and she didn't think she was missing much. Her passion was her music.

The morning after the symphony she called her aunt. Sunday morning was one of the few days she could generally count on finding her home.

"Hello, Aunt Bernice? It's Maddy. How are you?"

"Fine, dear. Are you calling to say hello, or do you have something on your mind?"

Maddy smiled to herself. Trust her aunt to cut right to the chase. "Well, I was wondering. This boy I've been dating, Brad? I think he's starting to get serious."

"My goodness. How do you feel about that?"

"I'm not sure."

Bernice cleared her throat. "Maddy dear. I know you're old enough to make up your own mind, but you must decide what is truly important: your music, or being someone's wife. He may accept your talent now, but once he's a doctor, that may change. And . . ." She paused.

"And what?"

"There's the religion issue to consider."

"Religion? What does that have to do with anything?"

"Madeleine, don't be so naïve."

Maddy tried to conceal her indignation. "The world is not the same place it was before the war, you know. I don't have to worry about the same things you and my father worried about."

"The world never changes, Madeleine. When circumstances become difficult, people become irrational. And even if that doesn't concern you, you should finish school before thinking about marriage."

Maddy did not respond. Bernice, as usual, read her silence as assent. "We'll be there for your recital, and can meet this young man then, yes?"

"I hope so. He has exams, but he's going to try to make it."

"Very well. Be sure to get plenty of rest."

"I will, thank you. Good-bye."

On an impulse Maddy dug into the bottom of her tiny closet, where she kept a box of mementos: the program from her first recital, her letters from Katherine, autographs of some of the famous musicians who had made an appearance at the school. At the bottom was her parents' wedding picture.

She had not looked at it in a long time. Now she scrutinized it, trying to distill from the expressions on their faces how they'd felt about each other. She could remember walking in between them, each of her hands in one of theirs, playing the game of "one, two, three," when on the count of three her parents would sail her out in front of them and she would hold on tight, knowing that she could fly through the air and that they'd never let her fall. She remembered the warm smile her father gave her mother each morning at the breakfast table, and the way the two of them would sneak a kiss if they thought she wasn't paying attention. Maddy knew with absolute certainty that when she was young, there had been love in her house.

After a while she put the picture away. Even after all these years, she couldn't look at it for too long without feeling an uncomfortable full-ness in her chest.

Her aunt was right. Brad had one more year of medical school, then his residency. She wanted to graduate and go on to some sort of career in music. They were both too busy to think about marriage yet. Soon it would be summer. She was going to spend it in Manhattan, room-ing with Katherine, in a sublet apartment in Midtown. Katherine had landed a summer job with the *New York Daily News*, and Maddy would spend the summer studying with a new teacher who, Mr. Auerbach swore, would do marvelous things for her technique.

"He's a dragon. A dragon's dragon, but a gifted one. If he doesn't scare you to death, you will blossom under his instruction," Mr. Auer-bach had advised. Maddy did not intend to let him intimidate her.

On a Saturday afternoon in mid-June, Maddy was at the corner market picking up the staples she and Katherine needed to get them through the week. She reached up for a jar of olive oil on the top shelf but couldn't quite get it. Slipping off her shoes, she stepped up on the ledge of the bottom shelf, and stretched her arm up as high as it would go.

"Can I help you with that?"

Maddy came down, olive oil in hand, embarrassed that she'd been caught climbing.

"No, thanks. I got it, after all."

"You live in the Bordeaux Apartments, don't you?"

"Yes," Maddy answered warily, slipping her feet back into her loafers.

"I do, too. I thought I recognized you. You're the piano player. I mean the pianist."

Maddy was eager to retreat. "I'm sorry if my playing disturbs you."

"Quite the contrary. It's beautiful. Like you."

Maddy went a shade pinker. He'd paid her this compliment as if he were talking about the weather. Did he really live in her apartment building? If so, how could she—or Katherine—have missed him? He was gorgeous: tall, broad-shouldered, with rough-textured curly black hair, and large gray, not-quite-blue eyes. His face was full and rounded, but all the features in it were firmly cut and masculine. Maddy caught herself ogling and tried to think of something to say.

"I . . . well . . ."

"I'm sorry if I embarrassed you," he said with obvious sincerity.

"Um, well. Thank you—"

"Gene. Gene Mandretti. I live in the penthouse. From my balcony I can see you when you and the red-haired girl are on your balcony, and when you play with the window open, I can hear you play the piano. But I don't want you to think I spy on you, or anything like that. I just love your music." He smiled at her. His teeth were white and even.

Maddy did not know how to react. He was a complete stranger, yet there was something familiar about him: the comfortable ease of his stance, and the careless charm with which he spoke. "Well," she said, completely at a loss, "you should come by sometime. We always have people dropping in for dinner, if you like spaghetti."

"I love spaghetti. I'm Italian." He said this while making stereotypical Italian hand gestures, and Maddy had to stifle a giggle.

"Madeleine Hoffman. Most people call me Maddy."

He put his hand forward, as did she, and they both laughed as she realized she was still holding on to the bottle of olive oil.

"Can I give you a hand home with your groceries? It's no trouble. I'm going that way, after all."

"Well, if you're sure you don't mind."

"No, it would be my pleasure," he said as if he really meant it.

They went through the checkout counter together and he picked up both bags of groceries, carrying the two of them easily. Maddy walked next to him, suddenly acutely aware of her own small stature. Everything about Gene was so . . . big. His eyes. His hands. The way he moved through space.

"So you're in New York for the summer?" he asked.

"How did you know that?"

"I know the Jasons, the couple you're renting from. They went to Greece for the whole summer. He's a professor at Columbia. He's the one who plays the piano. But not like you."

"And are you here for the summer?"

"No, I live here. I'm finishing up my degree at NYU. Then I'll go to work."

"What are you studying?"

"Business. Finance. The boring stuff."

"Are you really bored?"

"Not today." He smiled at her again. Maddy felt a peculiar tingle at the base of her neck.

Gene carried her groceries all the way to Maddy's door. Unsure whether Katherine was home or what state of dress she might be in, she insisted on taking them inside herself while thanking Gene profusely.

"Don't mention it. All it will take to pay me back is one spaghetti dinner."

"How about next week?"

"Great. Can I call you?"

"Sure."

"So, then, can I have your number?"

"That would help, wouldn't it?" She put down her groceries, fished around in the bag for the receipt, found a pen in her purse, scribbled her number on the back of it, and gave it to him.

"Until Saturday. About seven?"

"I'm looking forward to it. Ciao."

Buzzing with excitement, Maddy dashed into the apartment. Katherine was not there. Good. She wanted to keep this to herself. This feeling.

She ran to the piano and grabbed a pile of sheet music. It slipped through her fingers and fell to the floor. She sat down. She closed her eyes. Beethoven. It had to be Beethoven. Music that would sound the way she felt: music written to make everyone who heard it feel this way.

NINETEEN

"Oh, Katherine," Maddy wailed in despair, "you can't do this to me. I told Gene there would be a bunch of us here. Vicki and Allen have already canceled. He wants to meet you, and I can't have a man over alone. What will he think?"

"Oh, don't be such a baby. He can come over any night, can't he? He lives right upstairs. This is the first time I've been invited to cover the night police beat and I can't miss it. Call this guy up and tell him you're sick or something."

Maddy glared at her friend. She knew the police beat was an opportunity Katherine had been lobbying for all summer and that it was, truly, a great opportunity. *But what about my plans?* Why did she always come in last?

Katherine was starting to look a little guilty. "Listen, I'll make it up to you. And I'll call him right now if you want, to explain."

"No, thank you," said Maddy curtly. "Go and report on some hideous crime of some kind or another. I'll make the excuses."

Katherine hovered at the door, wanting to make amends but not willing to alter her position. When it became clear that Maddy was ignoring her, she stomped out.

Maddy picked up the phone and dialed Gene's number. She already knew it by heart.

"Hello?"

"Hi, Gene, it's Maddy. I'm sorry to have to cancel so last minute, but everyone has bailed out of my dinner party tonight. Katherine has to work, and my other friends were invited to Long Island for the weekend."

"And feeding me all alone wouldn't be a good idea, I guess."

"Oh, Gene, it's only that—"

"No problem. But is there rule against my inviting you out for dinner?"

Maddy glanced over at the kitchen counter, where a caesar salad awaited its dressing, garlic bread sat buttered, ready to be heated, and her homemade spaghetti sauce simmered on the stove.

"But I asked you—"

"I know, but things happen. Put the spaghetti in the fridge. Can you be ready in an hour?"

"Yes, but—"

"No buts. I've been looking forward to this evening all week. See you at seven."

He knocked promptly at seven. Maddy opened the door. She'd thought about his smile for seven days.

"Hi, angel," he said warmly, holding out his hand to take hers. His blue-gray eyes shimmered with amusement. "I sure am sorry to miss that spaghetti, but I'm not sorry to have you all to myself. Not too disappointed, I hope?"

"No, in fact, I'm beginning to think I'm glad it worked out this way. Where shall we go?"

"Wherever your heart desires. Atlantis? Mount Olympus? My chariot awaits your command," he answered as he pushed the elevator call button.

"Well, my plans fell through, so now you're in charge."

He brought her hand to his lips. He did not kiss it, so much as barely connect his mouth to it, right behind her knuckles. His eyes never left hers. Just when she thought she must snatch her hand away or faint, he released her.

He did not touch her again the entire evening.

They walked to a small French café nearby. He asked her a lot of questions about herself, and she found herself answering freely. It had taken Brad weeks to pry the same information out of her. Yet here she was, telling Gene all about her childhood in Shanghai, her mother's death, how she came to live with the O'Connors, her decision to live with her aunt rather than be with her father, and her desire to go to music school. He asked enough questions to keep her talking, but seldom commented, except for an occasional expression of sympathy. Gene listened intently, as if he were determined to remember every word; not only what she said but how she said it: every nuance of her voice, every gesture.

"And you never heard from your father again?"

"No. The two weeks we spent together when he came to New York, right before he went to Europe, are the last pleasant memories I have of him. It's funny though, how I sometimes think I see his face in a crowd. And I dream about being back at our home in Shanghai. A lot of them are bad dreams, but some happy times creep in as well."

"Was your aunt ever able to track him down?"

"She was able to get some information from her contacts in the Defense Department. More lies. He never worked for the OSS."

"What a bastard, if you'll pardon my saying so."

"Pardon given. What about you?"

"What would you like to know?"

"Did you fight in the war?"

"Nope. Wasn't drafted until forty-five, and hadn't even finished up at Fort Benning before Hitler caved."

"That was lucky. Well, let's see. Were you born in New York?"

"No. New Jersey."

"Brothers and sisters?"

"Two sisters."

"Do they have names?"

"Doreen and Lucia."

"Younger or older?"

"Both younger."

"You're not making this easy, you know."

"It's not where you came from that's important. It's what you make of yourself."

He said this in a tone not really in keeping with the conversation. Maddy wasn't sure how to continue. "I'm sorry if I was being too inquisitive."

"I'm the one who should be apologizing. Sorry. I'll tell you anything you want to know about me. Next question."

"You said you were Italian. Are your parents Italian? Born-in-Italy Italian?"

"Yes, they were. They're both dead now. My dad died a few years ago. Mom died last year."

"I'm sorry."

"Don't be. She never got over my dad's death. She wasn't a happy person."

"Oh." Maddy tried to shift the conversation to something a little less somber.

"Have you ever been to Italy?"

"Yes. When I was a boy."

"Did you like it?"

He told her stories about his summer in Italy. He described the wind in the cliffs on the seashore; the sight of old women, wrapped in black, coming out of church on Sunday; the houses put together from pieces of ancient Roman ruins. He made her laugh with a tale about trying to get a moody donkey to do what it was told, and described in detail the process of harvesting and pressing the olives that were the source of sustenance for so many.

"I'm glad I got there before the war. I hear it's ruined now."

"Do you want to go back?"

"No. My life is here." He signaled for the waiter to bring their check.

"What will you do when you graduate?"

"I'm going to join my uncle in the family business."

"Which is?"

"He owns some restaurants down in Jersey, some commercial real estate, and does some import business. He's hoping my education will help me come up with a brilliant plan for diversifying his portfolio."

"And will it?"

"I have some ideas. Shall we go somewhere else for dessert?"

"I couldn't eat another thing."

He got up, walked around to her side of the table, and pulled out her chair for her. *I can't believe how badly I want him to touch me,* she thought.

When dating Brad and the few other boys she'd been out with, she looked forward to a good-night kiss with a little prickle of anticipation, but nothing like this. She felt as if her entire body had been exposed to some sort of radiation, and only his touch would soothe her. Soothe her, or set her aflame.

As they walked back she tried to detect some sign that he felt it, too: this longing, this tantalizing tension. But he gave her no clues. Her heart was pounding by the time they reached her door. She went to unlock it, but one word from him stopped her.

"Angel."

She swiveled around to face him, leaning against her unopened door for support. Her mouth was so dry. He propped one arm up against the door, somewhere above her shoulder, and leaned down until his face was inches away from hers.

Maddy willed him to kiss her.

But he didn't. Maddy wanted to reach out and touch him, but her hands were riveted to her sides, trapped by the intensity of the look in his eyes.

Then he backed away. "Thank you for a wonderful evening."

She nodded, too shaken to speak.

"May I call you again?"

"Yes, of course," she faltered.

"Good night." But he made no move to leave. She did not know what to do. She turned around and found her key dangling from the keyhole. She unlocked the door, stepped into her apartment, and then checked behind her. Gene just stood there, motionless, gazing at her with those eyes. She felt an unexpected quiver of apprehension and reached for the open door.

"Good night," she said, and closed it. Rather than move away she put her ear to the door. The sound of his footsteps told her that he was gone.

"God, how crazy," she said aloud to no one. "He was a perfect gentleman. What on earth were you afraid of?"

She ran one hand over the top of her head and down her neck, unconsciously imitating a gesture of her father's. She wandered aimlessly toward the kitchen, put her purse down on the counter, and then walked toward the piano. She played until the sweat poured from her skin and her fingers shook with exertion. Then she realized that she was not afraid of Gene. She was not afraid of what he might do to her.

She was afraid of how she felt when she was with him.

Don't see him again, Maddy. You can't. You're only here for the summer, anyway. Brad is your boyfriend. Leave Gene alone, she lectured herself as she stepped into the shower. She turned the water on, cold, full blast, and stifled a yelp.

Katherine arrived home the next morning at dawn. She bounded into the room, long legs full of energy, as if she were ready to lead the Charge of the Light Brigade. Maddy was sitting on the couch, book in hand.

"Oh, Maddy, I can't thank you enough. It was fantastic. You wouldn't believe what goes on in Times Square at night. Why, there's a whole diff—what's wrong?"

"What do you mean? Nothing's wrong."

Katherine sat next to her on the couch. "I don't know. You look a little strange. Are you still pissed off?"

"Katherine!"

"Sorry. Ya hang out with the boys, you start to talk like 'em. Did you have to cancel?"

"Not exactly. Gene took me out to dinner instead."

"Did you have fun?"

"Yes."

"Is he going to call you?"

"I think so."

"Do you like him better than old Brad the Fourth?"

"No. I don't know. I mean, he's a friend."

"Did your first date with Bradley keep you up all night?"

"Oh, you idiot. I was waiting up for you. I was worried. Don't be a creep."

"I withdraw the question. Well, kiddo, Brad is in Europe touring the continent until August, right? So you're entitled to explore other options. Give this guy until Wednesday. Tuesday is too early to call. Wednesday says, 'I like you, but I'm cool.'"

"Now you sound like a beatnik."

"Harlem, baby. Harlem has the beat. Dave's gonna take me to a club."

"Oh, go to sleep," Maddy retorted, seriously annoyed. Annoyed with Katherine, and herself.

Gene did not call the next day. He did not call on Monday. He did not call on Tuesday, or Wednesday, or Thursday. Maddy's piano teacher lambasted her for her poor performance during the week. By Friday she was morose and difficult to live with. By Saturday she'd convinced herself that she did not care. He was just a friend, after all. A new acquaintance. Just a boy.

On Sunday morning, Katherine and Maddy were stretched out on the living room floor in their bathrobes, reading the *New York Times* and the *Daily News*. The remains of a bagel-and-cream-cheese breakfast lay strewn about the floor.

There was a knock at the door.

"You get it," both girls said simultaneously.

Katherine sighed. "Who could get in without being announced, anyway? Isn't there a doorman on Sunday?"

Maddy's head jerked up with a start.

"Oh, my God. Katherine. You get it. Please. I've got to change." She raced into the bedroom.

"Hey, what's your problem?" Katherine yelled after her. The visitor knocked again. She unfolded her legs and kicked through the papers on the floor.

"Coming. Hold your horses. Commm-ing," she sang out, resigned to her fate.

She yanked the door open, and her jaw dropped.

"Whoops. We weren't really expecting company."

"You must be Katherine," Gene greeted her. "I'm sorry we missed each other last Saturday."

"Yeah, me, too. That means you're Gene, right? Nice to meet you. Please excuse the glamorous attire." She indicated her bathrobe. "My tuxedo is being cleaned. Maddy is currently indisposed. She shall emerge momentarily. But please, come in.

"Oh, Maddy, it's a friend of yours," Katherine called out in a comical falsetto as she led Gene into the living room. Over her shoulder she asked him, "Would you like some coffee? There may be a cup left."

"No, thanks. I've had mine."

"Sports section?"

"Sure. Thanks."

Katherine tried not to gawk as Gene settled down on the couch and sifted through the sports pages. She tried to remember if she had ever seen such a good-looking man in her life, in civilian clothes, anyway. All guys looked good in a uniform.

"So do you think the Yankees stand a chance this year?" she ad-libbed, trying to make conversation.

"Do you care?"

"Sure. I'm a fan from way back."

They discussed baseball for a good five minutes before Maddy reentered, metamorphosis complete. She was dressed in a striped two-piece pantsuit. The cropped top revealed a hint of her midriff. The ponytail was gone. She wore red lipstick.

Katherine raised her eyebrows. "Well, it's about time. 'Scuse me, Gene, but I believe it's my turn in the shower. Come by again sometime when I have clothes on." She walked into the bedroom, shutting the door firmly behind her.

"She's an original," Gene commented, with a look communicating his approval.

"Yes, she is. And my best friend since I was nine."

"Well, I'm sorry if I came by at an inconvenient time, but I was won-dering—hoping—it's so beautiful out today, would you like to go sail-ing?"

"Sailing?"

"My uncle has a boat on Long Island. He's out of town, so he won't be using it. Would you like to come?"

The coy conversation that Maddy had been rehearsing all week fled from her brain. "I'd love to. Do I—"

"You won't need a thing. Well, a bathing suit, maybe."

"I'll be right back."

She dashed back into the bedroom. Katherine was sitting on the bed, a slightly amused, slightly envious expression on her face.

"No wonder you were pissed off," she said.

"Hush. We're going sailing."

"La-di-da. Have a great time. Nice new outfit, by the way."

"Katherine—"

"Hmm?"

"I may be late getting home."

"I should hope so."

Maddy made a face. She grabbed her swimsuit from her chest of drawers and stuffed it in her handbag, checked her image in the mirror, and dashed back to Gene.

It took a little over an hour for them to reach the boat dock where Gene's uncle's sailboat was moored in Long Island Sound. There was a picnic lunch already onboard and the boat—more like a yacht, a forty-foot, twin-masted schooner—was ready to sail.

Maddy had forgotten what it was like to move on the water in a small craft, in rhythm with the waves. She felt a heightened sensual awareness: the sun on her skin, the cry of the gulls, the taste of the bread in her sandwich, the chilling briskness of the water as she dove in for a quick, cool dip. She watched Gene as he worked the lines, waiting for him to stop and cozy up next to her. He didn't.

They made it back to Manhattan by nightfall. When they got to her door she thought, *This is it. Now he has to kiss me.*

But he didn't.

He invited her to dinner on Tuesday. On Wednesday they went to a free concert in the park. On Friday they went to a showing of impressionist paintings at the Metropolitan. He told her in advance that he could not see her over the weekend because he had to study for an exam, but they made plans to go roller-skating in the park the following Monday. Not once did he try to kiss her.

On the Fourth of July, Katherine and Maddy were getting ready to go on a picnic dinner when the intercom buzzed. The whole O'Connor clan was going out to Coney Island for an evening of fun and fireworks, and Maddy was always invited. Katherine, expecting her brother who was to come and pick them up, answered the buzzer.

"It's a Mista Brad Gordon, Miss O'Connor," announced the doorman. "Do ya want him sent up?"

"Brad? Here? Now?" Maddy blurted out, buckling the straps on her slingbacks with lightning speed.

"Sure, Marty. Send him up," Katherine replied, eyeing Maddy with amusement.

"But Brad's supposed to be in Europe with his parents until the end of the month."

"Guess your plans have changed. Don't worry, I'll make your excuses to Ma."

Seconds later Brad burst in and made straight for Maddy. "There's my girl," he exclaimed as he lifted her into the air. Katherine hooted. Brad put Maddy down and scowled at her.

"Who's this?" he asked abruptly.

"Never mind me. I'm the roommate and I'm leaving. I'll wait for Tim in the lobby. Nice to meet you, Brad."

He looked mortified. "I'm sorry. I didn't realize that we weren't alone. You must be Katherine."

"Where have I heard that before?" Katherine said, rolling her eyes then giving Maddy a wink. Maddy responded with a look that could only mean "shut up."

"Have fun." Katherine ducked out the door.

"Boy, am I glad she's gone." Brad pulled Maddy to him and pressed his lips against hers. She kept her mouth clamped tightly shut and wriggled free.

"Wait a second," she said, trying to sound cheerful. "You sure know how to bowl a girl over." He was her boyfriend. She should be happy to see him. And she was. Wasn't she?

"What happened to your trip?"

"I decided Europe wasn't big enough for me and my parents to be there at the same time, so I caught a flight back."

"Oh, Brad, don't tell me you're on the outs with your parents."

"So what if I am?" he chided her defensively. "I don't see your old man anywhere around."

"That's completely different."

"I don't think so. Some parents outlive their usefulness." Then he was at her again, kissing her cheeks with clumsy passion. "Let's get married, Maddy. Right now, this week, before my parents come home. Let's drive to Maryland and elope. Then they can't object, not if you're already my wife."

Maddy pushed him away. "What are you talking about? And what do you mean, your parents 'object' to me?"

Her question startled Brad out of his euphoria. "I thought you knew . . . They have misgivings. Because you're Jewish. But darling, it's never mattered to me."

She held out her hands as if to ward him off. "You mean, the reason I've never met your parents, other than that one night at the symphony, is because I'm Jewish?"

"I don't give a damn what they think. I love you. Please say you'll marry me."

"No."

Now he look jolted. "You don't mean that."

"Yes, I do. I don't want to be an outcast in my own family. And I don't want to get married yet. I want to finish school. I'm sorry to be so abrupt, but you really put me on the spot."

He looked as if he couldn't quite believe she was refusing him. "You'll change your mind, Maddy. I went about this the wrong way."

She shook her head. "I'm sorry."

"Don't be," he said, attempting to adopt a jaunty air. "I don't give up that easily. I'm going to stay with Theo for a few weeks, at his place in Newport. You can call me there when you start to miss me."

She walked him to the door. He kissed her on the forehead, and left.

Maddy slammed her hands down on the dining room table. Marriage? And that business about his parents. How could she have been so blind? So naïve? Her aunt had been right all along. *She would never be good enough. Brad's parents wouldn't even give her the chance to try.*

She thought about trying to catch up with Katherine and her family, but no longer felt in the mood for holiday festivities. Collapsing on the sofa with an exasperated groan, she put her feet up on the edge of the couch and glowered at the ceiling.

Another knock. She sat up. Could Brad be back so soon?

But it wasn't Brad. It was Gene.

"Hello, angel," he said as she opened the door. From behind his back he produced a dozen yellow roses.

"Oh, Gene, they're beautiful. But how did you know I was still here?"

"Well, I pay Marty to keep tabs on you. For a few bucks a week he lets me know about all the comings and goings in this apartment. He just called to tell me that Katherine took off without you."

Maddy gaped at him. Then she laughed. It was a joke. It had to be. "Creep. You had me going there."

Gene laughed, too. "You should have seen the look on your face. Okay, the real story is that I was going to drop these at the door. But, having come this far, I took a chance and knocked. Where's Katherine? Have you changed your plans?"

"Yes. No. I should try to catch up with them, I guess. How about you? What happened to your day of sailing?"

"Uncle Sal's arthritis kicked up. That's what he tells us when he's too hungover to go sailing. The rest of the family decided to skip sailing and go upstate. I wasn't in the mood for a big family day, so I passed. I was going to hang around and study. Unless you have a better idea."

Maddy's heart skipped a beat. How could she think that what she felt for Brad was love, compared to how she felt around Gene? What else could this be?

"I can pack a picnic. We can go to the park."

"Or come up to my apartment. We'll have a cocktail, then go for a special celebration."

"Can I have ten minutes?"

"See you in ten."

Maddy did not allow herself to think about what might happen that evening. She went into her room and put on a strapless white cotton sundress with a matching bolero jacket. She brushed her hair and put it up into a twist. She refreshed her lipstick. Then she went upstairs.

Gene opened the door as soon as she knocked, and looked her over from head to toe. "You are so beautiful."

Maddy could not answer. Her desire for him was so intense she thought he must be able to smell it emanating from her body like a wicked perfume. But she could not act upon it. She was incapable of taking that step.

"Welcome to life on top of the world," he said as he ushered her in and took her hand. "I have a surprise for you."

He led her into the living room. A wall of windows revealed a splendid view of Central Park and Midtown Manhattan. Long shafts of golden sunlight reached out from behind layers of rose-colored clouds to anoint the skyscrapers. And, in the center of the room, Maddy saw a glistening white grand piano.

She released Gene's hand and walked over to the magnificent instrument. "I didn't know you had a piano." Her voice trembled.

"It's a very recent addition. Got it last weekend. They had to practically take the whole thing apart and put it back together again to get it in here."

Maddy sat down and caressed the white leather bench. "It's too perfect."

"No. You—only you—are perfection." He handed her a glass of champagne.

Maddy seldom drank, but now she took a long sip of the effervescent wine. Within a few seconds she felt lighter, almost giddy. She took another sip, and looked up at Gene, trying to tell him everything without having to say anything. *Surely he will kiss me.*

"Play for me," he said, taking her glass away.

"What should I play?"

"Whatever you like. But you won't need this." He slipped off her jacket, barely touching her as he removed it, but Maddy felt her shoulders tremble. She thought for a moment, then out of her heart came the sensuous strains of Debussy's "Reverie."

She'd only played a few measures when she felt Gene touch the base of her neck with the forefinger of his right hand. It scorched her skin like a torch, but she did not stop playing as he continued to move his finger slowly down her spine. Her lips parted, as softly as a blossoming orchid. She poured her passion into her music, wanting so much more, afraid to ask for anything.

Gene's finger reached the bodice of her dress. Then she felt his whole hand, fingers and palm, slide underneath the fabric, and press against the skin between her shoulder blades. She arched her back and closed her eyes as her fingers fell away from the keys.

He was on his knees, behind her. He unzipped her dress, moved his hands lightly along the sides of her chest, and then cupped her breasts. She felt his tongue on her neck, moving in tiny increments. Delicate whimpers escaped her: sounds of helplessness, surrender, and delight.

Then he was next to her, straddling the piano bench. He cupped her delicate face in his large hands. "Do you want me, Maddy?"

She opened her eyes. "Yes," she whispered, her face burning with desire and shame.

"Tell me," he demanded, drawing closer. "Tell me that you want me."

"I want you," she breathed, and closed her eyes again. He traced the outline of her mouth with his thumbs. She was beyond thinking. She could experience only his touch, his scent.

"Tell me you want me to make love to you."

"I want you to make love to me." The words floated out of some murky, unfamiliar part of her. Her heart beat even faster. She could not open her eyes.

His hands slid from her face. He peeled down the top of her dress and caressed every inch of her naked torso, as if he were sculpting her body from clay. His hands came to rest below her waist. Then he leaned forward and, for the first time, kissed her mouth.

Her desire had become an unbearable torment. She writhed on the bench, only dimly aware of the release her body craved. She shifted her weight and flung her leg over the bench so that she, too, straddled it, and pushed herself up against him. Pressing her bare breasts against his chest, she kissed him back with passion that conveyed both a plea and a promise.

And then she was moving: moving through the air. She felt softness beneath her, and then an intense blend of pleasure and trepidation as he slipped off her underpants. She heard the sounds of clothes being removed and opened her eyes. He was on the bed, on his hands and knees, above her. She could see the movement of his chest as he inhaled and exhaled, and the small beads of sweat clinging to his shoulders. She saw all of him, ready and strong and full of desire.

"Is this what you want?" he asked again.

She had no voice. She nodded.

"Say it," he commanded.

"Yes," she said, and closed her eyes as he slipped into her. *Yes, yes, yes.*

She clung to him and heard herself make noises that could not belong to her as he ground her into the bed. She was no longer Maddy. Maddy had disappeared, overwhelmed by his power and the depth of her surrender. Her punishment. The sweet agony of her punishment.

She had journeyed to a dark place, a private place, a place of terror and truth. She knew, finally, where she belonged. And she knew that only Gene could take her there.

TWENTY

"I said call her and tell her that you aren't coming home."

Maddy lay naked on Gene's bed, sheets pulled up to her chin, trying to hide from the daylight and whatever reality had in store for her. Gene sat next to her, holding the phone by its cord, dangling the receiver a few inches from her face.

"Tell her you decided to go to New Jersey for the weekend. And then ask her to call your piano teacher and tell him you're going to miss a few lessons."

"I can't do that!" She sat up, ducking out of the way of the dangling receiver, clutching the bedclothes tightly up against her naked breasts. "If I miss a lesson, Aunt Bernice will have to pay for it anyway, and she—"

"Do you want me to call him?"

Maddy tried to read Gene's expression. She saw no threat there, but knew without a doubt that he would call her teacher if she did not do as he asked.

She took the phone. He dialed for her.

"Hello, Katherine?"

"Maddy, where the hell are you?"

"I'm sorry I didn't leave a note. I decided to go to Jersey for the weekend."

"Geez, kid. I was about to call the police. Did you and Brad have a fight last night? What's going on?"

"Oh, something like that. It's so stupid. I'll talk to you about it when I get back. I really don't want to go into it right now. But, well, would you call Mr. Laboucherd and tell him that I am not going to make my lessons today, or tomorrow?"

"You're kidding, right?"

"No, I need some time alone. I have to think about some things."

"I'll do it for you this once, but you'll have some world-class explaining to do when you get back here."

"You're the best. I'll see you tomorrow. No, I mean, Saturday." Gene was nibbling at her shoulder.

"Monday," he said in her ear.

"That is, I'll probably stay until Monday."

"Maddy, do you want me to come out this weekend? Are you going to be okay?"

"No, I mean, I'll be fine. I need some peace and quiet. I'll explain everything . . . when . . . I . . . see . . . you."

Gene snatched the phone out of her hand.

On Monday Maddy made it to her lesson with Mr. Laboucherd. She sat down at the piano in his stuffy studio on Madison Avenue and felt a yawning emptiness inside. Her fingers were stiff as she began playing her first piece. To her embarrassment the maestro stopped her almost immediately.

"Madeleine, you are a disappointingly inconsistent student."

She flushed crimson.

"This is why I seldom take women as students. They are slaves to their emotions. But you showed such promise." Lines of discouragement appeared on his aging brow.

"Anyone can play the piano, but only an artist can make music. We have a different soul, a different spirit. And in that spirit there is—there must be—passion. Passion that is impossible for a normal person to comprehend. But that passion must be mastered, for the music to be mastered. Your passion can be the source of divine elevation, or it can sow the seeds of your own destruction. If it cannot be tapped, you may as well be sitting at a player piano, watching a strip of moving paper crank out the music. But if you let your passion overcome you, if you do not master it, then you will never be a great artist.

"You have a gift, Madeleine," he continued, ignoring the tears trickling down Maddy's cheeks. "But you must prove yourself worthy of that gift." He walked toward the door. "I do not know if you are in love. I do not care. I will give you one week. If you are ready to become a musician, be here a week from today. If not, then go make some pretty babies." He strode out.

Maddy folded her arms across the keyboard, laid her head down, and sobbed.

She was supposed to meet Gene after her lesson, but after Mr. Laboucherd's lecture, she could not bring herself to go back to his room. She went, instead, to her own apartment, hoping to find some solace in the privacy of her own unrumpled bed.

At three o'clock she heard a knock on the door. She knew it must be Gene; he was the only one who could make it to the door unannounced.

She stayed completely still, afraid that the wild beating of her heart would be enough to reveal her presence. She heard him knock again. Then footsteps, and silence.

Her thoughts spun through her brain, an addled mass of shame and confusion. When she went to his apartment, was that only five days ago? She'd been convinced she was a woman in love. But the four days she'd spent with Gene hadn't been romantic. She'd felt only hunger: a greedy, insatiable hunger. Maddy brought her hands to her temples and squeezed, trying to press the pictures out of her mind. The ways Gene had taken her, the things that she'd done! And she'd wanted all of it, every thrusting, melting moment. And she wanted him still.

Passion. Her music could not come from the same place inside her as this insanity.

She dragged herself out of bed and into the living room. She would go to the park. She would buy a pretzel from a street vendor. She would escape from herself. She scampered back into her room, changed into a long cotton skirt, slipped her feet into a pair of flat sandals, grabbed her purse, checked for her keys, and left the apartment.

In the hallway she waited impatiently for the elevator. When it arrived she slipped in and pressed the button for the lobby. The door closed. It stopped on the next level down.

The door opened. There stood Gene.

"Hello, angel," he said, as he joined her in the empty elevator.

"Gene—what are you—"

He held his finger to her lips. Then he pulled the emergency STOP button on the control panel, and an earsplitting noise filled the small space.

"What are you doing?" Maddy shrieked.

Gene did not answer. He moved closer to her. Instinctively Maddy retreated, her hands covering her ears, trying to shut out the alarm bell. She stepped back until she hit the balance rail that traveled the circumference of the elevator. He lifted her up by the hips and planted her body up against the wall, precariously propped up by the small railing.

"No!" Her hands came away from her ears. She dropped her small purse and pushed with the full strength of both arms against his shoulders, trying to force him away.

His eyes, absurdly calm up to now, darkened with anger. "Don't fight me, angel," he said, in a voice all the more threatening because of its lack of emotion.

And she knew that she would not fight him. Her body was already beginning to betray her. The more he wanted her, the more overpowering her own desire grew.

He pinned her against the wall with his chest, dug under her skirt, and pulled off her panties. Seconds later he thrust up and into her and Maddy screamed, not knowing herself whether it was a cry of protest or pleasure. Then she closed her eyes, wrapped her legs around him, and dove again into their obscene madness.

When her spasms subsided Maddy could still feel Gene inside her, firm and demanding. The emergency siren continued to ring. He lifted her up and off him, and set her down gently. She grasped the railing behind her, trying to steady herself. She did not know what to think of him, or of herself. She dared not think at all.

Gene pulled up his trousers and pushed the emergency button back in, disconnecting the alarm. They rode the elevator in silence to the ground floor. When they reached the bottom, Marty, the ever-reliable doorman, was waiting for them, clearly worried.

"Get stuck?"

"Not at all," Gene replied suavely. "I banged the emergency knob by accident. We were actually going up, weren't we, Maddy?"

Maddy nodded, too ashamed to speak. She tried not to look at her panties, still lying in the corner where Gene had tossed them.

"You sure you're okay?" Marty asked again.

"Top-notch," Gene replied. "But thanks for checking up on us."

"No sweat," Marty assured them as the elevator door closed.

When they reached Maddy's floor, she picked up her panties and tucked them into her purse, trying to appear nonchalant, knowing it was a ridiculous effort. She stepped out of the elevator as if she did not expect Gene to accompany her. He did, and stayed right behind her as she unlocked the door to her apartment.

He followed her inside, slammed the door shut, grabbed her by the shoulders, and spun her around to face him.

"Never say no to me, Maddy. You are mine."

She stared at him, trying to reconcile the apprehension and exhilaration his words evoked in her. She thought he was going to kiss her, but instead he twisted her around, roughly, and brought her down onto the hardwood floor. She was on her hands and knees. He was behind her. He pushed her skirt up around her waist, revealing her wanton nakedness.

His tongue was inside her. She moaned, then gasped, as he suddenly pulled away and pushed her flat onto the floor, spread her legs apart, and lowered himself onto her body. She wanted to tell him, *No, not like this*. But then that part of her evaporated beneath the heat of his desire. *Yes. Take me. I am yours.*

At last Gene moved off of her. Maddy hid her face in her arms and stayed where she was, wishing she were invisible. He did not speak. She heard him pulling up his trousers, heard him walking to the bathroom, heard the sound of water running. She heard more footsteps, and then his voice.

"Come to my apartment for dinner tomorrow. Be there at six o'clock."

The door opened and then closed. Maddy stayed on the floor and curled herself up into a tiny, tight ball. She hated Gene at that moment. And she hated herself even more, for she knew that she would do whatever he asked of her.

TWENTY-ONE

Maddy listened at the door, trying to make sure that Katherine had already gone to work. She heard nothing. Breathing a sigh of relief, she unlocked the door and went into the apartment.

Katherine was sitting on the couch, reading. "Okay, kid," she said brusquely, slapping the thin volume shut and setting it to the side as Maddy entered the room. "Start talking. Where the hell have you been all night?"

"Aren't you late for work?" Maddy responded, lacing her fingers together behind her back.

Katherine rolled her eyes. "Yes, idiot. I am late for work, so spill the beans, and quick. Is it the pretty Italian playboy from the penthouse?"

Tears filled Maddy's eyes. She shook her head.

"Maddy, talk to me. We've never had any secrets—well, except about the fact that you're a piano genius. So do you have another secret life? I mean, first you're gone for four days, and you come back spouting, 'Guess what? Brad asked me to marry him, the nerve of that man,' then you're gone again. What gives?"

"Nothing," Maddy mumbled as she fought back her tears.

"I'm your best friend, Maddy. I don't care who you've got the hots for—unless, maybe, you've fallen for Marty the doorman, which would be pretty unforgivable. Don't tell me Brad came to town for another visit. Did he come to ask you to reconsider, using a new set of persuasive skills?"

Maddy did not answer.

"Fine. Don't talk. I can see I wasted my time. God, Maddy. I thought I was the crazy one."

Maddy wanted to tell her everything, but she did not dare. It would make it all too real, and it was too shameful to be real.

"Okay," Katherine snapped, reacting to Maddy's silence. "Have it your way. I'm going to work. But if you disappear again, leave me a note, okay? I can't afford to lose any more sleep." She stalked out and slammed the door behind her.

She walked into the bathroom and filled up the tub, then stripped, stepped into the scalding bath, held her breath, and sank low in the water. Gene's voice rang in her ears.

"Married? Angel, married is for diapers and cutting the grass and roast beef on Sunday. You think if I see you doing the dishes and sewing clothes and wiping up after the dog I'm gonna want to tie you to my bed? You're fantastic, Maddy. Outside you're so beautiful and delicate, but on the inside—when I heard you playing your piano, I knew that I could set all that fire inside you free. And I'm not gonna screw up what we've got by getting married."

"But what if I get pregnant?"

"There are ways to handle that which don't involve marriage."

Maddy shuddered despite the heat of the water, just as she had when the words came out of his mouth. She thought about what Katherine had said before she left. Brad wanted to marry her. Brad loved her.

Next she heard Mr. Laboucherd's words echoing in her brain: *"Master your passion, or go make pretty babies."*

It did not take her long to find Theo's number. Long-distance information, in Newport. *Newport. America's Cup. Sailing. Sailing with Gene. Don't stop to think. If you stop to think you'll be lost.*

"Hello, this is Madeleine Hoffman. May I speak to Bradley, please?"

She waited for an eternity. Twice she almost hung up the phone, but didn't. She had to escape from the ugliness that Gene had summoned from within her.

"Hello, Maddy?"

She'd almost forgotten how soft and deep his voice was. "It's me."

"Darling, to what do I owe this pleasure?"

"I've thought about what you asked me. And I do want to marry you. Today. I want to be your wife. I'll make your parents love me. You'll see. I'm not afraid. I'm not afraid of anything."

Her words came out in a torrent. When she stopped there was silence on the line.

"Brad?"

"Oh, God, Maddy. Do you mean it?"

"Yes." *Don't stop to think.*

"Okay, I can get to Grand Central by one o'clock. We can take the afternoon train to Baltimore, and get married tonight. Do you want Katherine to come, or anything? Should I bring Theo?"

"No, just you and me."

"What about your aunt and uncle?"

"They're in California. They won't object. They'll be happy if I'm happy."

"You'll be happy, Maddy. I promise. I love you."

"I love you, too."

"Until one?"

"Under the clock."

"I love you," he told her again before he hung up.

"I know," she whispered, "I know."

She put the receiver back on the phone. She would pack, and spend the day at the public library. She would not take a chance that Gene might find her. For the first time in weeks, she felt calm.

Katherine came home at six. She called out Maddy's name. Silence.

"Figures," she groused to herself.

She threw her purse on the couch, kicked off her shoes, and ambled into the kitchen to see if there was anything still edible in the refrigerator. There was a note on the counter. She picked it up.

Dear Katherine,

I've eloped with Brad. We're getting married in Baltimore.

I'll be in touch. Please tell Aunt Bernice.

Love always,

Maddy

P.S. You told me to leave you a note.

Katherine plunked down onto the floor. The piece of paper fell from her fingers. "Holy shit. Holy, holy shit. Maddy, I hope you know what you're doing."

Later that night, at a small roadside motel outside Baltimore, Bradley Harrington Gordon IV carried Madeleine Hoffman Gordon, his new bride, across the threshold of their room.

"I promise, Maddy, in a few days we'll go on a real honeymoon. We can go to Paris, Vienna—anywhere you want. I couldn't get enough cash in one day, without—well, you don't need to worry about that."

"I don't care where we are. I just want to be with you."

They kissed. Gradually, his tongue crept out of his mouth and touched her lips. When she did not pull away, he pushed the tip of his tongue gently into her mouth. She sighed.

He pulled away from her face and brought her head to his chest, holding her tightly against him. The top of her head reached up to his Adam's apple.

"I can't believe you're mine, Maddy. Mine forever."

She shivered.

"Are you cold?" Brad asked, pulling back so he could see her face.

"No, silly. I'm a little nervous, I guess."

"Don't be. We're married, right? So do you want to go and freshen up?"

"I guess so. Where's my suitcase?"

"Oh, right." He dashed out the door and was back in an instant.

"Looks like it might rain tonight," he said, sounding pretty nervous himself. He handed Maddy her small bag.

Maddy took off her clothes and examined herself in the bathroom mirror. She could not believe she looked exactly the same as she did five days ago. Her life had exploded on the Fourth of July. What a joke. Funny, her parents were married in July.

She picked up a wash towel and rinsed her face with cool water. Unlike Gene's voracious demands, Brad's awkwardness made her self-conscious. Maybe that was good. She wanted her wedding night to be different than . . . all that. Completely, totally different. She'd borrowed a long, kimono-style robe from Katherine's closet to wear on her wedding night. It had been a gift from Katherine's only surviving brother; he'd brought it home for her from Japan, after the war. Maddy knew that Katherine would forgive her for taking it, given the importance of the occasion.

She reached into her bag and pulled out the exotic garment. The green silk rippled out of the suitcase like a waterfall. She wrapped the robe around her naked body, tied the sash around her waist, splashed on some perfume, and opened the door.

Brad was sitting up in bed. He was wearing a full set of short-sleeved pajamas.

"You are so beautiful," he said as she emerged, his eyes filled with tenderness.

Maddy came to him shyly, wanting to please him, but afraid to do anything that might reveal that she was not an innocent bride. She crawled onto the bed and lay down next to him, trying her best to send him a wordless invitation.

He rolled over on top of her and kissed her forehead, her nose, then her mouth, then her neck. He kept on kissing her until he reached the belt of her kimono with his lips. With trembling fingers he undid the loosely tied knot. The silk slipped to her sides. He moved up so that they were face-to-face again, and this time she could feel his erection rubbing insistently up against her thigh. She kissed him, tenderly holding on to his shoulders, and then reached around to stroke her fingers along his back.

When he pushed his way up into her she started to cry hot, silent tears. Brad felt wetness on his chin and stopped moving.

"Oh, Maddy, I'm so sorry! It'll get better. Please, don't cry."

She shook her head, trying to make him understand, knowing that she could not explain anything. "Please. I want to."

Brad looked doubtful, but he was still aroused. He entered her again and she arched her back to meet him. He came immediately, thrusting with sharp, sudden movements, emitting small grunts of pleasure.

"Are you okay?" he asked when he'd finished, his words drifting down from somewhere above her head.

Maddy sniffed. Her eyes were closed. "I'm fine. Would you please hold me?"

He stretched along beside her and put one arm underneath her. With the other hand he caressed her tear-stained face. She rolled over and pressed against him, until every inch of their bodies was touching. Then they were silent, for a long time, comforted by each other's presence, resting in the quiet cradle of the night.

TWENTY-TWO

"I don't believe it!" Bernice cried, exhibiting an uncharacteristic loss of control. Archibald Mason looked up from the financial pages as his distraught wife entered the parlor of their suite at the Los Angeles Hilton.

"What's bothering you?" he asked calmly, without actually setting the paper down.

"That was Katherine O'Connor on the phone. She called to tell us that Madeleine has gotten married. *She eloped.* Yesterday, with Brad what's-his-name, the boy from Harvard Medical School. It's impossible."

Archie put the paper aside. He was a stout, serious, and clever man, to whom sex meant little, good food meant a lot, and money meant just about everything. He'd never shown much interest in Maddy, but he'd never been unkind to her, either; she was simply one more variable in his wife's well-organized life. He cast about for an appropriate response.

"Well, I'm sure he'll be a good provider. And didn't you tell me he comes from money?"

"Don't be vulgar. Madeleine doesn't need a good provider. She has us. What she needs is independence. And what she does not need is to be treated like a pariah by some blue-blooded Boston anti-Semites."

"Now Bernice. It may not be as bad as all that. Don't let your own bigotry get the best of you."

She gave him a look of total dismay and dropped into a chair. "She's exactly like her mother, after all. There must be a genetic explanation for this."

Archie gazed fondly at his wife. "Messed up your plans, did she, dear? Children will do that."

She glared at him. He returned to the financial pages. "Oh, look. GM's up two points. I love America."

Across the world, Mr. and Mrs. Bradley Harrington Gordon III were enjoying a late afternoon tea in their suite, in an elegant hotel in the most fashionable part of London. The tuxedo-clad butler served them, then bowed, and presented Mr. Gordon with a telegram.

"Why, it's from Brad," he said, tearing open the message.

"An apology, I hope," sniffed Mrs. Gordon.

"DAMN."

"Bradley, your language!"

"Francis, the boy has gone mad. He's eloped! Married the little Jewish girl. This is outrageous."

"Oh, dear God, no," his wife whimpered, her face as pale as the lilies on the table in front of her.

Bradley III started roaring and stomping around the room like a wounded bear. "And there's more. He wants money for his honeymoon. Over my dead body. First he snubs us, now this. He's gone too far this time. If he wants to live his own life, then let him."

"And I always wanted Brad to have such a beautiful wedding," Francis moaned. "Why would he do this to us, Bradley? Why would he want to hurt us this way?"

He went over to her, his concern for her momentarily taking precedence over his anger. "Don't cry, dear. Perhaps they won't stay married long."

She began to cry in earnest.

A week later Brad sat in an elegant office in a historic brownstone in downtown Boston, glaring at the dour face of Henry Walthen Waters Jr. He'd been the attorney for the Gordon family since the day his own father had passed away, nearly twenty years ago, long before Bradley IV was old enough to cause trouble.

Waters disliked this young man. He'd disliked him ever since Bradley IV had enlisted in the navy, on the very day after the draft board had issued his meticulously engineered exemption from military service. Luckily for the insubordinate runt one of Waters's law partners was able to pull some strings and got Bradley IV assigned to a supply depot in San Francisco. The war was over soon after he joined up, but Waters never forgave the boy. He abhorred disobedience, especially among the children of his wealthier clients. It made for such messiness, like the business he was dealing with now.

"But he can't cut off my trust money. It's mine. Grandfather left it to me."

"Yes and no. Under the terms of the trust established by your grandfather, the principal will be distributed to your children, and if you have no surviving heirs, then to—ah—the children of your father's first cousin, I believe, but that's really of no relevance at the moment. The interest income is yours to spend as you see fit, but not until you reach the age of thirty, or when you finish your education, whichever comes first. No dilettantes in the Gordon family. Up until this point your father has paid for your education out of his own pocket, although he could have, as trustee, authorized payment out of the trust for such a purpose. However, until you finish medical school—and your residency, at which point you will be twenty-eight—until that time, your father, as trustee, is within his authority to deprive you of all access to the accrued interest in your trust fund, including any money required for your tuition for medical school."

"He won't pay for me to finish school?"

"Not unless you are willing to divorce your wife."

"The bastard." Brad punched one fist into the palm of his other hand.

"Please, Bradley. You're speaking about your father. He doesn't want you to throw your life away following the whimsy of youth. You have an important career ahead of you. An important place in society. The right sort of wife—"

"I have the right sort of wife, thank you," Brad interrupted, eyes blazing. "My parents are absurd. They don't know Maddy. They wouldn't even invite her to the house for dinner, because they didn't want to 'encourage' me. I don't give a damn if she's not from the right sort of family, or if her father was a pickle salesman from Hong Kong. Tell my dear old dad I'll finish school without his help. And that I won't be naming my son Bradley V." He stalked out.

That evening he explained the situation to Maddy. She listened quietly.

"Don't worry," she said as he finished, placing a hand on his knee. "I can ask Aunt Bernice for the money. She'll pay for your medical school."

"No!" He pushed her hand away. "I won't take her money. I don't want her help, thank you."

"But she's paying for Katherine's school, and mine."

"Don't you see? You let people do something for you, and then they own you. Pushing and prodding, telling you what to do, then bemoaning your ingratitude. My parents have done this to me all my life. And when I got into trouble, they were always there with their apologies, their bribes and excuses. If I can't finish by myself, then I'm finished, anyway. I don't need your aunt and uncle to step into my parents' shoes."

"Then will you let me help you?"

"How?"

"I can get a job."

"No. Impossible."

"But Brad, how else?"

"I'll take a year off and do lab work. I'll borrow the money."

"But that will delay your graduation, and your freedom. If it weren't for me, they wouldn't have disowned you. Please, let me help. I'm your wife. If you can't take my help, then what kind of marriage do we have?" *And then I can quit school. I wouldn't need to explain anything.*

"But I don't want you to give up your dreams."

"I don't have any dreams, Brad. Oh, I wanted to play the piano, but I don't have what it takes to be a real musician; I learned that this summer. I was a talented prodigy, but I can't—I don't want a musical career."

She looked him in the eyes, and tried to make him believe what she was saying, trying to make herself believe it, too. "I just want to be your wife." *I just want to be safe.*

Brad was weakening; she could tell. After all, her offer would give him no more than what a bunch of the other fellows at the med school already had: a supportive wife, helping to make ends meet until medical school was over, the residency finished, the bills paid.

He eventually agreed. They moved into a small apartment near the medical school in downtown Boston. Maddy got a job at Filene's Department Store selling ladies' sportswear. Every day she got up early and rode the subway to work, enjoying a sense of productive usefulness that she'd not experienced since her childhood days, living in the busy O'Connor household.

At first she saw some of her friends from the New Music School, but the life of a student was at odds with the hours and responsibilities of a working wife, and she soon lost contact with them. She received one letter from her teacher, Mr. Auerbach, in which he expressed his disappointment about her decision to withdraw, worried that he was to blame; perhaps a summer with Mr. Laboucherd had shaken her confidence. Maddy threw the letter away and never wrote back.

Bernice was extremely displeased with Maddy for ignoring her advice about Brad, and doubly so when her niece dropped out of music school. Given her displeasure, she did not feel obligated to soften the harsher edges of the new life her niece had created for herself. Bernice believed that consequences built character. She wished the newlyweds well and gave them one nice check as a wedding present, but other than that she left them to their own devices.

Katherine came to visit at Christmas. She took in the tiny, shabby apartment, the skinny, half-decorated Christmas tree, and the dime-store furniture piled high with medical books.

"Cute place. Is Brad joining us for dinner?"

"No, he's doing an obstetrics rotation, and won't be home until sometime tomorrow, having delivered a few babies of various colors, shapes, and sizes, all in time for Christmas."

"That should give us some time to catch up."

"Would you mind if we decorate the tree while we talk? I wanted to finish it last night, but Brad was so tired."

"Sure, if you tell me where you want the ornaments to go. As you know, I have no artistic eye. I can pithily plant punctuation marks in a paragraph much more easily than I can discern the discordance of an awkwardly placed ornament on a Christmas tree."

"Okay, Miss Pulitzer. You can sit there, unwrap, and hand me things."

They worked peacefully for a while. Maddy started to hum. That was all the room Katherine needed.

"Maddy, I don't get it. I've known you since we were kids, but I've always felt that I was one step away from knowing who you really are. Like some part of you was all locked up. I figured it was on account of your parents; that would've been tough on anybody. But when I heard you play at your first recital, I figured it out. Behind all that sweetness— which believe me, I envied—there was this power. When you finally let it out you were happier than I'd ever seen you before. And then, instead of staying on the path that could get you what you wanted, you get spooked, and settle instead for what you think you should want."

"That's not fair," Maddy interrupted hotly. "Don't criticize something because you don't understand it. We can't all be globe-trotting career girls, you know. I love Brad and I'm proud to be his wife. He's kind, handsome, and intelligent—"

"And arrogant."

"Katherine!"

"Come on, Maddy. Don't ask me to pretend otherwise. Anyone who's been telling his parents where to get off as long as he has suffers from a big, fat arrogant streak. Now he's married you and pissed them off some more. Don't you ever worry that his wanting to marry you had as much to do with how he felt about *them* as how he felt about *you*?"

"How dare you suggest that Brad doesn't really love me!" Maddy was furious; how could Katherine have conjured up that ugly question, the one that sometimes slithered like a deadly snake out of the darkest corner of Maddy's own mind? Why did Brad marry her? Why had she married him? Go away, questions. Go away, snakes. Go away, Katherine, if necessary.

Maddy climbed up on the stepladder and busied herself with the ornaments. She'd felt this kind of rage only once before, on the day she'd last seen her father. She was afraid that if she didn't calm down, she could, and would, throw Katherine out of the house.

"You're just jealous, Katherine," Maddy accused her friend, on the verge of angry tears. "You're jealous because you're afraid you won't ever have what Brad and I share."

"You can think that if you want to, Maddy. But since I don't understand it, I'm not sure how I'm supposed to be jealous of it. I'd like to see you save a part of your life for yourself. Maybe you don't have to go for the famous concert pianist routine, but why do you have to give up your music altogether?"

"Oh, you sound like my aunt. I can't have that and this, too, Katherine, for reasons . . . reasons that I can't explain."

"Can't or won't?"

"As you like."

"Look, Maddy, I didn't come up here to ruin your Christmas. I only—"

"You wanted to try out a little of your psychology training on an interesting subject. Well, don't bother, Katherine. I'm happy, and I'm not crazy. Believe me or don't."

"Okay, okay. I'm sorry. I won't bring it up again." The two worked in silence for a while, both uncomfortable with the tension their discussion had created. Just when Maddy thought the argument had blown over Katherine asked a question that almost made her fall off the ladder.

"You haven't, by any chance, heard anything from our old neighbor, Gene Mandretti, have you?"

Maddy felt her cheeks flush. She kept her back turned as she replied. "No, I haven't. Why?"

"Because he came to find you the night you eloped. I showed him your note, and I could tell he was angry, but he stayed so quiet, like a volcano about to explode. It was pretty frightening. He struck me as, well, dangerous."

"Don't be ridiculous. If he did have some feelings for me he kept them to himself. And he hasn't contacted me at all." She stepped back down to the floor. She felt sick. But it was true. She hadn't heard from Gene. She'd walked out of his life and he had let her leave, without a protest. Good. She had exactly what she wanted: Brad and a calm, well-ordered life.

"Okay then," Katherine was saying, clearly relieved by Maddy's confirmation. She stepped closer to her friend.

"Well. I've spoken my piece. No more bad behavior. I promise. Need some help with the tinsel?"

Katherine's smile helped clear the air. It always had.

When Brad graduated from medical school he was offered a residency at Stanford. Maddy made friends with the wives of some of the other residents, and hid the pangs of envy that struck her when, one by one, they each got pregnant. Brad didn't want to have children until he'd finished his residency; they were young, he said. They should wait until they could afford to give their children the best of everything.

After his residency Brad was offered a position at a hospital in San Francisco. He wired to Boston for his long-awaited trust payments, and he and Maddy bought a beautiful house overlooking the bay. And on the day they found out that he'd passed his medical boards, he kept the condoms in the nightstand drawer.

But no babies came.

Gradually Maddy began to fill the emptiness of her life with small rituals. It began in simple ways; she always put the coffee on before heading down the driveway to pick up the newspaper. She always brushed her teeth before brushing her hair. She went to the grocery store on the same day every week, and went down each aisle, from right to left, pausing to make sure she did not need anything else before moving on to the next one. She had the car washed on Thursday afternoon, and had her hair done on Friday morning. The strictness with which she adhered to her small routines helped numb her mind and constrict her emotions. It made the wait for a baby bearable.

For her birthday that year Bradley surprised Maddy with a piano. She found that she could play, when requested, without triggering any internal turmoil. She limited herself to cheerful contemporary songs, and always played using sheet music. Her strategy had worked. She'd put the genie back into the bottle.

But still, no babies came. The lack of children began as a small absence, like the missing piece of a jigsaw puzzle. But over the years it grew, until it was a great, unmentionable gulf that lay between them. And they each wondered, at times, if they recognized the person across the abyss.

PART FOUR

TWENTY-THREE
SAN FRANCISCO, 1960

Maddy walked through the tall, colorful archway marking the official entrance of Chinatown and was instantly transported from the lofty ambience of San Francisco to the frenzied, crowded streets of her childhood. Men huddled in doorways or squatted in corners, swapping stories, spitting, smoking, playing cards. She smelled fish and ginger, garlic and incense; admired the triumphant colors of the ravishing silks; and heard the incomprehensible but familiar sounds of Chinese voices scolding, laughing, and cajoling. This chaotic, noisy place was her refuge. There were times she even thought she caught a glimmer of a happy memory, reflected in the eyes of a child who was there with a parent, exploring the sights and sounds and smells of Chinatown.

She headed toward an alchemist's shop. Hundreds of drawers, each marked with unintelligible Chinese characters, were filled with unimaginably exotic ingredients used by the oriental pharmacist to ward off evils ranging from warts to lung disease. They contained powders that fought impotence, snake blood that cured cancer, pollens to help with liver ailments, and the roots of plants that produced a tea guaranteed to bring forth healthy sons from a barren womb.

On more than one occasion Maddy had succumbed to temptation and brought home a concoction purported to enhance fertility, knowing her actions would become a source of ridicule if Brad discovered that she gave a second's thought to such nonsense; but the unfailing faith of the Chinese in these ancient remedies was sometimes persuasive when Western science offered no solution.

"The two of you together present an awkward combination, that's all. Irregular ovulation and a slightly low sperm count, which, when combined, makes things more difficult, but not impossible. Just keep trying" was the verdict of the fertility specialist she'd finally persuaded Brad to consult. After that, their lovemaking, which had never been inspired, gradually became an agonizing chore.

Then Maddy turned thirty and, frightened by the possibility of a childless future, raised the possibility of adoption. Brad hadn't merely refused; he'd acted as if she'd accused him of committing a crime, and barely spoke to her for two weeks.

She did not bring it up again.

Maddy walked inside the alchemist's shop and was surprised to find another non-Asian customer inside. The few white people she saw wandering around Chinatown were generally tourists. They gawked with a combination of curiosity and badly concealed disgust, taking pictures of the strange vulgarities like whole roasted ducks hanging in the store windows and curbside cooks serving boiled dumplings to men who squatted in place and gobbled them down using chopsticks. Tourists were careful not to touch anything that might be home to a wayward microbe.

This woman was in the shop to do business, and she wasn't being pleasant about it; she was yelling at the proprietor, who withstood the woman's verbal onslaught with indissoluble dignity.

But that voice. Although deepened with age and dried out by liquor and cigarettes, Maddy still recognized that voice.

"Amelia?" The question escaped like an involuntary reflex.

The woman turned. Her hair was too blond, and her makeup too loud. Her narrow face was lined, her once-luminous skin now sallow, but it was still the same face that had tormented Maddy as a child.

"Martha? Jesus bloody Christ. You're supposed to be dead!"

Walk out. Let her think that you're your mother's ghost.

Amelia took a step closer. "Well, I'll be damned. It's you. What was I thinking? Martha would be shriveled up like me by now. Quite the re-semblance, though. Imagine two old friends like us running into each other in a place like this. How's your darling father?"

"He's dead."

"Is that so? Well, we'll all be dead soon enough." She turned back to the alchemist, who was measuring a beige powder into a small box. "You telephone me when you get more, you understand? I'll pay dou-ble." She brushed past Maddy and left.

Maddy did not move. *Why did you lie to her? You don't know that he's dead.* The proprietor hurried over to her.

"You okay, miss?"

She nodded. "Just surprised. She's someone I knew a long time ago."

"You are very much younger. Her daughter-in-law, maybe? Maybe her son die in the war, making you widow? Very sad."

"No. Nothing like that." *She's the wicked stepmother. From a land far, far away.*

To her consternation the man reached for her wrist and felt her pulse. "You sit down. Drink water. Rest awhile. Big shock."

He pulled her over to a narrow wooden chair. Maddy sat down. It was then that she realized her limbs were trembling. She took the water offered her and drank it quickly.

"Feeling better, miss?"

"Yes, thank you. I'll go now."

"You didn't come in to buy something? Again something to help babies grow? It didn't work last time?"

She felt an inexplicable wave of nausea, and had to wait before she could answer. "No, it didn't. Thank you for the water. I have to get home."

"Wait a moment more. Have some tea."

"No, thank you." *Amelia. How long had she been in San Francisco? What was she doing in this place?*

"Why was that woman so angry? What did she want?"

The man shrugged. "She is very bad sick. Wants special Chinese medicine, very expensive, very hard to get. But no medicine can help. She is rotting from inside."

"She's dying?"

He nodded. "Soon."

Amelia, dead. What secrets would she take with her? There was so much that Maddy didn't know, so many pieces missing. Would knowing make any difference? Would it help her escape from the echoes created by the emptiness inside her?

She got to her feet. "Do you think—could you please give me that woman's phone number? She's . . . we're sort of distantly related."

He looked skeptical. "Mrs. Langtry is a relative of yours?"

"In a way, yes. I should have asked for her number before she left, but I was so surprised to see her."

The Chinese gentleman made his way slowly over to the counter and copied a number on a piece of paper. "Be careful," he warned as he handed it to Maddy. "The fangs of a dying snake still carry poison."

Amelia admired the massive diamond ring on her left hand. Poor Richard had been so generous. So shy. So trusting. So homely. So very rich, and so pathetically unlucky.

Amelia Langtry, widow of Reggie Simmons and ex-wife of Leo Hoffman, married her third and final husband, Richard Langtry, in December 1943. Richard met Amelia while he was waiting to be shipped out. Social barriers that might have otherwise deterred their courtship were eradicated by the war. They were married within two weeks.

Then Richard died, and she was once again a widow. Amelia found it laughably ironic that she had a kamikaze pilot to thank for her freedom, although it was an observation she kept to herself. Luckily for Amelia, her aged in-laws liked her. The elderly Langtrys were at the stage in life when they believed what they wanted to believe.

She lived with them on their estate in Connecticut while Richard was away at war, then stayed on after they received the news of his death, consoling them over the loss of their only son. Within five years of their son's death they both passed away. The bulk of the estate went to nieces and nephews. But Amelia was, as the Langtry family lawyer had explained, "quite well taken care of."

She traveled. She went to Europe and viewed with disappointment the remains of a war-ravaged continent. She went to Mexico, Brazil, Bali, and Hawaii. She lived well, and took a lover only when she wanted one. She was not a dance hall girl anymore. She could look back on the poverty, the flophouses, the unsatisfying sex, and the dance tour that had ended in Shanghai as if she were watching a movie starring someone else.

When the doctors in New York told her how ill she was, she came back to San Francisco, where she'd twice succeeded in turning her luck around. No one could tell her anything about her chances of survival. She'd beaten those odds long ago.

Amelia bunched her napkin into a tight little wad. Why had she agreed to see Madeleine, for chrissake? What could she have to say that Amelia could possibly want to hear? She wasn't going to sit still for any goddamn tongue-lashing, that was certain. And she hadn't waited for the little snit to ambush her, either. She'd gathered all the ammunition she might need before agreeing to meet her former stepdaughter. *Just tell me what happened to him.*

Of all the men she'd been with, Leo was the only who'd ever really mattered. She should have known back in Shanghai that he loved his wife too much for him to take their brief affair seriously; she should have known that losing Martha would break him. But Amelia thought she'd have another chance to be with Leo if she stayed around to pick up the pieces. No dice. She drained her martini and beckoned the waiter over to order a second.

Maddy walked into the restaurant and saw Amelia talking to the waiter. Her determination dissipated with every step she took toward the table. *What were you thinking, you idiot? What makes you think she would ever tell you the truth about anything? Leave before she sees you—*

Too late. Madeleine started to raise her hand in greeting, felt foolish, and touched it to her small hat instead, needlessly checking the security of its position. *Go on. This was your idea.* She made her way over and slid into the booth across from Amelia.

"Thank you for coming."

Amelia ignored this. "I can't imagine we'll be sharing a meal, so you may as well have a drink. I can recommend the martinis."

"I don't really drink very much."

"Suit yourself." The waiter brought Amelia's drink. Maddy ordered a soda. Amelia raised her glass. Her hand was shaking slightly. "You said all you wanted was to ask me a couple of questions. I'll answer yours if you answer mine. First. Respect for your elders and all that crap."

She's nervous? Maddy had not expected that. Not from Amelia.

"What do you want to know?"

"What happened to him?"

Him. Her father. Of course. "I don't know. I wasn't completely truthful when I saw you in that shop. He might be dead, but maybe not. I haven't seen him in fifteen years."

"Oh. And here I thought you were going to tell me some gruesome story about how heroically your father died in the war."

What was behind that sarcasm? Curiosity? Relief? "No, he didn't die in the war. I saw him once, briefly, when he got back from Europe. But that's all I know."

"Don't tell me he left you all alone? Didn't stick around to play with his grandchildren, any of that?"

"Does that surprise you?"

"No." She reached into her purse for a cigarette, and lit it before she spoke again. "Your turn, my dear. But don't make things difficult for me, or for yourself."

"I want to know why things happened the way they did, when you took me with you to New York."

"Christ, as if I knew the answer to all that. Your father didn't treat me any better than he did you. I tried to do him a favor. Get him out of Shanghai before the whole place blew up and the Japanese shot whoever was left just for the hell of it. Then he dumps you on me and stays put. I never knew why, either."

"What do you mean, do him a favor? I thought—I thought you and my father were—"

Amelia blew out a cloud of smoke with a derisive snort. "Were what? Madly in love? Planning to run away together the minute your mother died? No. He slept with me to get some information he needed about my husband's business, then politely excused himself from my bed, which in those days was not the usual treatment I received."

"Then why did you take me with you?"

Something approaching regret briefly deepened the wrinkles on Amelia's face and doused the bitterness in her eyes, giving Maddy a glimpse of the worn-out, dying woman she was; but the Amelia she knew flashed back before Maddy could feel any compassion for her.

"You should just be glad that I did. I did you a favor, too. You could've been dead before you were ten."

I was. I am. "Amelia, you never did me any favors."

"Well, I'm about to do one for you now. Your husband is cheating on you."

Maddy stood stock-still, staggered by the foulness of the accusation and the effrontery it took to make it. Her anger finally rescued her voice. "Nothing about you has changed, has it? You lie just to hurt people. Well, you can't hurt me anymore, and I'm not going to sit here and listen to your horrid accusations." Maddy grabbed her purse and started to slide out of the booth.

"Suit yourself, but walking out of here won't change the truth. He's a surgeon, right?"

That was enough to keep Maddy in her chair. "How—no, anyone could find that out. Easily."

"True, but at this point, why would I care? I've got my own problems." Amelia kept talking, offering no sympathy, just an explanation.

"A few years ago someone hired a private detective to find out what you were up to. The guy was very good at his job. He wouldn't tell me who was paying him, and I didn't have much to tell him, but he left me his card.

"I called him up right after you called me. For the right price he was willing to come back and prepare a quick update for me on the life of Madeleine Hoffman Gordon. Everyone's secrets are for sale, Maddy; you're no different. And he discovered that you're in a dead marriage. A wasteland. But now you have a reason to get out. Start over."

"I don't believe you."

"Ask the guy yourself. Here's his card. I told him to talk to you."

Maddy snatched the card out of Amelia's hand and stormed out.

Barely conscious of what she was doing, she was four blocks away before she remembered that she'd parked her car with the restaurant valet. She searched her purse for her valet ticket. It was in her wallet next to the card Amelia had given her. She threw the detective's card in a wastebasket on the corner and went back to retrieve her car.

Lies. She's never told you anything but lies. As soon as she got in her car Maddy drove back to the intersection where she'd thrown the card away. With a wild squeal of brakes, she stopped at the curb and jumped out with the engine running. A group of surprised pedestrians waiting to cross the street watched her as she dug the card out of the trash bin. Back in the car she tossed it on the seat, peeled off her soiled gloves, and roared away.

A wasteland. What would Amelia know about marriage? About making a life with someone? *No one hired an investigator.* Dying snakes still have fangs, all right. She never should have met with that woman. *I hope you die soon, Amelia, and very, very painfully.*

She drove out of the city on a road that ran along the cliffs of San

Francisco Bay. Pulling in to an area carved out for motorists to stop and enjoy the view, she cut the engine and picked up the card again. Richard Bates. He would tell her whatever Amelia had paid him to say. There was no point in calling him.

Maddy got out of the car with the card in her hand. A stiff breeze threatened to blow her hat away, so she removed it. She walked to the railing at the edge of the cliff, hat in one hand, the business card and a few hairpins in the other. The ocean was gray. Gray and empty.

She opened her hand. The hairpins fell to the ground. The wind caught the card. She watched as it twisted and flipped, taunting her with its macabre dance until it reached the water and vanished into the white-tipped waves.

Please be there, Brad. Please be there.

"I'm sorry, Dr. Gordon is not on call tonight. Would you like me to leave a message? He'll be back in for his rounds in the morning."

"No, I'm sorry . . . I must have misunderstood. Never mind."

She waited, awake and alone in the darkness of their bedroom, for him to come home. When she heard him come in the front door she almost went downstairs to confront him, but her limbs were locked in place. *You could ignore this. Lots of women do.* It didn't mean that he would leave. Whatever was going on could blow over, if she waited and said nothing.

He entered the room and headed over to the sitting area where Maddy had, as usual, laid out his pajamas and left a small light on for him so he could throw his clothes over a chair, dress, and then find his way to bed. She watched as he took off his jacket, then his tie. *Had he undressed like that earlier tonight?*

She sat up and flipped on the overhead light.

"Who is she, Brad?"

He blinked at her, surprised. "Are you still awake?"

"Who is she?"

She could tell by the look on his face that he'd heard her the second time. "What the hell are you talking about?"

What had she expected? An admission? An apology? Not this. Not anger. Self-doubt flooded Maddy's mind. Was she wrong? Had she fallen into some trap Amelia laid for her?

No. She knew. She'd seen the truth in his eyes before he'd hidden it behind his indignation. She *knew*.

"You weren't on call tonight. I called the hospital."

"For God's sake, Maddy, I took Bill's shift. He probably forgot to change the list. What's gotten into you?" He stalked into the bathroom. Maddy got up and followed him.

"Who is she, Brad?"

He ignored her and went to the sink, splashed water on his face, grabbed a towel, rubbed his face for longer than it took to dry it, then flung the towel into the sink before spinning around to face her.

"Do you have any idea what it's like for a man to feel competent everywhere but in his own bed?"

Maddy bit back the words that leapt into her mind. *Do you have any idea what it feels like to never feel competent at anything?* She knew that tears were pouring down her face but could not feel them. Her vision blurred and she reached for the doorjamb to steady herself. The world had split open again, leaving her no safe place to stand.

"It doesn't matter," she said, more to herself than to her husband. Nothing mattered. Nothing at all.

"Doesn't matter? What wonderful words of wisdom. Let me ask you this, Maddy. Were you a virgin when you married me?"

The question caught her completely off guard. A hot blush of humiliation flooded her face. She stumbled out of the room as Brad's vindictive words sliced through her.

"I suppose you are going to tell me it doesn't matter, after nearly ten years of wedded bliss, when you've been such a good little wife. Did you think I wouldn't notice that you didn't bleed, Maddy? Of course I noticed. But I loved you. God, how I loved you. But why did you marry me? What were you running away from?"

He was shouting now. Maddy reached blindly for her chest of drawers and began throwing clothes on the bed as he continued to berate her.

"You know the worst of it? My parents were right. 'Marrying a woman who does not come from a good family is like taking a time bomb to your bed, son,'" he continued, mocking the stern, pompous tone of his father's voice. "'Sooner or later, that lack of a pedigree will explode and you'll be hoist with your own petard.'"

Maddy dropped to the floor and put her hands over her ears. Brad leaned over her, breathing hard. "Her name is Caroline," he finally said, and then left.

By the next morning Maddy was on a Pan Am flight bound for New York.

TWENTY-FOUR

Bernice met Maddy at the gate. It had been nearly a year since they'd seen each other. Bernice looked stern. Unchanged. Just what Maddy needed to see.

"Thank you so much for coming to meet me."

"Well, this is a bit unusual, Madeleine. Can you give me more details about your sudden decision to come to New York?"

"When we're in the car, if you don't mind."

It did not take long to gather Maddy's bags. There was no driver to assist them. Maddy had never quite figured out the pattern behind her aunt's small economies, although she was sure that there was one.

"Ready for dinner?" Bernice asked as she started the car.

"No, thank you. I'm really not very hungry."

"I've taken a room for you at the Plaza. I assumed you'd have people to see, and I'm sure you don't want to be stuck all the way out in New Jersey. Traffic in and out of the city is getting worse and worse. Thank goodness I seldom need to go in. Archie doesn't mind all the socializing. I abhor it."

Despite her weariness, Maddy had to smile. She could imagine her uncle happily wining and dining his biggest clients, unencumbered by the restraining effect of Bernice's disapproval of his expanding expense account, and the expanding waistline that went with it. What a funny pair they were. Archie, having lived to make a fortune, relished spending it. Bernice often behaved as if the money didn't exist.

Maddy pulled herself back to the conversation. "Katherine's in London for a few weeks, but I suppose I should drop in on Mrs. O'Connor."

"I'm sure she would love to see you. So tell me, what's this all about?"

"I found out . . . I'm afraid Brad has found me something of an inconvenience as of late."

"How ludicrous. You're a terribly supportive wife. Ridiculously so."

"I'm not sure he feels that way. I guess we need a break from each other."

"I see," Bernice commented, giving Maddy no clue about what she really thought. For once Maddy was grateful that intimacy did not come naturally to her aunt. She didn't really want to discuss what had happened.

"Well then, why don't you go see Katherine? Take the *Queen Elizabeth*. She's in port, leaving day after tomorrow. I'll be no comfort. I'm up to my eyelids in conductivity formulas. Don't worry about the ticket. I think I owe you a birthday present, anyway."

"I don't think I'm in the mood for a long trip."

"Think about it. Where shall we stop for dinner?"

When Bernice had what she thought was a good idea, she seldom let go of it. Dinner evolved into an hour-long opportunity for her to persuade Maddy to visit Katherine in London. The trip would give Madeleine a chance to sort herself out, she said. A change of scenery would be good for her. "Call me tomorrow, after you've slept on the idea. I'll make all the arrangements."

The next morning Maddy woke with the odd sensation that she was back in her old home in Shanghai. As she pushed away the bedclothes the pain hit her. She was not home: not in Shanghai, not at her aunt's in New Jersey, not in her house in San Francisco. She was alone. *The little albatross.*

She snatched the phone off the nightstand and asked to be connected to London. Katherine was not in her room. Maddy left a message with the desk clerk. "Coming on the *QE*. See you in five days." She didn't care if it was a good time for Katherine to have a visitor or not.

By the end of the day Maddy had seen the inside of virtually every exclusive shop within a six-block radius of the Plaza. She'd bought everything she needed for an ocean voyage and sent all her packages straight to her suite. Bernice and Archie were to meet her for lunch the next day before she sailed, but she was on her own for the night. She should go get some rest, or pop in and see Mrs. O'Connor.

But there was something she needed to do before she left Manhattan.

She flagged down a taxi, gave the driver the address, and deflected his attempts to make conversation as they made the trip across town, fighting the remains of rush-hour traffic.

There it was: the apartment building where she and Katherine had lived together for part of the summer, a lifetime ago. The double glass door to the lobby was propped open. She crossed the street and peeked in.

The doorman looked up.

"Well, if it ain't Miss Maddy Hoffman. What're ya doin' back in the old neighbahood?" he asked with a grin.

She recoiled in surprise. "Marty, I can't believe you remember me."

"Oh, I don't forget pretty ones, like you and ya friend. The redhead."

"You must mean Katherine."

"Yeah. And, you was friends with the boss, too, which don't hoit."

Maddy's heart hurtled into her stomach. Her mouth went dry.

"The boss?"

"Gene Mandretti. He owns the place. This buildin' and who knows what else. So what brings ya back? If you're lookin' to catch Mr. Mandretti, he lives out on Long Island, but he still comes in occasionally. I could give him a message."

"No, thank you. I'm sure he wouldn't remember me. And I'm not staying. That is, I'm leaving for London on the *Queen Elizabeth* tomorrow."

"No kiddin'? Life's been treatin' you okay, then, huh?"

Maddy nodded, anxious to retreat. Why had she come here? What was she thinking?

"So, good seeing you, Marty."

"Right. You still see the redhead? Tell her hi from me."

"I will." She fled.

That night Maddy did something she'd never done before. She bought a bottle of gin at a package store. Back in her room she ordered a pitcher of lemonade from room service, and proceeded to get very, very drunk.

Around midnight Gene Mandretti walked into the lobby of the apartment building where Marty was still on duty.

"Evenin', Mr. Mandretti," Marty greeted him, with his usual chatty chipperness. "Saw an old friend a' yours today."

"Oh? Who's that?" Gene asked, not really interested but always careful.

"That cute little brunette what used to live here one summer. Maddy Hoffman. You rememba her?"

The elevator bell rang. The door opened. Gene did not move. The door closed. The elevator disappeared back upstairs.

"No kidding. You sure about this?"

"How could I not be sure? She's the only lady you ever paid me to keep tabs on. Comes walkin' right in here, pretty as you please. Prettier, even."

"Where is she?"

"Funny you should ask. She mentioned that she's goin' to London, tomorrow, on the big *QE*. What a coincidence, huh? Almost ten years ago, exact, since she lived here."

"Thanks, Marty. Too bad I missed her."

Gene Mandretti rode the elevator up to the penthouse. He unlocked the door, tossed his jacket over a chair, and picked up the phone.

"Hi, Tina. I know it's late. Listen, we've had an interesting opportunity develop . . . I know you hate it when I say that . . . I'm afraid it may mean travel for a few days. London. No, you can't come this time. It's all business. I'm leaving tomorrow, but I'll stop by for breakfast. Have Max get a suitcase ready—tell him some black tie and business—he'll know what to pack. I love you, too. Kiss the kids for me. I'll see you in the morning."

He dropped the phone back on the hook. He had some business in London to take care of, all right. Some unfinished business.

TWENTY-FIVE

Maddy took a long, slow sip of her ginger ale, relieved that her stomach had stopped fighting back. Her headache was gone. The wobbly feeling in her legs had disappeared. She would live after all.

"Never again," she said out loud to herself, her vow lost in the strong breeze that blew along the deck as the mighty ocean liner churned through the Atlantic. Lunch with her aunt and uncle had been one of the worst ordeals of her life. Not having any experience with hangovers, she made a terrible choice of what to eat. Her eggs benedict stayed put for barely ten minutes before her gin-ravaged tummy revolted, and Maddy subsequently spent a good part of the meal in the ladies' room.

She hid in her cabin during the bon voyage festivities, trying to avoid the noise and commotion that only made her head pound more. It was well past seven o'clock when she finally emerged, thankful for the calm seas, and the polite, experienced valet who was ready with advice for what he assumed was seasickness. "Please, step out and allow me to unpack your things. You should go get a little fresh air. Keep your eyes on the horizon. That will help," he'd suggested, and the therapy was working.

"I never want to taste gin again. Or lemonade. Ugh. Pity. I like lemonade," Maddy told the stars. Perhaps by the time the late supper was served she would feel like eating something. Some bread, maybe. A little soup. Not a challenge for the *Queen*'s chef who, it was said, could produce virtually any dish requested by a passenger within twenty-four hours.

Feeling decent for the first time since she had come aboard, Maddy went for an exploratory tour of the ship. The *Queen Elizabeth* was the biggest cruise ship in the world, proclaimed the brochure she'd picked up in the lobby. Not a penny had been spared in refurbishing her majesty once her days as a troop transport ship came to an end. Maddy spent well over an hour roaming, then decided she was hungry enough to find some food, and sufficiently recovered to bear the company of her fellow travelers.

Back in her stateroom she was amazed to see a large vase of yellow roses glorifying the vanity. She dug around in the bouquet for a card, careful not to prick herself. Nothing. She called the ship's florist.

"Hello, this is Mrs. Gordon in suite twelve. I have some beautiful flowers here, with no card. Could you please tell me who sent them?"

"Certainly, madam." He was back in an instant.

"A fellow passenger sent you the roses, madam, and the sender asked to remain anonymous."

"There must be a mistake. I don't know anyone onboard."

"Well, it is a large ship. Would you like the flowers removed?"

"No, thank you. They are lovely. But thank you for your help."

"My pleasure. Good night."

Maddy inspected the bouquet again, as if careful scrutiny would force the roses to disclose the identity of the sender. Did she really know someone onboard? Not likely. The florist must have made a mistake. She shed her suit and donned a black evening gown, for dinner on the *Queen* was strictly black tie. On an impulse she gathered her hair up into a twist. The style exposed the smooth white skin of her neck, making her feel elegant and feminine. Her mirror image registered her approval, and she went in search of supper.

The maître d'hôtel greeted her with cordial civility at the door to the dining room.

"Ah, yes. Mrs. Gordon," he repeated after she gave him her name. "Your table is ready. Please, come this way, madam."

He escorted Maddy to a small table for two, set for an elaborate supper. A bottle of champagne sat chilling in a stand beside the table, and two crystal flutes waited to be filled. The host held a chair out for her but Maddy did not take a seat.

"Excuse me, but I don't think I'm supposed to be sitting here."

"Oh? This table does not suit you?"

"No, it's fine. Beautiful. But I'm fairly sure that I'm to be seated at a group table, and I didn't order any champagne."

"That is not a problem. May I?" He pulled the chair out a bit farther. Hesitant, she sat down.

"Your companion will join you shortly, Mrs. Gordon. I need only notify him that you are here."

"But I'm not expecting—" Wait, could it be that Brad found out she was traveling on the *Queen*? Did he think their quarrel would end so easily?

"Thank you," she said, switching thoughts in midsentence, surprised at her own mixed emotions. Did she even want to see her husband? Could she forgive him? What could she tell him about her past? And why did he bring it up now, after all this time? If he would only agree to adopt a child . . .

She was rehearsing their conversation in her head when she heard a voice behind her.

"Hello, angel."

Maddy took in two huge gulps of air. Yellow roses. Only one man in her life had ever given her yellow roses.

She felt his lips touch her neck, briefly. A shiver ran through the length of her body.

He sat down across the table from her. Ten years had added a touch of fullness to his face, and a few small lines had surfaced around his eyes, but the rest remained the same.

Maddy put her hand to the bodice of her dress to reassure herself that she was not as naked as she felt. "Gene, what are you doing here?"

"I'm looking forward to dinner with you. You were kind enough to tell Marty how to find you. Ten years is a long time to wait, but you were worth waiting for. You're even more beautiful than you were the last time I saw you."

Maddy's senses stumbled through the flustered maze of her brain. She tried to move back from the table. She tried to pull her eyes away from his. She could do nothing.

"You can't do this."

"Can't do what?" countered Gene amiably. "Can't meet an old friend for dinner? Can't offer a beautiful woman a glass of champagne?" He signaled to the waiter, who hurried over.

Maddy stayed silent while the waiter served their wine. Once their glasses were full, Gene lifted his.

"To you, Madeleine Hoffman, the most fantastic creature God ever placed on this earth." He took a sip. Maddy did not touch her glass.

"My name isn't Hoffman. It's Gordon. I'm married. You know that."

"Married?" Gene looked around, pretending to be shocked. "Where's your husband?"

"He's in—he's in London. He's waiting for me there. I'm going to meet him."

"You're lying, Maddy," Gene said soothingly, as if he were comforting a small child. "He's in San Francisco."

"How did you—what makes you say that?"

"Angel, you didn't think I'd let you walk out of my life and disappear, did you? I've kept track of you over the years. And all it takes is a simple call to the hospital to see if Dr. Gordon's on duty, which he is. Unless he's cozying up to some nurse somewhere."

"You're a bastard," Maddy retorted, and found the willpower to rise.

"Where are you going? We're in the middle of the Atlantic Ocean."

"I'm going to whatever part of the ship you're not on."

She left the table. In two strides he was next to her. "I'm sorry if I upset you," he said quietly, holding on to her arm. "All I want is an explanation. Our last parting was rather sudden, don't you think? I will make a scene, if that's what you want. But it would be easier if you'd just, please, sit down and join me for dinner."

She shook her head adamantly.

He did not let go. Instead, he pulled her around to face him. He leaned down until his forehead nearly touched hers. "I love you, Maddy. I've loved you for ten years. I never thought I'd have this chance. There's no one in the world who wants you more than I do. No one." He released her.

She stood mute, immobile. Fear and confusion danced across her face. Then she turned her back on him and walked away.

The knock came sometime after one o'clock. She'd been telling herself for hours not to move, not to make a sound when it came. She closed her eyes and tried to will him away. He knocked a second time. "I'll just tell him to leave," she lied to herself, pulling on her long satin robe.

She opened the door and saw him standing there. Before she could speak he moved into the room.

"Gene, you can't—I just wanted—no, please—"

He held her face in his hands and kissed her under her eyes, next to her mouth, on her chin. One hand went to her hair, and he wove his fingers through the loose tresses.

"Tell me that you don't love me. Tell me that you never loved me," he demanded, his voice caressing her as skillfully as his hands.

"I don't love you. I've never loved you," she pleaded, closing her eyes.

"You're lying, Maddy."

And then it was gone; everything was gone. The ocean and the ship and the stars were gone; Brad and Bernice and Katherine were gone. All of the pain was gone. There was no one, and nothing, anywhere, except Maddy and Gene.

TWENTY-SIX

"Water, water everywhere," Maddy murmured as she gazed out over the endless acres of empty sea. "It's like being in a different world."

Gene came over and positioned himself right behind her.

"I don't want to talk," she said.

"I didn't ask you anything."

"I know. But you were thinking about it."

"About what?"

"About whether you could ask me why I ran away, why I married Brad Gordon."

"That's right."

The morning sun had barely crept over the horizon, painting the ocean a pale blue gray. The color of Gene's eyes. She looked up into them. "Are you hungry?"

"Not yet."

"Would you like some coffee?"

"You'll do anything to change the subject, won't you?"

She turned back to face the ocean. "Yes."

He wrapped his arms around her and let his chin rest on her shoulder. Maddy could not believe how comfortable she felt in his arms.

"Angel, we don't have to talk at all. We can spend the next three days the same way we spent last night."

"I'm not sure I could take three days like last night."

"Well, we could take little breaks for dining and dancing. Maybe even sleep a little."

The mention of the word set Maddy to yawning. "Sleep would be nice," she said. "Now that I've seen the sunrise."

"Your place or mine?"

"Mine. Alone. I won't get any sleep if you're there, too."

Leaning against him, she could feel his body tense, but he kept his tone light. "Very well, sleeping beauty. Since I know you can't jump ship until we reach England, I'll risk letting you out of my sight, but only if you promise to meet me for lunch. You skipped out on me at dinner, remember."

"Oh, I promise. I'll be famished by noon."

"Okay. I'll walk you back."

He kissed her at the door to her cabin, a long, deep kiss that was both possessive and reassuring. Once she was alone in her room, she touched her lips with her fingers, marveling at how long the sensation stayed with her. How could she feel so completely connected to someone she'd known for such a brief period of time, so long ago? Someone she really knew very little about. Someone she'd been sure was so absolutely wrong for her, and probably still was.

She knew that he'd reentered her life at the worst possible moment; she'd never felt more vulnerable. Lost, in the middle of the ocean, betrayed by the man she'd relied upon to love her and take care of her—

Just as she'd been when she was seven years old.

"God, don't be so neurotic," she muttered, aggravated with herself for drawing the parallel. She needed some sleep.

Sleep came quickly, heavy and dreamless. When she woke up it was nearly noon. She took her time getting bathed and dressed, then went to the dining room to meet Gene.

During the meal they found a surprising number of amusing, meaningless things to talk about. After their solicitous waiter brought them their coffee, Gene attempted to bring up the topic that Maddy had ducked earlier that morning.

"Are you ready to talk now?"

"Not really. I don't know what explanation would make any sense. At times the answer was so clear to me, and there were other times when being married to Brad . . . It felt like I was living someone else's life, as if I had woken up in the wrong bed, in the wrong house, at the wrong time. I was scared, I guess."

"I understand that. I've grown up a lot over the past ten years. It took me a long time to realize how overwhelmed you must have been by what we experienced together, and how it must have terrified you. I was pretty overwhelmed myself. I just handled it differently."

Overwhelmed. That didn't begin to describe what it had been like. But last night had been different: as if there might actually be something left of the two of them once the flame burned itself out. Maybe.

"So what now?" she asked.

"Now we spend three days making up for lost time. The rest can wait."

They discovered that there was no better way to drop off the face of the planet, to live a separate life, to become a different person in a different place, than onboard an oceangoing cruise ship. Completely removed from the rest of the world, each day was a fresh palette for them to use their imagination. They spent many hours in bed. They ate their meals on the private balcony in Gene's stateroom. They also tried badminton, bingo, and shuffleboard. Once Gene tried to show Maddy how to use a rifle to shoot the clay pigeons sent soaring off the rear deck by a uniformed steward, and to her astonishment she knocked two of the twenty she shot at out of the sky. They went to the ballroom to dance, swaying to the gentle rocking of the sea, or twirled to the pulsating rhythms of the Cuban band that cranked up in the cocktail lounge near midnight.

The weather held, and so did their good mood, until the morning they were due to arrive in Southampton. Then the clouds covered up the sun. The sea changed from blue gray to a brownish green. They went up on deck after breakfast, trying to find a place to themselves, away from all the other passengers vying with one another to be the first to spot the coast.

"So where do we start?" she asked at last, her tone of voice matching the downcast color of the day.

"Well, first, why don't you tell me why you're here without your husband."

"We had a fight."

"Because?"

"He wasn't getting what he wanted from our marriage. Perhaps we both went into it for the wrong reasons."

"And those were?"

Maddy shrugged, without taking her eyes off the sea. "Why didn't you ever try to get in touch with me?"

"You mean, to try and persuade you to leave the man you married and come back to me? It was pride, at first. I wanted you on my own terms. I was young. I was selfish. So I sulked. Then I eventually went on with my life."

"And I went on with mine." She turned to face him. "What happens next?"

He grasped her shoulders. "I know what I want. I want you back in my life. I don't ever want there to be a time when I can't reach for you. But I'm married, Maddy. I'm married, I have two children, and I won't get a divorce."

Of course he's married. You're married. Neither of us should be here. We never should have done this. Her stomach lurched in a way that had nothing to do with the movement of the ship.

"Don't think you should've told me this three days ago?"

"Would it have mattered?"

Yes. No. I don't know. She couldn't answer. She felt piece by piece of herself shutting down in response to the pain shooting through her. She wobbled. Gene put his arms around her and held her close.

"Will you go back to him?" he whispered into her ear.

"I don't know."

"What if you couldn't? What if you couldn't go back?"

"I don't know. I don't know anything. I can't make sense of any of this."

"Can I see you in London?"

"No. This isn't . . . It isn't right, Gene."

He pulled away from her slightly and lifted her chin with his hand. "Please come back to me, angel. If you give me a chance, you'll understand. Don't judge me by rules created for other people. Just believe that I love you."

Don't judge me. Her old piano teacher's scolding reverberated in her mind. *Artists are different. We have a different soul, a different spirit.* She shook her head, unable to do or say anything else. *No. It's a lie. Lies built on lies built on lies.*

Gene took out a handkerchief and tried to dry her eyes. She pushed his hand away. He put his handkerchief back in his pocket and withdrew a slim velvet box. She did not make a move to accept it, so he opened it for her. It was a necklace, made of yellow diamonds and emeralds, set to form a garland of roses. Even in the overcast light that surrounded them, the jewels in the necklace sparkled with their own brilliant fire.

"Take it, please. I want something of mine to be near you when you're away from me."

"No."

He didn't argue any further, but he reached for her again, and she didn't struggle this time. She rested her head on his chest, listening to his heartbeat. They stayed that way for a long time, and then, when the rest of the ship had begun the hurried drill that meant an imminent approach to shore, he released her, and handed her a slip of paper.

"Call me when you get back to New York," he said simply. And he walked away.

Maddy was one of the last people off the ship, for she spent a good long time in her suite, sobbing, childishly wishing the voyage had never come to an end. Summoned by a fourth and rather forceful knock from the deck steward, she washed her face, put on some makeup and her sunglasses, and headed to where she hoped Katherine was waiting for her.

The sight of her old friend standing on the other side of the customs gate, waving and smiling, set Maddy off again. Katherine arranged for the luggage to be delivered and bundled Maddy off to a taxi. She prattled on as if Maddy were not crying her eyes out on the seat beside her, talking about London, about the historic sites they were passing, about the people with whom she worked at Reuters. By the time they reached the hotel, the elite Grosvenor House, Maddy had calmed down.

Katherine bustled her into the room, tipped the bellhop, and then sat down in the overstuffed chair that filled one corner of the suite's small sitting room. She kicked off her shoes and lit a cigarette.

"Do you smoke?" she asked, offering Maddy one of hers.

"No, thanks," replied Maddy, subdued.

"Neither did I until recently, but it's difficult to be taken seriously if you don't in this game. It's part of the window dressing. I can drink like Hemingway, too. Irish genes are good for something, I guess. Your turn. What's going on?"

Maddy told her. She started at the beginning. Katherine asked her a few questions, but mostly let her talk. She related every detail of her story. By the time she finished Katherine was lighting her fifth cigarette.

"Holy shit," she said as she got up to open a window, for the room was getting quite smoky. "I always knew that truth was stranger than fiction, but this takes the cake."

"Gee, thanks."

"Well, I don't know what you expect me to say. I'd ditch the both of them. Sounds like you could use a fresh start, Maddy."

Maddy had to laugh at her candor. "Is life always so simple for you, Katherine?"

"Life is simple, Maddy. Human beings are the only things that complicate it."

"How profound."

"Laugh if you want," Katherine said as she flopped back into her chair. "Look, I feel for you. I really do. I feel badly that you put up with

Bradley the Fourth for ten years, and I feel even worse that you've fallen for a world-class bastard, although the latter is a bit more understandable. You want my advice? Dump 'em both. You want my sympathy? You got that, too. You want a place to run away to? I'll be here for at least a couple of weeks. We can stay at the Grosvenor compliments of your aunt, or at the crummy crash pad I rent on my minuscule salary. I love you, Maddy. You're my oldest friend in the world. I'm here to help."

With this, she put out her cigarette and bounced out of her chair. "So are we doing dinner tonight? Maybe dinner and a show?"

"That would be nice."

"Great. I'll call you."

While unpacking her hand luggage Maddy heard something fall on the floor. It was Gene's necklace. *How did he do that?* She started to cry again.

That evening dinner and a show was followed by drinks and a little music. The next day Katherine took off from work and they did the requisite sightseeing: the Tower of London, Westminster Abbey, and Buckingham Palace. On the third day, Maddy wandered about on her own, shopping and seeing the city. That night she met up with Katherine at a small pub near Fleet Street.

It must have been a journalists' haunt; it seemed like every other person there had a complimentary word to say to her friend. Maddy was pleased at first, but one hour and two pints of hard cider into the evening she felt an all-too-familiar, unflattering wisp of jealousy creep into her thoughts.

"How come you're the center of attention tonight?" she asked as another of Katherine's acquaintances wandered back to the bar for a refill.

Katherine gave her a piercing look. "Maddy, there are two goals in my business: getting to the truth, and getting to the top of the heap. The first is gratifying, the second is essential, because when you're there, you can go digging farther and faster for the former. I impressed some old hands this week because I goaded a vain member of Parliament into contradicting himself on record. Everyone loves to see a politician humiliated, so I picked up a few kudos. But in a couple of days that won't mean a damn thing, and if I can't break a big story soon, I'll never be able to convince my boss to let me go to Latin America."

"Would it be so terrible to stay in London?"

"Terrible? That depends. Most male reporters think I should quit whining and be grateful to have escaped the social column. Can you imagine me writing about fashion?"

Maddy nearly choked on her drink. "No," she finally got out.

"Me, neither. And while London is fine, it's not where I want to be. And I can't make them let me go unless and until I have some leverage. That means a lead on a huge story over there, or enough accolades to make them listen when I threaten to quit if they won't send me. 'Too dangerous for a woman' is the bullshit excuse I get. They'll let someone else cover Havana who doesn't know the culture, who doesn't even know the fu—flipping—language, but they won't send in a woman.

"So yeah, at this point there are a few people in the business who know me, or at least know what I'm capable of; but most of the time it burns me up that their attitude toward women gets me stuck in places like fu—oh, what the hell, *fucking* London, covering the opening of Parliament, when I should be where the real action is. Does that answer your question?"

"Yes, ma'am," Maddy answered meekly. "I'm sorry if—"

"Oh, to hell with being sorry, Maddy. Regrets slow you down, like leaky galoshes. Better to brave the weather and get your feet wet."

"You sound like your mother."

"Aye," responded Katherine in a full-on Irish brogue, "and a wise woman she is."

By her third day in London, Maddy was beginning to think she would survive all she'd been through during the past ten days. Then came Bernice's telegram.

Please come home immediately. There has been an accident.
Bradley is dead.
B.

TWENTY-SEVEN

Katherine accompanied Maddy on the plane trip home, insisting that she was due a vacation anyway, and that her mother would kill her if she found out that Katherine had let Maddy make the trip alone.

Bernice picked them up at the airport, and it was from her that Maddy learned the details of how her husband had died. He'd driven his car off a cliff, at night, while driving on the Pacific Coast Highway. There was alcohol in his bloodstream at the time of death, and the weather had been, as was usual for that time of year, damp and foggy. Suicide had been ruled out, not only because he'd not left a note, but also because he had, despite the critical nature of his injuries, tried to crawl away from the car before it exploded. He escaped the inferno, but died before the rescue crew could reach him.

"A horrendous accident," Bernice concluded, telling the story as if she were reporting it to a medical conference rather than to the widow of the man who'd died. "Especially at a time like this—not that I expected you two to reconcile, but still—this was no way for things to end."

Maddy was nearly catatonic. Everyone treated her delicately. They had no way of knowing that guilt, as much as grief, was the emotion eating away at her. Down in the untouchable part of her mind where a frightened seven-year-old girl still lived, Maddy knew that she had killed Brad by reaching for Gene, by taking what she wanted, just as surely as she had killed her own mother.

To Maddy's relief, Bernice stepped in and made all of the necessary arrangements. "You don't have to do a thing," she told Maddy firmly. "Burials are arcane, anyway. A waste of perfectly good real estate. Still, if you want to go, I'll go with you, and Katherine will come, too. But I won't have those people putting you through any more nonsense. You've suffered enough at their hands."

Maddy went to the funeral. She sat in the front of the crowded church, flanked by Bernice and Katherine, her guardians against the Boston establishment. Bradley Harrington Gordon III kept his eyes fixed straight ahead, his complexion the color of ancient granite. Bradley's mother wore a hat with a black veil that covered her face. It was impossible for Maddy to believe that she'd been a member of this family for ten years, and had never been a part of it at all. It was impossible to believe that Brad was dead.

The service continued at the gravesite without incident. Once Bradley's coffin had been laid in the ground and the final benediction made, Maddy, Bernice, and Katherine headed straight to their car. Before they'd taken more than a dozen steps they heard Katherine say, "Wait, Maddy. Here she comes."

Maddy turned to see Mrs. Gordon approaching. The older woman walked slowly, uncertainty plaguing her every step.

"Do you want me to stay?" Bernice asked.

"No, thank you. Please wait in the car. You, too, Katherine. This is something I have to do myself."

Her two companions obeyed.

Once they'd gone Mrs. Gordon moved more quickly, visibly relieved to have Maddy to herself. "Thank you for coming, Madeleine," she said when she was close enough to speak in a hushed tone. She raised her veil. Her eyes were puffy, and her skin showed blotches of red beneath her makeup. She'd probably been crying for days.

Maddy simply nodded.

"I know you would have preferred for this to happen in San Francisco. That's where your life is. My husband takes charge of these things. Rather like your aunt. They've had some interesting conversations over the past few days, as you might imagine."

Maddy found herself smiling at Mrs. Gordon's attempt to lighten the air between them. Neither of their smiles lasted very long.

"Bradley called me the day before he died. I was so surprised, and so pleased. Ten years ago I had to choose between my husband and my son. You know the decision I made. I abided by it, though at times I've hated him—my Bradley—for it, and myself for giving in to him so easily.

"Bradley told me that you had quarreled. He said you left him because he'd . . . because he refused to try and adopt a child."

"That's not true," Maddy exclaimed.

"It doesn't matter, dear. I'm not here to blame you. I'm here to apologize. I always thought that Bradley married you because he hated us. Now I know that he married you because he loved you. I'm sorry, as was he, that he could not give you what you wanted."

"But you can't—it wasn't that way—"

"It's all right. At times like this, one sees more clearly what matters and what doesn't. At least, I think women do. We can't just write off the people in our lives the way men can. The way my husband can. We suffer for it. I don't want you to suffer any more than you have to."

Maddy did not have the strength for another denial. Mrs. Gordon leaned over and kissed her on the cheek. "There," she said, on the verge of breaking down herself. "I should have done that ten years ago. If I had, maybe we wouldn't be here now." Her self-restraint in tatters, she stumbled back across the lawn in the direction of the long black limousine that waited to carry her home.

"What did she say?" Katherine asked as Maddy joined them in the car. Bernice listened in stern silence while Maddy choked out her answer between sobs.

"She said she was sorry that she'd let Brad's father cut us off from the family. That she wished things could have been different. And she said . . . she said that Brad called her, before he died, and told her that I left him because he wouldn't let us adopt."

"Did you?" Bernice asked, still ignorant of the true story.

"No, it's not true. Why would he say that?"

"To make you look like the bad guy," Katherine explained, "so his parents wouldn't blame the failure of the marriage on him."

"Oh, God," Maddy moaned, resting her head against the window. "Why am I always, always crying?"

Late that night, when they were all back at Bernice's home in New Jersey, Katherine came into Maddy's bedroom. "Listen, Ma sent something with me, to give to you. You know Ma. She has her own way of doing things. Well, she's had all these letters from your father, letters he sent years ago, back when you started living here with your aunt. I guess you didn't want them at the time, so you sent them back, and he sent them all on to Ma, and told her to give them to you, if she ever felt like you'd want to see them. I never even knew she had them.

"Ma thought that everything was hunky-dory between you and Brad in California, and she never wanted to upset the applecart by sending you these. But yesterday when I was home she handed them off to me, and told me to give them to you, because it might be a good time for you to hear what your father wanted to tell you."

She cleared her throat. "Ma says he loved you, and at a time like this, it might make you feel better. So here they are."

She handed Maddy a manila envelope.

"I can't believe this," Maddy said, looking at the thing as if it might blow up in her hands.

"Yeah, well, me neither, but that's Ma for you. And she might be right, you know. I hate to admit it, but she usually is."

"Thank you, Katherine."

She shrugged. "Don't thank me yet."

Maddy dumped the envelope's contents out on the bed. Inside were the letters she'd received over fifteen years ago. Scrawled across each was the word REFUSED, written by her own hand. All except one.

She picked up the fat envelope. The postmark indicated it had been sent in 1948, well after the others, from Washington, D.C. She ripped it open. Page after page spilled out. Maddy picked up the first one and began to read.

Dear Maddy,

I won't ask your forgiveness, for I don't deserve it. I'm hoping it might help you to understand why I've done what I've done—not to forgive me for it, but to understand it—if you hear my whole story.

Only two people in the world have known everything there is to know about me. One was a man in Shanghai, a

Chinese by the name of Liu Tue-Sheng. The other person who knew me best was your mother. If I had told her everything sooner, perhaps our lives would have turned out differently.

I came from a peasant family in a small village in Hungary. My father was a blacksmith, but when I was ten a teacher came to our village and discovered that I have a gift for learning languages . . .

Maddy read and read and read. She read about how her father was taken in by a foster family in Budapest, and how the first Great War ruined their country and their lives. She read about how her parents met in Paris when he was there on business, about how he was blamed for a counterfeiting scandal, and why he'd killed a man. She read about his decision to flee to Shanghai, about why he'd become involved with the gangster, Liu Tue-Sheng, and what that mistake eventually cost him.

He told her how he'd been recruited to work as a spy, and how that decision made it impossible to come back to her until after the war was over.

Near the end of the letter, he wrote:

At first I told myself that I was protecting you by sending you away. The truth was that I was afraid of failing you, as I had failed your mother. You were right, Maddy. I am a liar and coward. But you must understand that I do love you.

She had to stop reading for a long time. Then, finally, she picked up the last page.

I think, if I did give you anything at all, it was your musical gift. Your mother and I together gave it to you. She was the musical one. And you do have a gift, Maddy. You owe it to yourself to use it. It would have made your mother so happy. She was so proud of you. As am I.

You will not be able to contact me after you receive this letter. I will spend the rest of my life, however long that may be, trying to do something worthwhile for what is left of the human race. I suppose in some ways it's easy for me to take this step because I'm going back to the only arena in my life where I've been successful. But I do love you, my little princess, for what it is worth. I do love you.

When Katherine came in the next morning, she found Maddy sitting on the floor, her father's letters spread around her, still dressed in the clothes she'd worn the previous day.

"Hi," she said uncertainly, not sure whether she should be interrupting. "Do you want some breakfast?"

"I've got to get cleaned up first. Get out of these clothes."

"Did you sleep at all?"

"Not really. I guess I dozed off a little. I feel okay, though."

"Good. So what's in all those letters?"

Maddy picked herself up off the floor. "I think he did love me, Katherine."

"He had a strange way of showing it."

"I know. But he didn't leave me because he didn't care, Katherine. He left because he was lost. And I . . . I know what that feels like."

"I know you do, Maddy." And then Katherine did the only thing she could think of; she gave her old friend a big hug.

TWENTY-EIGHT

Maddy didn't tell Bernice about the letters from her father until after Katherine left for London. Sitting at the breakfast table, her aunt listened patiently.

"I would take everything he said with a grain of salt, Madeleine," Bernice said when Maddy was finished. "He was nothing if not a very capable liar."

"But there's more. I saw Amelia in San Francisco."

"Who?"

"Amelia, my former stepmother. She lives there. We ran into each other. She told me some things about what happened between her and my father. And it's the same story he told me in his letter."

"What does that matter now?"

"It means she lied to you, Aunt Bernice. She lied to us, to keep me from forgiving my father. To keep me away from him."

"Which was not a bad outcome, Maddy."

"How can you be so sure?"

"Maddy, when you're trying to purify a formula, you have to isolate and exclude the impure ingredients to protect the final product. It's no different with human beings. So many unanticipated events can adversely affect the outcome. One controls what one can."

Something in her tone of voice planted a long-overdue realization in Maddy's head. "You knew, didn't you? You knew that she was lying about the extent of her affair with my father, about everything."

"No, I did not know that."

"But you wanted to believe her, didn't you? You didn't want me having anything to do with him."

"And was that so wrong? Was I to stand by and watch him destroy your life as he had destroyed your mother's? Was I not entitled, no, *required* to protect you from that man?"

"Did he really destroy my mother's life? What if she loved him? What if, up until the end, he did make her happy?"

"Madeleine, he abandoned you. And then what forced him to disappear off the face of the earth, might I ask, if he was so determined to reconnect with you? Where is he?"

"I don't know. But if you helped to keep him away from me, then I expect you to help me find him. Or at least find out what happened to him."

"What would be the point? Haven't you been through enough?"

"That *is* the point. I've been through enough not to be afraid of what I could find out."

"I can't imagine how one would go about looking for him."

"Surely your contacts at the Defense Department could come up with something."

"It's not that easy. One doesn't just go peeking through the Pentagon's personnel files."

"You must know someone who can open a few locked doors. Please."

Bernice gave her an exasperated look, but Maddy knew that she'd won. "I'll try," her aunt ultimately agreed. "I can't promise anything, but I will try." Then, as if proceeding to the next agenda item at a business meeting, she changed the subject.

"Will you be going back to live in San Francisco?"

"No."

"That sounds very final."

"It is. I'll go back and pick up a few things, arrange to get the house sold, and that's it. There's nothing left for me there."

"You're welcome to stay with us, of course, until you get your bearings."

"Thank you. I will. Until I get a job, at least."

"A job? What sort of job do you have in mind?"

"I'm going to play the piano."

"Now, dear, you don't need to work just to earn money. Do something that will give you a sense of accomplishment. Focus your efforts on something a bit more practical."

"I know it's not practical. But it's my passion."

She did not call him until a month after Brad's death, and it took several tries before she found him at the number that he'd given her.

"Hello?"

The sound of his voice sent tremors of desire rippling through her body. "It's me. Maddy."

"Maddy, I've been so worried! What took you so long to call? Have you been in London all this time?"

"Actually I've been home for a while. I had to come back. Brad was killed in a car accident."

"Oh, my God. I'm so sorry. Why didn't you call me right away?"

"I didn't want you to get involved. Things were difficult enough."

"But I want to help. When can I see you?"

Now, screamed her body. *Right now*, cried her broken heart. "Gene, I can't. It's not right. And I would always want more of you than I could have."

"You don't know until you try," he said, sounding like a disappointed little boy.

"But I don't want to try. I don't want to be your mistress, or whatever it is I'd be. I have to make a new life for myself."

"Can I at least see you, so we can talk this over?"

"No. If I saw you I'd feel the same way I always feel when I see you."

"Doesn't that tell you something?"

"Please, don't. This is hard enough as it is."

"I can't lose you again."

"That's the stupid part. You never have. I just can't live by your rules."

"You'll change your mind."

"I don't think so. Gene?"

"Yes?"

"I need to know something. On the ship you said that you'd 'kept tabs' on me. Does that mean . . . did you ever hire a private detective?"

Silence.

"Richard Bates?"

"I'm sorry. That was years ago. I didn't want—"

"Don't ever spy on me again."

"I promise. Maddy, please—"

"Good-bye, Gene." She hung up the phone. She felt a dead weight descend upon her chest. She did not know how she would ever feel happy again.

"Work will take your mind off your other problems" was Bernice's advice. Maddy was prepared to listen. She knew that she could never make up for the ten years of lost time. But the music was still there, if she could find a way to let it out. She wanted to find a place for herself, and she knew her music was the key.

She couldn't just walk into Carnegie Hall and start playing. Maybe a nightclub? But so few remained. Television enabled musicians to wander into people's homes with the push of a button, and Technicolor magic brought dazzling, full-scale musicals to the movies. But surely, somewhere in New York, someone must still appreciate live music.

Maddy started to make the rounds of the older clubs still in business, asking if anyone needed to hire a house pianist, someone who was versatile enough to accompany the guest artists, and good enough as a soloist to entertain the clientele between headliners. She kept hearing the same answer: "Sister, the only place that could use someone like you in this day and age is a jazz joint."

And so Maddy discovered that in the heart of Manhattan, from Fiftieth to Fifty-ninth Street, from Seventh to Third Avenue, there remained a small nest of the smoothest musical environment ever invented: the jazz club. Teens had flocked to rock 'n' roll, but to those who appreciated it, nothing could replace the sense-surrounding strains of live jazz.

She'd played a little jazz in music school; it was a form of music very suited to her ear, and she was confident in her ability to follow another musician's lead and then improvise quickly, to help create a raft of musical notes in a rushing river of harmonious sound; but a discouraging chorus of "no openings," "no, thank you," "let me take your name" was all she received as she trudged from club to club.

Then, one Friday night, a call came.

When the phone rang it was nearly nine o'clock. Maddy did not make a move to answer it; any call received at that hour was normally from one of Archie's contractors in California. But she responded quickly to Bernice's rather grouchy summons.

"Madeleine, there's a telephone call for you. A Mr. Silvers. He says it's urgent."

Curious, Maddy set aside the book she had been browsing through and went to the phone.

"Maddy Gordon? This is Matt Silvers, at the Blue Door. I've got a gig for you."

"A what? Oh, wow. That's great. When?"

"Tonight, sugar. As soon as you can get here."

"Tonight?"

"Honey, I can go to the next person on my list if you can't do it, but you made a good impression on me when you came in last week, and it's an all-male trio you need to back up. A classy kid like you would be a nice touch. Interested?"

"I'm sorry. Which club is it?"

"The Blue Door. On Fifty-second."

Maddy remembered it. It wasn't the nicest, but it was far from the seediest. The club was located in the basement of an old brownstone building, behind a blue door that gave the place its name. "When do I have to be there?"

"When can you get here?"

"In an hour?"

"Make it less." He hung up.

Maddy made it to the club in less than forty-five minutes. The crowd was still light. She recognized the man standing at the hostess station as the man for whom she had auditioned, and hurried over to him.

"I'm Maddy. Where do I go?"

"Glad you could make it, sweetheart. Let me take you back to meet the group. You'll have to play it by ear tonight, sister. Do what Casper tells you to. He's the lead, on sax. You got a good sound; you'll do okay. And thanks."

The next four hours went by in a whirlwind of music. With no time to prepare, all Casper wanted her to do was listen and improvise: play in the background, leap in when the groove got slow. Even playing on the club's shabby upright piano, Maddy was in heaven. She could feel the emotion of the crowd, felt the music pulsing inside her. It was a little like, no, it was a lot like great sex.

"Terrific," Casper told Maddy at the end of the evening. "Man, we were lucky to get you on such short notice. Where do you play?"

"At home," she laughed, wiping the sweat off her face with a napkin.

"No kidding? Aw, sister, c'mon. Did you take this gig behind your agent's back, or what? Got somebody who'll want a piece if he finds out?"

"An agent?" Maddy asked blankly. She'd never even thought about getting an agent. What a dimwit she was.

"This lady doesn't need an agent," interjected Matt, stepping onto the small platform that constituted a stage. "She's got a job. Here. She's the house pianist."

Maddy gave him a dazzling smile. "How much are you paying me?" she asked sweetly, as Matt grimaced and the band members broke into guffaws.

"Don't let him tell you we play for love," Casper warned as he put his horn away.

But Maddy would have, if they asked her to. She would have played for free. She'd found where she wanted to be.

The next day she found an apartment in the city, not far from the club. It was more like an overgrown studio than an actual apartment, but it was the first place she'd ever lived in that was all hers: not paid for by her aunt or her husband, not shared with a roommate. It was hers alone.

Bernice thought the whole plan was some sort of disturbing psychological response to Brad's death, and said so. Maddy tried to explain to her that the marriage to Brad had been the mistake; this was what she should have done years ago. This was who she was. She was sure.

Each new artist with whom she played helped her to reach further; the responses to her solo gigs during the week were fantastic. Matt Silvers knew he had a find on his hands, but he kept that fact to himself. He asked Maddy to sign a contract. She did so gladly, grateful for the opportunity.

After a couple of weeks her new lifestyle began to take a bit of a toll on her. She slept until late in the afternoon, but still woke up feeling exhausted and nauseous from the long nights spent nibbling on pretzels and inhaling other people's cigarette smoke. But the exhilaration she felt by the time she was onstage filled every tired cell of her body with adrenaline, and all discomfort was forgotten.

One evening, when she had been working at the Blue Door for about a month, Maddy started up a conversation with one of the waitresses, a pretty young blonde who wanted to be an actress. Charlene knew every story about every Broadway and Hollywood starlet who had allegedly been discovered in a sandwich shop, a country club, a department store, or on the beach. "I check out the customers really well. If there's a show biz somebody here, I'll sniff him out," she confided as Maddy helped herself to a handful of olives from behind the bar.

Charlene made a face. "Maddy, I ain't never seen nobody eat olives by the handful that way. Except my cousin Josephine, when she was pregnant. It was hilarious. No martini was safe for miles."

"Well, I'm not pregnant," Maddy responded playfully, as she helped herself to another handful.

The idea stayed with her as she drove home. She thought about her nausea in the mornings, or rather, in the afternoons, when she woke up. Her periods had always been irregular, and since she and Brad had not needed birth control . . . It was silly. It was impossible.

Before going to work the next day she slipped into a nearby clinic and asked for a test. Two days later, a nurse called her.

"Congratulations, Mrs. Gordon. You're going to have a baby."

TWENTY-NINE

Gene Mandretti lived in a roomy house on the north shore of Long Island, with his wife, the former Tina Rose Marro, and their two children. Gene's uncle, Salvatore Mandretti, worked with Tina's uncle, Frank "Papa" Carbolo. Sal and Frank had grown up as friends in the same shabby neighborhood. Through hard work, perseverance, and a little old-fashioned luck, they'd both risen to positions of achievement within their shared profession. Frank was the head of the Carbolo crime syndicate, one of the most powerful of the Five Families of the New York Italian mafia. Salvatore was his chief lieutenant.

Salvatore was not well educated, but he was observant, and practical. He knew it was no joke that Al Capone, Waxey Gordon, and a handful of other smaller figures had gone to jail, not for murder or extortion, but for tax evasion. Salvatore also knew that neither he nor his lifelong friend Frank Carbolo would be able to keep the Internal Revenue Service accountants off their asses forever.

Sal's little brother, Tony Mandretti, had been one of Papa Carbolo's bodyguards. He'd died during an attempt on the don's life by a rival gang. So Sal took Tony's widow, his son, Geno, and his two daughters into his own home. He got the boy a good education at a fancy prep school, then sent him to an even fancier college. He made Gene keep out of trouble. Sal figured that the Carbolos didn't need another hit man or another bill collector. What they really needed was a business-man to run the finances and keep them all out of jail.

Gene graduated from business school in 1951, the same year that Senator Estes Kefauver's well-publicized hearings on the operations of the New York Underworld triggered an unprecedented effort by the Internal Revenue Service to convict hundreds of suspected mafia mem-bers for tax fraud. The timing was perfect.

"We need to get better at hiding the money coming in," Gene ex-plained the first time he was asked to meet with Papa Carbolo. "You buy a yacht, the IRS wants to know where you got the money; we have to make it look like it was all earned legally. To do that we have to diversify into legitimate businesses. Illegal money can generate legal money, lots of it, making the origins of the initial capital easier to disguise."

"But won't we have to pay more taxes?" Papa Carbolo spoke like a beaten-up boxer, for his nose had been broken several times before he'd developed into a man no one would dare assault unless he wanted to die.

"Some. But that's better than going to jail, and paying a few taxes lays the groundwork for the rest of our enterprise, which, on the out-side, appears legitimate. Remember, they only use the tax code as a weapon because they can't get us any other way. If you can make the money look clean, you've disarmed them. Make the paper trail compli-cated enough, they'll give up and go pick on someone else."

"You think you can do all this?"

"I know I can."

Carbolo shifted his attention to Sal, who'd been listening politely the whole time.

"He's a smart boy. You done good to bring him to me."

Salvatore beamed.

Gene was as good as his word. Within four years, three different Family-owned corporations held investments in, among other things, commercial and residential real estate, a cigarette vending business, and a waste-removal service. Through these various ventures they were able to launder the vast sums earned through their more nefarious enterprises.

Papa Carbolo was pleased. He was so pleased, in fact, that when his niece, Tina, came home from college for Christmas, took one look at Gene Mandretti and fell in love, Papa suggested to Sal that such a union had all the earmarks of a match made in heaven. The old friends were delighted when Gene and Tina reacted positively to their matchmaking plans.

By the fall of 1960 Gene had fulfilled everyone's expectations, and did so in a way that kept his name from being associated with the lords of the mafia. He was a very successful businessman with a loving family. He had everything he wanted.

Almost.

That year Gene decided it was time to go into the entertainment business. Not the brothels that had been the Family's bread-and-butter for years, but legitimate entertainment. Who knew how many martinis were consumed in one night? Who knew what the bills would be for dry-cleaning tablecloths, for tuning a piano, for publicity? How could the IRS argue with well-kept receipts?

He had a specific place in mind. There was a little jazz club on

Fifty-second Street, between Fifth and Madison. It had been around for years, had a good reputation, and the owner, a man by the name of Matt Silvers, liked to gamble. In fact, he owed money to one of the bookies in the area. It was not a Carbolo operation but there were, Gene explained at the Family's quarterly board meeting, times when it made good sense to pay off someone else's debt. They could acquire the Blue Door and the whole building it was in for pennies on the dollar by bailing Silvers out and giving him enough to start a new place. Somewhere else.

"But jazz?" Papa Carbolo asked quizzically. "It ain't music, even."

"That's the beauty of it. Whether we have a hundred people a night or twenty, it won't matter. We either make money, or we use the club to wash it. Either way, we win."

"Okay, Gene. You ain't taken a wrong step yet. We'll go with it."

According to the corporate bylaws, a vote on a new investment required approval by a majority of the board of directors. In reality, Papa's was the only vote that counted.

Two weeks later a rather agitated Matt Silvers asked everyone on the Blue Door staff to stay after closing. All the regulars assembled: Charlene and Theresa, the waitresses; Jimmy, the doorman; Tex, the bartender who wasn't from Texas; Al, the cook; Luis, the busboy; and Maddy, the house pianist. They all sat and listened as Matt explained that he'd sold the Blue Door.

"But the new owners, they won't be makin' any changes, at least not right away. You'll all be able to keep your jobs for six months. That's part of the deal. I didn't want to leave you guys high and dry."

Six months won't mean that much to me, Maddy thought as she processed the news. She would only be able to play at the Blue Door for a few more weeks; an unmistakably pregnant woman playing the piano in a nightclub went beyond the bounds of good taste. At four months her belly looked like she'd swallowed a small cantaloupe whole, but luckily the latest fashions helped hide her expanding waistline. Nothing was more forgiving than a trapeze dress.

As the group broke up, Matt approached Maddy.

"Listen, sweetheart, one of the new owners wants to meet you. They know you're my ace in the hole."

"Sure. Have him call me."

"Well, he's here now. Upstairs, in my apartment."

"Now? Oh, Matt, I'm bushed."

"Yeah, well, as a favor to me, could you go up and say hello? He came in and heard you play tonight. He said you were fantastic."

"Okay, okay," Maddy replied, flattered out of her exhaustion. "I'll go. What's the guy's name?"

"Ah, darn. I don't remember. But he's a real charmer. You'll like him."

The small brownstone had been divided into two apartments. Matt lived in the one on the first floor, so that his bed was directly above the Blue Door's stage. "No tenant would stand for it," he explained, "and I'm almost never home when the music is playing."

The door was ajar. Maddy went in without knocking.

"Hello? Is anyone here?" she called out.

The door closed behind her.

"Hello, angel."

Maddy flinched. "Gene? You—don't come near me. I'm leaving."

"Wait, Maddy, hear me out."

"No, damn it, I thought you would at least respect my—oh, my God. You bought the club?"

"I bought the whole building. Got a good deal, too."

"Oh, you son of a bitch," Maddy yelled at him, using one of the colorful phrases she'd picked up from her new circle of friends. "I thought you said—how could you—"

"I called your aunt's secretary and asked about you. She was happy to tell me that you were becoming a jazz sensation. And Mason Industries isn't exactly an unlisted number."

"But you said—"

"You told me not to call you, and I didn't. I'm not trying to be funny, Maddy. I'm only trying to be able to see you on your terms."

"My terms? I can't see you at all. I quit."

"You have a contract."

"So sue me. Anyway, I won't be able to play for more than a few—" she stopped, horrified at what had almost come out of her mouth. She'd promised herself that Gene would be the last person in the world to find out about her baby.

"Why, Maddy? Why won't you be able to play?" he asked, moving closer.

"Because I'm going on a trip."

"Where?"

"To Brazil, to study samba. Oh, God, Gene. This isn't what I want—"

"Yes, it is, Maddy." He wrapped his arms around her shoulders. "I have a present for you."

"I don't want it."

"Wait until you see what it is, before you say no." He dropped his arms. "Go look on the coffee table."

"No."

"Maddy, I'm not going to let you out of here until you go look on the table. Come on, it's in the envelope."

She sighed heavily, not sure how much more she could stand. "Fine. But whatever it is, I'm not keeping it." She walked over and picked up a large envelope. Inside was a document. She pulled it out and began to read.

"You can't do this," she said within seconds.

"Yes, I can. I own the place."

"But I don't want it."

"Why not? A lot of the big jazz artists have—or had—their own clubs: Goldie Hawkins, Eddie Condon, Jimmy Daniels. You hold in your hands a lease to the Blue Door, for ten years, at what I would call an outstanding rate. The landlord will also pay the salary of the manager of your choice, within the stated limit. But I decide who keeps the books. You artistic types are notoriously bad in that department, and part of the rent comes from your profits."

"I don't know anything about running a club."

"You won't have to. You handle the music. The manager will handle the business. I'll handle the finances. The important thing is it will be yours."

"No, it won't be. It will be yours," she said stubbornly.

"Ours, then. But it will be your music. Music you can share, music no one can take away from you."

"Gene, I—"

"Just sign it."

"I have to think."

"No, angel, no. You don't have to think. That's the last thing you need to do." He moved closer. She spun away from him. He put his arms around her anyway, and his hands came to rest on the firm mound of her stomach.

Gene was already a father. His fingers knew the truth.

"Maddy, how could you not tell me—"

She pulled away from him. "This is not your baby. This is *my* baby. This has nothing to do with you."

"Nothing to do with me? You don't think—"

"It's Brad's."

He stepped back. "Are you sure?"

"Yes," she lied, holding her chin up defiantly. "I've counted. There's no way this baby could be yours."

"I see."

Maddy could not tell what he was thinking. "So," she said crisply, determined to leave before she started to cry, "I guess we can tear this up—"

"No," Gene said sharply, grabbing her wrist. "This doesn't change anything. Maddy, I will take whatever part of you I can have. If I can't share you, at least I can share your music. I promise you, I'll never ask anything of you that you are unprepared to give. Please, sign it."

Maddy contemplated the pen he had placed in her hand. Could she do it? Could she somehow keep the Blue Door, and her baby, and have Gene for a business partner? Maddy put her hand on her stomach protectively. She was so alone. The alternative was to go back to her aunt Bernice and admit she'd failed: to give up.

She signed.

Maddy's baby was born in the spring: a beautiful baby girl with black hair and blue eyes. "Just like her grandfather," remarked Bernice coldly, not at all happy about the apparent resemblance to Leo Hoffman. She'd kept her word about investigating the man's fate, but the short paper trail she'd uncovered led to a dead end. The navy would only confirm that he'd worked in intelligence during the war. For Maddy, the knowledge was a comfort. She'd found one twig of truth in the nest of deception in which she'd grown up. It helped.

Maddy named her daughter Martha Anne Gordon: Martha, after her mother, and Anne, to honor her best friend, Mary Katherine Anne O'Connor. She called her child Annie. Maddy did not get in touch with Brad's parents. She did not want to open that pandora's box again.

When Annie was a month old, Maddy moved into Matt's old apartment over the Blue Door. She hired a nanny, an old Polish woman named Tia, who came with a list of references as long as her arm. Business at the Blue Door was good. Maddy was able to book many well-known musicians into the club, and even pop down and play herself when she felt like it.

Bernice was horrified at her lifestyle. Maddy did not care. She was happy. She loved her work, and had most of the day to spend with Annie. She was overwhelmed with love for her child, and she wallowed in the unconditional adoration that Annie gave her in return. She felt stronger and more capable than she'd ever felt before.

Gene never pressured Maddy. Their conversations were infrequent and strictly business. When Maddy was scheduled to play he sometimes dropped in to listen. He never stayed long.

On the afternoon of Annie's first birthday Gene showed up unannounced, his arms full of presents. After Gene and Maddy watched the baby smear herself with cake and plow through her gifts, Maddy put Annie down for her nap, and Gene took Maddy in his arms.

Maddy had the Blue Door, and her music, and her baby. She also had a piece of Gene. She decided that was enough.

PART FIVE

THIRTY
BERLIN, 1963

On a street corner in West Berlin an old man waited for a bus. He was sitting on a wrought-iron bench, reading a newspaper. At six o'clock it was already quite dark. There was little traffic at that hour; most Berliners were home for dinner by then. The air was frigid. The man wore an old leather coat, and his head was wrapped in a hat lined with sheepskin. Cracked leather gloves barely covered his hands.

A few feet behind the old man, attached to the outside wall of a small tobacco shop that had been closed for at least an hour, was a public telephone. At a few minutes after six, the phone rang.

The old man ignored it. After a dozen rings the phone went quiet, but within a few seconds it began to ring again. The man looked back at the phone and scowled. A gust of air formed a cloud of condensation in front of his face as he sighed. He got up off the bench and looked down the street to see if his bus was coming. It was not. The phone kept ringing.

With a cantankerous grunt the man folded his paper, tucked it under his arm, and shuffled over to the phone. He picked up the receiver.

"Ja?"

"Is that you, Walter?" asked a man's voice.

"Nein, nein, this is not your friend Walter. This is a public phone, at a bus stop. You have the wrong number."

"I know this is a public phone. My friend was supposed to be there, waiting for my call. Is there anyone else there? A husky man in his fifties? Brown hair, glasses?"

"No. There is only me, an old man waiting for the bus."

"Well, I guess he got tired of waiting. I don't blame him. I can't wait any longer, myself. I have to get going. Good-bye."

The old man heard a dial tone, and then hung the receiver carefully back on the hook.

His bus arrived. He rode it for ten blocks, then alighted near a small coffee shop. He went in and ordered a cup of coffee. As he waited, he pulled out a pen, and doodled on his paper napkin.

The coffee arrived, and he drank it, slowly, taking his time, reading the newspaper he still carried with him. When he finished he wiped his mouth on the napkin, crumpled it up, and stuffed it inside the empty cup. He fumbled through his pocket for an appropriate amount of change, dropped it onto the table, and with a solemn "danke" gave his thanks to no one in particular and hobbled out the door.

After he had gone the waiter came over to clear his place. He saw the napkin in the cup, and made a face.

When he got off work that night the waiter walked home, as usual. As usual, he walked by a small office building, the front of which was guarded by two American military police. They were dressed warmly against the cold, and stood well within the frame of the door to stay out of the wind.

As he crossed in front of the doorway the waiter reached in his coat pocket and pulled out a pack of cigarettes. The old man's napkin fell out of his pocket onto the sidewalk.

"Hey, you, pick that up," ordered one of the soldiers in very bad German.

"Pick it up yourself, asshole," the man shot back, not breaking his stride.

The guard rolled his eyes, stepped forward, and, with a couple of mumbled curses, stooped down to scoop up the paper. He shoved it in his own pocket.

The napkin changed hands again, twice, before making it out of Germany. The message it carried was decoded at a military base in England. The message was then reencrypted and transmitted by wire to the Central Intelligence Agency in Washington, D.C.

This wire was personally decoded by the deputy director for Eastern European covert operations. "Shit," the man said as the translation became clear. "SHIT, SHIT, SHIT."

He then called his own boss, the assistant director, who then called the head of the CIA and asked to see him immediately.

There was no easy way to deliver the message. "We've had an emergency communication from Chameleon. His cover is blown. He's trying to get out," the assistant director blurted out, not even bothering to sit down.

"Oh, Jesus H. Christ." The director put his head in his hands. "Well, there goes the most successful mole operation in American history. Fifteen years. Damn it to hell! Any details?"

"Not yet, sir."

"Anything we can do to help him?"

"We don't even know where he is, sir."

"Has he been caught?"

"Not as of yesterday, at least, not according to anything we've been able to pick up. Even if his cover was badly blown, I doubt they'd advertise. Too damn embarrassing."

"And if he's caught?"

"He knows what to do. And he will. He'll take the pill. I know this man."

"Oh, Christ, I hope so." The director gazed with mournful resignation at the phone on his desk. "Well, I guess I better call the president. If Khrushchev calls him up all pissed off, Jack will have my ass in a sling if he doesn't know what it's all about."

"Yes, sir. Sorry, sir."

"Keep me posted. God help the son of a bitch. He's done one hell of a job."

"Yes, sir. Thank you, sir." He hurried out.

The director shook his head, then picked up the phone. "Peggy? Get me the White House."

THIRTY-ONE
NEW YORK

Assistant United States Attorney Ryan Matthew Sullivan leaned forward on his desk and looked impatiently at his watch. He was excruciatingly punctual, and therefore completely intolerant of tardiness in others. The two FBI agents he was supposed to meet with, Kevin Royster and John "Jimmy" Jamison, were already ten minutes late.

Well, he thought. *They will learn.*

Sullivan's physical appearance was somewhat at odds with his stern professional reputation. He had a round, boyish face, accented by an embarrassing splash of freckles across his nose. Tall and lithe, he could easily be mistaken for an athlete, or a poet. More than anything else he was unmistakably Irish, and he owed his looks and his career choice to the law-and-order Irish family into which he had been born.

His great-grandfather had been a magistrate in the old country. His grandfather had been a policeman in Boston. His father had been a special agent for the Bureau of Alcohol, Tobacco and Firearms, and had waged war against the bootlegging gangs of New York City and Chicago during Prohibition.

Sullivan knew from an early age that his mission in life was to do what his father, and his father's father, had both done before him. He was going to get the bad guys. And he knew that the very worst of all the bad guys belonged to a shady organization known as the Italian mafia. Some people said that the mafia didn't exist, that there was no such thing as organized crime. But Ryan Sullivan had been raised to believe in the existence of the mafia the way some children were raised to believe in miracles, or the invincibility of the Yankees.

He joined the police force in New York when he was seventeen. After his stint in the Pacific he went back to the force, using his G.I. benefits to pay for night school. With a college degree he landed a job at the Federal Bureau of Investigation, where to his disappointment he spent five years investigating alleged Communists, because J. Edgar Hoover, longtime director of the FBI, confidently pooh-poohed the whole concept of organized crime. So Sullivan decided to quit the Bureau and become a prosecutor.

Ryan Sullivan was in his third year at New York University Law School when the New York State Police stumbled into a meeting of the heads of all the major crime families in America. He gloated over the press coverage, relishing every detail. Over fifty known gangsters had gathered at a private estate in Apalachin, New York, and they fled when the police showed up. Among the "guests" apprehended in the raid, fifty had police records; all were Italian or of Italian descent, and nearly half were related by blood or marriage. There was no way to argue that it had been anything other than a meeting of the mafia bosses.

In the face of this public relations disaster, Sullivan thought, Hoover would have to do something. The hounds of vengeance would be released, and he intended to be at the front of the pack.

But still, Hoover stalled.

Upon his graduation from law school Sullivan was hired as an assistant prosecutor by the Manhattan District Attorney's office. The pay was lousy, and the work seldom glamorous. He worked more on assault, battery, and theft cases than anything that smacked of organized crime, but he learned a lot. He got to know the cops: who could be trusted, who couldn't. He got to know the politicians: who was honest, who had a reputation for being on the mob's payroll. He saw how the mafia bosses let underlings take the hit for petty offenses to keep themselves out of jail, and he observed that the mafia soldiers did so willingly. By dealing with the crooks in the trenches, Ryan began to get a handle on how the mob made its money. He began to know his enemy.

When John Fitzgerald Kennedy was sworn in as president Sullivan applied for a job as a federal prosecutor with the Department of Justice, in Attorney General Robert Kennedy's Organized Crime division. Robert Kennedy had been chief counsel to Senator John McClellan when the senator spearheaded an investigation of the mafia's alleged infiltration of the country's biggest labor unions. During that time the younger Kennedy had not hidden his belief in, or his fiery contempt for, the mafia. Sullivan had finally found a hero.

He got the job as an assistant United States attorney. After two years in Washington, D.C., Sullivan was assigned to the Organized Crime division's brand-new New York field office. His mission, like that of his peers, was to crack the mob. By February 1963, he was where he'd always wanted to be.

It was slow going. By and large, the mafia chieftains learned from their mistakes. The code of silence remained unbroken. It was virtually impossible to get information. The bosses were much more likely to get killed by one another than to land in jail for any serious offense.

But Ryan Sullivan had a plan.

Two men showed up at the open door of his small, spartan office. One was fair-haired and slim; the other had a Mediterranean complexion, dark hair, and the stocky physique of a wrestler. Both wore the FBI "uniform": dark blazer, straight black tie, and white shirt, topped off by a bristly military-style haircut.

"Come in, gentlemen," said Ryan, before either man had a chance to say hello. "I've been waiting for you."

Jamison responded for both of them. "Gee, Mr. Sullivan. Sorry about the time. Traffic is hell at this hour."

"New to New York?" Ryan inquired pleasantly.

"No, sir," Jamison answered. "Lived here all my life."

"Then you should be prepared for the traffic. Next time get an earlier start."

Jamison and Royster exchanged glances. The new prosecutor was an even bigger hard-ass than they'd anticipated. They took their seats across from Ryan.

"We're going after the Carbolo Family," Ryan told them, as soon as they'd settled into their chairs. "I want to fill you in on the target of this particular investigation."

He handed each of the men a folder. "This is a background report on Gene Mandretti. I think he is the key to the Carbolos' money-laundering operation. I want him tailed for the next three weeks. I want to know where he eats, sleeps, pisses, drinks coffee, and buys cigarettes, what he eats for breakfast and how often he does it with his wife. You can choose two agents from the pool to help you, but choose well. This is no typical—"

Royster interrupted. "Who is this guy, exactly?"

"He's the nephew of Frank 'Papa' Carbolo's right hand man, Salvatore Mandretti, and married to Papa Carbolo's niece. Went to Williams College and then to NYU Business School. Serves on the board of several of the Family's privately held corporations."

"How do you know he's on the team? They're always using blind family to hide assets," Jamison observed.

"I don't. Call it an educated guess. The first Carbolo-held company wasn't incorporated until a year and a half after little Geno here graduated from business school. Over the past eight years the IRS boys have been able to tag nearly a hundred of the underbosses from the other four mafia families for various forms of tax fraud and evasion. They haven't touched the Carbolos. Why? Financial sophistication. That sure isn't Papa's strong suit. I think Geno is the brains behind the cleanliness of their operation. Here are photos and start-up information, home address, etc. Come back in three weeks. Call me with any questions. I want a daily log."

"Okay," Royster said, with a sigh of resignation.

"I don't require enthusiasm, Mr. Royster, just competence. I've been told you are an excellent agent, despite your eccentricities. I don't expect to be disappointed."

Royster rose from his chair, not sure if he should feel insulted or flattered. "Three weeks," he said after a brief pause. "We'll be here."

The next time they came to Sullivan's office Royster and Jamison carried with them a stack of journals, several files of documents, and a book of photographs. They showed up on time.

"Well, what do you have for me?" Sullivan asked as they sat down, skipping all small talk.

"Well, it wasn't easy, I'll say that much," replied Royster. "It's like the man expects to be followed. He lost us on numerous occasions. I think he routinely takes countersurveillance measures, which I guess is actually an encouraging sign. Goes home to the little wife and two cute kids on Long Island most nights, but sometimes stays in the city during the week. Real snappy dresser. Has a driver, definitely a bodyguard type. Carries lead. The driver, that is."

"Any unusual patterns of behavior? Anything we can use?"

"I'm getting to that. The one place, other than home, he went to once a week was this jazz club, in a building owned by the Family, on Fifty-second Street. Went in early, between seven and eight. Came out late, around midnight."

"Any chance there's a meeting going on?"

"Could be. It's a small place, and the one time I sent Peyton in after him for a peek—he's the other agent helping us on this—he didn't see Geno boy anywhere, so there's got to be a back room of some kind, although we couldn't find any sign of a back entrance."

"Who else was there?"

"That's the odd part. No one. No one we could identify, anyway." He began flipping through the notebook of photographs. "We got a shot of everybody who works there: bartender, busboy, doorman, manager, two waitresses, and all the musicians. The piano player is one hell of a looker. It appears she lives in the building. Looks like everything but the club's been converted to one big apartment. No sign of a husband. Here she is." He handed the open book of photographs across the desk to Sullivan.

He saw a beautiful woman: slender, with black hair, ivory skin, and a heart-shaped face. She was holding on to the hand of a little girl, who was concentrating on her feet, trying to navigate the steps that led from the door to the sidewalk. The woman was smiling down at her, and pushing her own hair out of her face with her free hand. Hadn't he seen her somewhere before?

"Check her out," he told the two agents.

"Who, the dame?"

"Yes. What's her name?"

"Madeleine Gordon."

"Get me everything you can on Madeleine Gordon. By the end of the week I want to know her better than her own mother does."

"Can I ask why?" Jamison inquired, full of curiosity.

"Isn't it obvious? Gene goes to this place once a week. No one else we know shows up to see him. She lives in the building, which is owned by the Family. My money says she's Geno's 'special friend.' Good start. Let's see where this leads." He handed the notebook back.

"We aim to please," Royster said, not bothering to disguise his sarcasm as he gathered up their files.

Jamison finally spoke up. "Didn't you tell us that this guy is married to Papa Carbolo's niece?"

"That's right."

"Brave son of a bitch then, ain't he?" opined Jamison. "One portrait of a suspected mafia mistress coming up."

The three men met again two weeks later. This time Royster could not hide his excitement as he tossed his treasure onto Sullivan's desk. "Here's the report."

"What does it say?" Sullivan would read it later, cover to cover, underlining items, taking notes, and preparing a list of questions. First he wanted the investigators' informal impressions.

"Well, it was pretty easy, really. Had Jamison call her up, usin' his best 'been to Princeton' accent, and he told her that he was a freelance journalist doing a piece for the *New Yorker*—'Jazz in the City'—and wanted to interview her." He gestured to Jamison. "Give him the scoop, Jimmy."

"We met at a little coffee shop down the street from her club. She was pleasant and cooperative. Not at all what I expected. I mean, she's pretty classy. Anyway, her maiden name is Hoffman. She had two years of classical musical training at the New Music School in Cambridge, but quit to marry Bradley Gordon, a doctor, whom she met while he was at Harvard. They moved out west and lived in San Francisco, but she moved back to New York when her husband died in a car accident three years ago.

"I asked her about her family, and she got a little evasive; said her parents died in the war. I laid on some sympathy, you know, 'So you're all alone in the world?' and that kind of thing. She told me she had a daughter, which we already knew, as well as an aunt living in New Jersey. Then we talked about jazz. She's had an impressive list of musicians in her place—"

Royster chimed in. "We talked to a few people at the New Music School, including an old guy named Auerbach, who was very sorry to see her quit. Said she was an incredible talent, blah, blah. Also told us that her husband's family is loaded, and that her aunt in Jersey is none other than Bernice Mason of Mason Industries."

"Hang on a second," Sullivan mused aloud. "Didn't Archibald Mason . . . wasn't he the one who dropped dead of a heart attack on the floor of the New York Stock Exchange the day his company went public last year?"

"That's the one. Stock hit the market, quadrupled in an hour, and the poor ol' guy's ticker blew out when he realized how much money he was making, leaving his wife a very wealthy widow. Which means Mrs. Gordon doesn't have to work, unless she's on the outs with her aunt or her husband's family."

"Interesting. What else?"

"Here's the kicker. Check out Mrs. Gordon's 1961 tax return." He picked up the report and flipped to one of the last pages, pointing and talking. "Declared income of over eighty thousand dollars, based on salary and the club's net."

"That's a pretty big number."

"Yeah, especially since it's a pretty small place. Nice, but no Copacabana. Becomes even more suspicious when you check out her bank account. Either she keeps cash under her bed or the money goes elsewhere." He sat back, a smug look on his face. "Or it doesn't exist."

"I think we have what we need, gentlemen. Let's see if we can arrange to meet Mrs. Madeleine Gordon and ask her a few pertinent questions. Every man has a weakness." Sullivan picked up another picture of Maddy and examined it closely. "Every man has a weakness," he repeated. "Maybe this woman is Gene Mandretti's."

THIRTY-TWO

On a clear and breezy Thursday afternoon Maddy left her favorite hair salon and walked toward Fifth Avenue to buy some new clothes for spring. She was half a block away from the shops when she saw a man she recognized. It was Bob Carlson, the journalist who'd interviewed her a few weeks earlier for a piece in the *New Yorker*. Maddy waved cheerfully as she approached him. "Well, hello again."

"Hi, Mrs. Gordon. Gosh, was this lucky running into you like this. Do you think you could talk to me for a few minutes? I have a few more questions for you."

Maddy sneaked a peek at her watch, but there was really no hurry. "Okay, if you like."

"Great."

Another man came over and joined them. He was tall and slim, with reddish hair and a sweet, friendly face. Maddy smiled at him.

"Is this a friend of yours?" she asked Carlson. He said nothing. The other man spoke.

"Mrs. Gordon, I'm Ryan Sullivan, with the United States Attorney's office. This gentleman works for the FBI. We need to ask you some questions."

This must have something to do with my father, Maddy thought, for no clear reason. *My father the spy.*

The redhead took her by the elbow. "We'll walk over to the park, if that's all right, and find a comfortable place to chat." His expression was friendly but serious. Maddy allowed herself to be led across the street.

They headed for a bench where another man sat: a stocky Mediterranean type. He grinned up at Maddy as they approached. The look in his eyes put her on the defensive.

"Royster, keep your eyes open," the redhead ordered.

The man called Royster heaved himself up off the bench. "Nice day for a walk, isn't it?" he commented, and sauntered away.

"What's all this about?" Maddy demanded.

"We'll get to that," replied the tall redhead mildly. He took the seat vacated by Royster. "Please, sit down."

Maddy did as she was asked, growing more alarmed by the minute.

"Tape running?" the redhead asked the man Maddy knew as Bob Carlson.

"Yes, sir."

"Okay. April 17, 1963. First contact with racketeering suspect Madeleine Gordon—"

"What did you just say?"

"My name, in case you missed it the first time, is Ryan Sullivan, and I work for the attorney general's Organized Crime division. Mr. Jamison, whom you met as Bob Carlson, is an agent with the Federal Bureau of Investigation. You are currently under investigation, because evidence has come to light suggesting that you are involved with an organized crime syndicate."

"That's ridiculous. There must be some mistake."

"I don't think so. Do you know a gentleman by the name of Gene Mandretti?"

Maddy look startled but didn't answer. Sullivan proceeded to interrogate her. "Speak up, please. We'll need your answer to register on the tape. Do you know Gene Mandretti?"

"Of course I do. He's my landlord."

"Is that the full extent of your relationship?"

"Yes. Well, we're friends, but it's essentially a business relationship."

"I see. Mrs. Gordon, I think I should explain to you what is involved here. Jamison, let's have the tax return."

Jamison knelt down, opened his briefcase, pulled out a document, and handed it over.

"Do you recognize this as your tax return for 1961?"

She glanced at it. "I wouldn't know. I don't do my own taxes."

"Is that your signature?"

"I guess so. I sign the papers but I don't really check them over. I have no idea how to read one of those things. Gene—Mr. Mandretti—has his accountant handle the club's finances."

"How much money did you make that year?"

"I paid myself a salary of twenty thousand dollars. Mr. Mandretti tells me the club is profitable, but not remarkably so. I don't really play for the money, Mr. Sullivan. Maybe that's hard for you to understand—"

"Do you have any idea what the club cleared, over and above your salary?"

"Thirty thousand, something in that range. I think that's what the accountant told me."

"Not eighty thousand?"

"Heavens, no."

"Then why does it say one hundred thousand on this filing?"

"I—let me see that—how do I know this is mine?"

"Believe me, you're the taxpayer responsible for this. The club is leased, isn't it? From a corporation that Mr. Mandretti helps run?"

"That's correct."

"He's using your club to wash funds."

"What's that supposed to mean?"

"It means you're helping make money from gambling rackets, prostitution, drug sales, and extortion look like it was earned legally. It's called money laundering. And that tax return makes you an accomplice. The one you filed two days ago is even worse. You claim nearly one hundred and ten thousand dollars of income from the club's operations."

"I don't believe you."

"You'll believe me when I have you arrested."

Maddy sprang up from the bench. "You can't do that! I don't know anything about this—"

"That's not what this document indicates. Please, sit back down."

"I'm leaving."

"Mrs. Gordon," Sullivan continued patiently, "if you leave, the next time we see each other will be at your arraignment. There will be someone waiting for you at your apartment with a warrant for your arrest."

"No."

"I'm afraid so. And I know that would prove upsetting to your little girl."

The mention of Annie made Maddy's knees grow weak. She fell back onto the bench.

"Now," Sullivan asked her, "how well do you know Gene Mandretti?"

"Not very. I mean, I've known him for about three years. Since he bought the building from Matt Silvers, the man who hired me."

"How often do you see each other?"

"Not often. Once a week at the most. Sometimes not even that. He comes by the club."

"Do you meet in your apartment?"

Maddy looked at him, trying to decide if he meant what she thought he meant. "No, we do not."

"Mrs. Gordon, Gene Mandretti is married."

"I know that."

"He's married to the niece of Frank Carbolo, who is head of one of the five mafia families operating in the New York area."

"What are you saying?"

"The mafia. The mob. Gene Mandretti's uncle, Salvatore Mandretti, is the number two man in the Carbolo Crime Family. We think Gene is instrumental in helping to hide the Family's illegally obtained assets. We know he's been using your club for that purpose. We need more information. We need your help."

"And if I don't want to help you?"

"Then you will go to jail."

Maddy wanted to deny everything this man was telling her, but every accusation hit her like a punch in the stomach. It explained so many things that she'd been willing to ignore: the driver who seemed to double as a bodyguard, Gene's reluctance to talk about his family, the large quantities of cash he carried with him, and why he sometimes carried a gun, hidden in a holster that he wore under his jacket. The first time she'd seen it and balked, he calmly explained that he needed protection when he went into certain "ugly" parts of town where he owned investment property. The next time he came to see her he brought a gun for Maddy to keep in her apartment. After all, she was an attractive woman, living alone in the nightclub district. For her own protection she should have a gun and know how to use it.

Sullivan's revelation even made sense of the elaborate secret staircase that Gene had installed: he'd had an old service staircase reworked and expanded, so that it led from her office in the club to the uppermost floor of the building. Privacy, he'd said.

Gene was involved with the mafia. That's the reason he teasingly kept her from "bothering herself" about the Blue Door's finances. She'd been blind. Willfully, deliberately, stupidly blind. What was it that Mrs. O'Connor used to say? *I knew it in my bones.*

Sullivan was talking again.

"We need you to tell us everything you know about Mandretti. If you cooperate fully, I can probably keep you from being charged, but if you don't come across the bridge, then you may well end up in prison."

"But I haven't done anything!"

"That's not what this document suggests. And it will strike some people as odd that you don't keep track of what your club is earning. A trial is a very public forum, Mrs. Gordon. I'm offering you a chance to avoid that type of notoriety."

An uneasy silence ensued. When Maddy spoke there was no antagonism left in her voice. "What do I need to do?"

"Excellent. We're going to start with some questions. If I find out that you're not being truthful, then you will go to jail, directly to jail, you will not pass 'Go,' and you will not collect two hundred dollars. Is that clear?"

She nodded.

"So I'll ask you again. What is the nature of your relationship with Gene Mandretti?"

He already knew the answer. That made it easier, somehow. "He's my . . . my boyfriend."

"That's a good start. How often do you see each other?"

"As I said, about once a week. Sometimes less."

"And you meet in your apartment?"

"Most of the time. Gene had a sort of a secret staircase built, from my office in the club to a room on the top floor. He comes into the club; I meet him upstairs."

"Do you ever go out in public together?"

She shook her head. "Not anymore. He's very careful."

"If I were cheating on Papa Frank's niece, I'd be careful, too. Has he ever discussed any aspect of the Blue Door's finances with you?"

"No, other than to tell me that we're doing well."

"I need for you to copy documents for me. Anything you can find: receipts, payroll records, names of suppliers. Anything relating to anything bought by or sold at the club. And we'll be planting some microphones."

"Microphones? Where?"

"In your little rendezvous chamber."

"*What?*"

"Not the bedroom, unless you two talk a lot in the bedroom. Does he ever use the phone?"

"Sometimes."

"Okay. So we'll bug the phones, too."

"When is all this going to happen?"

"Very soon. Gene is smart. If he gets a whiff of trouble, he'll cover his tracks, and quick. Some plumbers will come in to fix something in your apartment. You'll show them how to get upstairs without being noticed." ·

"Where will you be listening?"

"We won't be far."

"What should I do?"

"Absolutely nothing. If he gets an inkling that we're setting him up, this will blow up in our face. But if he has no idea that we can hear him, if he trusts his environment, he's likely to say something, sooner or later, that we can use. So do nothing different, is that clear?"

"I think so."

"Fine. Agent Jamison will walk you home. And we'll be watching you, too, so don't try to make a break for it. Papa Carbolo is not an understanding man, and if Gene finds out you're helping us, well, chances are you'll wish you were in jail. Your only choice is to cooperate, and be careful. You can contact one of the agents, or me, if you feel you're in danger."

"Thanks," Maddy said bitterly.

"I'll be in touch." He walked away.

Maddy pointed to the briefcase. "Is that thing off?"

"Yes."

"So what *is* your name?"

"John. Everyone calls me Jimmy, though."

"Okay, Jimmy. You know the way home."

Neither said a word until they were a couple of blocks from the Blue Door. "I'll be leaving you here," Jamison said politely. "We'll be in touch."

"So you've said. Before you go, I'd like to know, do you think that man—Sullivan—does he believe me? Does he believe I knew nothing about all this?"

"If he believed that, you wouldn't be here."

"Do you believe me?"

"What I believe doesn't matter," he answered, unable to look at her as he said it.

She let out a deep sigh. "Well, that's honest, I guess."

Maddy went home. Annie had woken up from her nap and was playing in the kitchen, where Tia was fixing dinner for the three of them. It was five o'clock. She would have dinner, play with Annie, bathe her, put her to bed, and then go to the club. She must go on as if nothing had happened. As if nothing had changed.

But it was all different. Everything was ruined. All she could do now was try and save herself—and her daughter.

THIRTY-THREE

Maddy looked around fitfully as the phone rang. She was sure, or at least, she hoped she was sure, that no one had followed her to Grand Central. Still, the thought that Gene might discover that she was helping the FBI tied her stomach into agitated knots.

"Sullivan here."

"This is Madeleine Gordon."

"What's wrong? Has Mandretti—"

"Nothing like that. But I need to talk to you about all this."

"Can you get free this afternoon?"

"Yes."

"Okay. Are you familiar with Chinatown at all?"

"Of course."

"There's a restaurant on Mott Street, the Dumpling House. Do you think you could get there within an hour?"

"I think so."

"Okay. I'll see you there."

He was already there when she arrived, sitting in a booth in the corner. He waved her over as she came in.

"Thanks for coming," she said stiffly. He gave her a warm smile. It didn't fit him, somehow. It was someone else's smile, briefly displayed on Sullivan's face, and then gone again.

"No problem," he said as she sat down. "I know how difficult this must be for you."

"Fat chance."

"Okay, I had that coming. Listen, I was an agent before I was a lawyer. I've been in the trenches. I know what it's like to sweat it out—"

"Do you have children?"

"No, I'm not married."

"Then pardon me for saying so, but you don't know a damn thing."

He could see the exhaustion in her eyes. He did not argue.

"Are you hungry?" he asked, artfully changing the subject. "Do you like Chinese food?"

Maddy laughed. It seemed like such an irrelevant question. "To be honest, I haven't been hungry in weeks. But I do like Chinese food. I was born in China. But you probably know that already."

"No, I didn't know that. What were you doing there?"

"Being born."

"Got me. Allow me to rephrase the question. What were your parents doing there?"

Maddy paused. She was going to give a pat answer: my father's business brought the family to Shanghai, etc., etc. But she found herself telling this man, her accuser, a brief version of the truth.

"Did your father ever come for you?"

"Not until it was too late. Too late for us to accept each other, I guess. I stayed for a while with a foster family, and then my aunt found me. You know the rest. I told Bob, I mean, Jimmy, everything else."

An impatient waiter hovered nearby. Maddy and Sullivan ordered. After that they sat in silence. Maddy dipped her chopsticks aimlessly in her water glass and stirred.

"I don't know if I can keep this up," she said softly, concentrating on the motion of the water.

"Because you're in love with him?"

She took a moment to reply. "No," she answered at last, tasting the truth of her words as she spoke. "I suppose I was at first, at least, I thought I was. But our romance, if you can call it that, it's always been like living out some kind of fantasy. It was something I . . . I guess you could say I needed. And when you told me the truth about him, well, it made too much sense. That's all it took to shatter the illusion. I'm not sorry for him, or for myself. I'm just furious with myself for being so stupid."

An intense sense of awareness spread through Ryan as he listened to her. *What if she's telling the truth? What if she's innocent?* But he said nothing. This case was too important, and she was too vital a link. She was the mistress of a mafia kingpin. She was the enemy.

"Why did you want to see me?"

"I want to speed things up. I'm going to go crazy. I can't put up with this tension. I'm a wreck. And I'm worried that something will happen to Annie."

"Can you send her away? To your aunt's?"

Maddy smiled ironically. "For a few days, I suppose that would work. My aunt is not a very maternal person. And she'd wonder why. No, I want this all to end. There must be something I can do."

"Not really. You've done a great job so far. These past three weeks have been really productive. We've copied all the documents that you've secured for us, and we have a good tap on the phone. He's called out several times to some key people. Nothing too important, but with time, something will give. All this takes is patience."

"And where did you, Ryan Sullivan, learn all this patience?"

She was getting under his skin. This was dangerous. "The hard way," he answered brusquely.

"I see." Their food arrived. She looked at her plate as if she did not know where it had come from, then slid out of the booth.

"Where are you going?" he asked, his voice betraying his concern.

"I'm not hungry. Thanks. Don't worry. I'll carry on."

"Maddy, wait." Neither of them noticed that he'd used her first name. He followed her out of the restaurant. When they reached the street he caught her arm, then dropped it.

"Maddy, I—"

She was waiting, waiting for something that he could not give her.

"I'm sorry," he said, as if that would help.

"Don't be. I got myself into this. You're just doing your job."

"Call me if you need another pep talk," he added, feeling foolish.

"I'll be okay."

Ryan found himself walking by the Blue Door that night. He knew it was a ridiculous thing to do. He told himself he was there to check up on the surveillance team. He could see Al Peyton's undercover car parked across the street. Let the boys think he came by to keep them on their toes.

He could hear the piano before he entered the room. A saxophone mingled its own melancholy voice with the music of Maddy's fingers. The blend was hypnotically beautiful, and the music stayed with him for hours, haunting him later as he tried to sleep. He thought about her expressive eyes. The shape of her shoulders. The sweet sadness that came gliding out through her music.

It was nearly morning before he fell asleep, and she was there, in his dreams.

Maddy never bothered to ask herself what she would do when it was all over, what she would do when the Blue Door and Gene and Ryan Sullivan were out of her life. She couldn't think that far ahead. All she could do was try and take one day at a time.

An early afternoon in mid-May found Annie and Maddy at the zoo in Central Park. Annie's favorite animals were the pigeons, and her favorite game was chasing them. Maddy sat on a bench and watched as her daughter's chubby little legs trotted with thundering speed in the direction of a clump of the dirty gray birds. Annie never caught one, but she never gave up.

A tall man, wearing a lightweight raincoat, sunglasses, and a felt fedora approached Annie. He held a bag of popcorn in his hands. Watching him, Maddy felt her maternal radar go up. She was ready to spring from the bench if the man came too close to her daughter.

He didn't. He stopped several feet away and started tossing popcorn to the pigeons. They gathered around him quickly, torn between their fear of Annie's treacherous toddler feet and their desire for such a tasty meal. Annie was fascinated by his success.

"My turn! My turn!" she burbled.

The man smiled and handed her the bag. Annie immediately spilled a quarter of it and the pigeons gathered around her greedily, happy to let bygones be bygones if she were willing to offer such a generous peace prize.

"Honey, that's for the birds, not for you. Don't put any in your mouth," Maddy called to Annie. The man was walking toward the bench. He stopped, looked at Maddy, and took off his sunglasses.

Maddy nearly fainted.

"Hello, Maddy," said Leo Hoffman. "May I join you?"

Moving as if in a trance, Maddy scooted over to make enough room for her father to sit down. "What are you doing here?" she got out at last. "Where did you come from? I thought you were dead. I mean, I assumed you were. We tried to find out, but there weren't any records—"

Leo smiled, that half-amused smile that Maddy still saw in her dreams. "Not dead. Just living someone else's life, behind the iron curtain."

"Still a spy?"

"Until quite recently. It's time for me to retire."

"Good God," Maddy groaned, sinking down farther into the bench. "My father is James Bond."

Leo laughed. Annie looked up from her pigeons when she heard him, then, satisfied that she was missing nothing, went back to the business of feeding the birds.

"I haven't seen the movie, but I have read a couple of the books recently. My work was nothing nearly so glamorous, I'm afraid. No, the spy business isn't exactly what Mr. Fleming describes."

Maddy stayed mute, still at a loss for what to say. Leo gave her some time to collect herself, and then he began to talk.

"I've been back in the country for a few weeks. I had some business to do in Washington. Then I thought I would come and see you."

"You could have called."

"Well, I wasn't too successful with that strategy last time, so I decided to try a personal reintroduction. The fact that you haven't yet seized your child and fled is, I admit, somewhat encouraging."

"No, Papa. It's a shock, seeing you like this, but I won't run away this time."

Leo let out a sigh full of grateful relief. "Thank you, Maddy."

They watched Annie for a while, who'd strewn popcorn all over the pavement and was using exaggerated stealth to try and pet one of the gluttonous pigeons. Each one managed to shimmy away from her just in time to avoid being touched.

"She's beautiful. What's her name?"

"Martha Anne. But we call her Annie. Aunt Bernice thinks she looks like you."

"No, she looks like you. And your mother."

"But she has your eyes. They're so blue."

Even this mild intimacy made Maddy feel dangerously exposed. "What do you want?" she asked, suddenly defensive.

Leo removed his hat. His hair was streaked with gray. Lines around his eyes testified to his age and the significant stress of his chosen profession. Still, he looked like the man Maddy remembered.

"I was only hoping to see you. I don't want to make you uncomfortable. I'll leave if you want me to."

"No, I'm sorry. It's that—I did finally read your letters. Mrs. O'Connor gave them to me when my husband died."

"I'm very sorry that you lost your husband," Leo said gravely.

"Well, I suppose it's one of the many things you don't know about me. We haven't exactly kept in touch."

"That is the greatest regret of my life." He said this without any drama; he was merely stating a simple truth.

She sighed. "It's not as if it was all your fault. I told you to go away."

"I shouldn't have listened. You were only fifteen. But there was so much pain there, for both of us, and my other path seemed so clear."

"Oh, Papa. That's how life works, I guess. One day a decision seems so straightforward, and the next day, nothing is clear at all." *Annie's life is all about pigeons and popcorn right now. I wish it would stay that way for her. Simple.*

"Maddy, this is probably asking too much, but I'd like you to consider, that is, to ask you if you might be willing to make some room for me in your life, on whatever terms you're comfortable with."

Maddy cringed, wishing he'd been there to ask her that question three months ago, before she had learned the truth about her lover, about herself. She wasn't sure how she could cope with Leo's sudden reappearance given everything else that was going on in her life. The sight of her father aroused so many conflicting emotions; there was so much pain there, and the scars ran so deep.

Her reaction was not lost on her father, although he had no way of knowing that her agitation was caused by anything other than his request. "This isn't something you have to decide right away. I can give you my number, and—"

For some reason this struck her as funny. "Do old spies have unlisted telephone numbers?" she asked, almost giggling.

He smiled back at her with a rueful grin. "Excellent question. Yes. At least this one does. Unlisted and under an alias. But I'll give it to you." He adopted a stage whisper. "I'm staying at the Carlyle, under the name Leonard Harmon."

And when I call you, Sullivan and his gang will be listening. "You must have my number already, or at least have figured out how to find me, right? James Bond style?"

"Using tools no more elaborate than the phone book. That's also how I found out that you play the piano at a jazz club."

"Well, I waited too long to make a go of a career in classical music, but somehow jazz was the right choice for me. At least I used to think so."

"But that's changed?"

"Well, there's Annie. It's not really the life a mother should lead. She'll get older, and I'll have to do something else."

Leo could tell she was lying. He decided not to push.

"And what about you?" Maddy asked him. "What's next?"

"I don't know. In part that depends on you."

Maddy had no time to respond, for Annie decided that she'd had enough of the pigeons. "Oh, dear—there she goes—come on!" She flew after Annie, who was trundling down the sidewalk in the general direction of the bear cage.

The child kept them going for over an hour before slowing down, a signal to Maddy that she was ready for her nap, and sure enough, Annie's head had collapsed against her mother's shoulder before they reached the exit.

"May I walk you home?" Leo offered. "I'd be happy to carry her." As he reached for Annie, Maddy recoiled and jerked away. They stared at each other, he embarrassed by his own thoughtless audacity, she startled by her reaction to it.

"I'm sorry, I—"

"Oh, Papa. Do you remember the first time you came and met me at school here in New York? The day after you brought me back to the O'Connors' from Amelia's place? When I thought you were already gone?"

"Of course I do."

"That's how I feel right now, the same way I did when I walked out of the building and saw you standing there. Even after all this time, I want so much from you, but I'm so afraid." A lone tear crawled down one of her cheeks, and she tried to rub it off on Annie's hat. "I don't know if I'm ready for this—"

"Here, let me," Leo handed her his handkerchief, and then reached for Annie again so that Maddy could use it. This time Maddy let him take her. The child's eyes opened briefly, but she didn't really wake up.

"Do you want to stop for some coffee? Water?" Leo asked his daughter.

She shook her head and wiped away another tear. "No, I'll be all right. But it's okay if you want to walk us home."

"Nothing would give me greater pleasure," he answered, and was rewarded with a wan smile.

This one moment is more than I deserve, Leo thought a little while later as he placed Annie in her crib. He and Maddy crept out of her room before he spoke again.

"I'd love to come and hear you play at the Blue Door. I'll sit in the back. I don't want to make you feel uncomfortable."

"I'd like that. Not tonight, though. Maybe tomorrow. I'm doing a solo gig, I mean, a solo performance, tomorrow, if you think you could make it."

"Nothing could keep me away. I'll be there."

Leo showed himself out. He saw a brown, two-door Chevrolet that was parked across the street. Leo had been keeping tabs on Maddy for several days in order to find a convenient way to approach her. The brown car had been there the whole time: not always in the same place, but always nearby. And there was always someone in it.

Leo had spent years training himself to observe such things. His professional instincts made him wary. Then he chided himself. This was New York, not Eastern Europe. The Russians were unlikely to snatch him off the street, even if they eventually found out his real identity. That part of his life was over. He deliberately turned his back on the car and walked away.

After Leo left, Maddy sat in her room staring at the walls for well over an hour. Her father. Her father. After almost eighteen years. To think of all the times she'd thought she'd seen his face in a crowd, or had awoken to the sound of his laughter as it slipped away in a dream. He'd always been with her, in some way. If he was willing to try, then so was she.

But first she needed to straighten up the mess she'd made of her life. There had to be a way out, no matter what Sullivan said. Gene was planning to come over tonight; tonight she would end this charade. She would prove her innocence to Mr. Ryan Sullivan, and rid herself of Gene Mandretti.

She dialed Bernice's number.

Later that evening the phone rang in Leo Hoffman's suite at the Carlyle. He let it ring several times before picking up.

"Hello?"

"This is Bernice Mason. I would like to say welcome back, where have you been, and all the usual rubbish, but I think I'll skip the formalities. Madeleine called me a few minutes ago, and explained that she talked to you earlier today."

"That's right. I met her in the park, with little Annie. It was very pleasant, or at least I thought so."

"If it was so 'pleasant,' would you explain to me why she's asked me to take Annie for a few days? The child is on her way over now, with that Polish nanny of hers. Madeleine said she needed some peace and quiet. She sounded extremely distraught. I think your sudden reappearance has disturbed her very deeply. I'm disgusted that you would consider it appropriate to leap back into her life, like a jack-in-the-box. I must ask you not to see her again."

"But when I left them Maddy was fine. She asked me to come by the club tomorrow. I don't know what happened. I'll go and see her—"

"For God's sake, don't upset her any more than she is already. You must have given her a dreadful shock. Just stay away from her. Stay away from my family."

"She's my daughter, Bernice."

"As if that has ever mattered to you." She hung up.

Leo put the phone back on the hook. Something was not right. The Maddy that Bernice had described had nothing to do with the poised young woman he'd seen this afternoon. Maybe Bernice was lying, trying to make him leave Maddy and Annie alone.

Or maybe there was something going on in Maddy's life he needed to find out more about.

Maddy took special care dressing that evening. She spent a long time brushing her hair, and put on the emerald-and-diamond necklace that Gene had given her on the *Queen Elizabeth*. That was one piece of information she did not share with the FBI: that her affair with Gene had begun in June 1960. There was no way she was going to let anyone know that Annie was his daughter. Especially not Gene himself.

She was not performing that night; Gene would come early, and expect to stay for hours. She had dinner delivered from a bistro down the street. She put a bottle of champagne on ice. She put on her makeup. And she waited.

He arrived at eight and greeted her with his usual sensuous embrace. They had dinner and talked about what they usually talked about: the club, Annie's latest accomplishments, what news she'd had from Katherine. Maddy did not mention her father. She floated through the evening like an actress in a play: not missing a cue, laughing at the right times, as charming as she could be.

After nibbling at dessert she mixed a pitcher of martinis and poured one for each of them. Gene liked his liquor.

She watched him as he took his first sip, nodding his approval. *Now,* she thought, *before he starts . . . before he gets what he came here for.*

"Gene, tell me, is the Blue Door making money?"

He acted as if he were surprised by the question. "Sure it is, angel. You pull 'em in like bees to honey."

"Well, how much of it do we get to keep?"

"What do you mean?"

"You know, after taxes. Income taxes. I may not be a financial genius, but I know there are ways around paying your taxes. Doctors love to get paid in cash, so they don't have to report every dime. It helps make up for all the times they don't get paid at all."

"What the hell is she tryin' to do?" barked Royster, *listening from the FBI surveillance post set up in a building on the next block. "Didn't Sullivan tell her not to try and make him talk? This is gonna backfire. Shit. Stupid bitch. Call Sullivan. Tell him this whole operation may blow any minute."*

"Maddy, Maddy, the doctor's wife," Gene responded, with a touch of sarcasm. "What other bad habits did ol' Doctor Brad teach you? Good thing his brakes failed when they did, or you'd be in jail with him for income tax evasion, instead of here in my arms, where you belong."

His words triggered a terrifying train of thought. "How did you know his brakes failed? The car exploded."

Gene looked at her with a mixture of irritation and defensiveness. "Well, Maddy, his car went over a cliff. Something must have been wrong with the Cadillac."

"How did you know he was driving a Cadillac?"

"Why am I getting the third degree?"

Maddy's heart raced. She'd not connected what Sullivan had told her about Gene with the circumstances surrounding Brad's death. But it made too much sense not to be true. *"What if you can't go back to him?"* Gene had asked that last morning on the *Queen Elizabeth*. She'd taken his question to mean *"What if he doesn't want you back?"* But that wasn't what he meant at all. He meant that he could have Brad taken out of the equation. Gene had made sure that she had no husband to go back to.

"You killed him. You killed Brad, so you could have me."

"Okay, I may have wanted the man dead. There was a time I wanted to see both of you dead. But isn't it a little far-fetched to go accusing me of murdering your husband? Not to mention unkind."

"You didn't murder him yourself. You had your fairy godfather do it for you: your uncle Sal."

Gene's expression turned deadly serious. He put his drink down on the coffee table.

"Who have you been talking to, Maddy?"

"No one," she said, looking away. "I'm not as dumb as you think I am. Your uncle is Salvatore Mandretti. Everyone knows he's connected to the mafia."

"Who's been talking to you about the mafia?"

"No one, Gene. I put two and two together, that's all."

"Is there something you need to tell me? Has someone been asking you questions about me? About my uncle? About my family's business?"

She forced herself to meet his gaze. "No."

"Good. And if anyone does, you'll tell me about it, won't you?" He reached out and grasped her jaw tightly, too tightly.

"Stop," she demanded, the words muffled by his grip on her chin. "You're hurting me."

"You'll tell me, won't you, Maddy?" he repeated, not releasing his grip. "Because I would never want anything to happen to you, or our daughter."

Her eyes grew wide. With a surge of strength she tore his hand away from her face.

"She is *not* your daughter. Don't bring Annie into this."

"That's bullshit, and you know it. She's got Mandretti written all over her. And if you and Brad didn't have a kid for ten years, I'm not going to believe he planted one right before he died."

Maddy's eyes filled with tears of fury. "You're a bastard."

"I know I am, Maddy. The last time you told me that was the night I got you back into my bed. Don't kid yourself, angel. This ain't no sweet romance. You give me what I want, and I give you what you want. What you've always wanted. It's what you want right now."

"Don't touch me."

Gene grabbed her wrists. "I told you once before, Maddy. Never say no to me."

"Looks like we're in for a show," Royster hollered to Jamison. *"You reach Sullivan yet?"*

"Got Sully on his car radio. Sullivan? This is Jamison. You read me?"

"Loud and clear."

"You better get over here. She's going off script, trying to get him to spill something, and he's getting mighty damn suspicious. Something's gonna blow."

"Uh-oh," interrupted Royster. *"Sounds like we got a situation on our hands."*

"What's that?" Sullivan asked, *unable to catch what Royster was saying in the background.*

"Well, it seems Mr. Mandretti wants some—uh—you know—and Mrs. Gordon isn't cooperating."

"Shit," said Royster, still listening. *"She's really gonna fuck this up if she starts playin' hard to get now."*

"I'm on my way," Ryan responded, *and drove his car like a rocket in the direction of Fifty-second Street.*

Maddy twisted out of Gene's arms and ran toward the door. He tackled her before she reached it. She stopped struggling and lay beneath him, noiseless, passive. When he climaxed she looked at his contorting face with detachment.

Gene got off of her and walked back to the coffee table to reclaim his drink. Maddy sat up on the floor. She felt uncannily calm and clearheaded. She watched Gene as he picked up his martini, drained it, and put down the empty glass. He kept his back to her.

She would not let him threaten Annie. If there was one thing she could do with the rest of her screwed-up life, she'd protect her daughter from the monster who'd fathered her.

She got up, tried to straighten her skirt, and then walked over to the small foyer table next to the door. She kept Gene's spare cigarettes in the drawer. And her gun.

"Cigarette?" she asked sweetly, as if she'd just made love to the man she adored.

"Why certainly, my love," Gene replied, in a fair imitation of Cary Grant. He turned to face her. Sullivan burst in as she lifted the gun from the drawer. He saw it in her hand.

"Christ! Don't shoot!"

"What the fuck?" yelled Royster. "Sully's in the apartment!"

Gene took a step forward. "Who the hell are you? Fuckin' shit—I don't care who you are, you're a dead man."

Maddy held her gun straight out in front of her, and shot him.

The bullet opened a small, red wound in the side of Gene's chest. He looked down at the hole in his body, then up at Maddy.

"Angel," he said, and fell forward, dead.

Ryan Sullivan snatched the gun from Maddy's hand and shot another round into the wall. His eyes raked the room. He saw Mandretti's coat jacket hanging over a chair and raced over to it, searching for the gun he desperately hoped was there. It was. Using his handkerchief, he placed it in Gene's right hand, shouting as he did so.

"Royster! Jamison! I had to shoot. I think he's dead."

"Oh, Jesus Christ. What next?" cried Royster. "Sully went and blew the asshole away. What the hell is he thinking?"

"We're getting out of here," Ryan shouted again to the invisible ears. Maddy stood transfixed, staring at Gene's corpse and the red stain rapidly spreading on the carpet beneath it. He took her hand. "Come on, Maddy. We have to go." Half dragging her behind him, he headed out of the apartment and down the stairs.

Gene's bodyguard stood on the first floor landing, his gun pointed up at them.

"Would you mind telling me where Mr. Mandretti is?" he asked, in a voice as menacing as his weapon.

"He's dead," Maddy said, pushing her way past Ryan. "I killed him."

"Don't!" Ryan tried wildly to reach for her and aim his gun around her at the same time.

"You fuckin' bitch." The bodyguard fired. The bullet caught Maddy in midstep. She tumbled down the stairs.

Ryan got one round off, but his shot went wild. He plunged down the stairs as he heard another shot and flinched, expecting to feel pain, for he knew the bullet was aimed at him. But he felt nothing.

In front of him the bodyguard's knees buckled, and the big man fell over. Another man stood behind him. An older man, someone Ryan had never seen before.

"I'm Leo Hoffman. Maddy's father. My car's across the street. Let's get her out of here. And then you can tell me what the hell is going on."

THIRTY-FOUR

Leo sat in the hospital waiting room, desperate for the surgeon to bring him news of his daughter. He heard rapid footsteps coming from the wrong direction, and half expected to see Bernice with Annie in tow. Instead, he saw the haggard face of Ryan Sullivan.

"How did it go?" he asked, as soon as Ryan fell into a chair. His own interview with the city police had taken place hours before, and was mercifully brief. His CIA credentials had thrown them for a loop. They happily handed him over to the FBI, whose agents were both irked and confused by the sudden appearance of a CIA man in the middle of their failed sting operation. The FBI and CIA higher-ups were having joint conniptions in Washington, trying to figure out what Leo could say to whom, and about what. Eventually, he would have a lot of explaining to do. But he wasn't worried, not for himself.

"Better than I expected, actually," Ryan answered, heaving a sigh. "No one challenged my story. The police were happy to give the whole matter over to the Bureau. The tape backed up my story. I said 'don't shoot' to Mandretti, who then told me I was a dead man. I said my first bullet hit him in the chest, and the second one went wild. The ballistics test proved I'd fired one of the guns, and his was in his hand, so the self-defense story stands up reasonably well, as long as she doesn't contradict me. I'll catch hell—more than likely I'll get the sack for botching the whole investigation. But I don't care. It was worth it."

Leo studied him: this man who had first jeopardized his daughter's life, then tried so hard to save it. Ryan told him the whole story as they sped to the emergency room. Leo had seen the remorse and panic in the younger man's eyes then, and now he was trying to keep Maddy from being charged with murder. Ryan Sullivan was in love with her, though he doubted the young man yet realized it himself. He was desperately in love with her.

Leo still remembered how that felt.

"I have some friends in Washington who owe me a favor," he said. "I may be able to help you. About the job, I mean."

Ryan nodded, then shrugged. "Thanks," he said. "But it won't mean anything . . . if she . . . you know." He could not finish.

Bernice stormed into the waiting room.

"Who are you?" she demanded of Ryan.

He dug in his breast pocket and flipped open his credentials. "Assistant United States Attorney Ryan Sullivan, Organized Crime Task Force. You're Bernice Mason, Mrs. Gordon's aunt, aren't you?"

"I am. How did Madeleine get hurt? And *shot* of all things? Was it some thug from that nightclub?"

"Not exactly, Mrs. Mason," replied Ryan, regaining some of his professional demeanor. "Your niece has been assisting us in an investigation involving organized crime activities in the New York entertainment industry. A target of the investigation caught wind of the fact that she was cooperating with federal authorities, and threatened to kill her. She was shot by his bodyguard while trying to escape him."

Bernice sank into a chair, bewildered. "I don't believe it."

"I'm sorry, sorrier than I can tell you, but that's the truth, Mrs. Mason."

"Why would she get involved in something like that?"

Ryan did his best to keep his guilt at bay as he tried to answer the question. "She's a brave woman. She had access to important information, and she wanted to see justice done. She's a hero."

The surgeon entered the room, depriving Bernice of the opportunity to grill Ryan any further. "I know Mr. Hoffman," he said, after removing his surgical mask, "but I don't think I've met either of you. I'm Dr. Hartstein."

"How is she?" Ryan asked speaking for all of them.

"We won't know for sure for several hours, but I think she'll make it. The bullet missed her lung by a fraction. Splintered some ribs, but no spinal trauma. She should be okay."

"When can I see her?"

"I have to talk to her."

"I must see her."

The doctor held up his hand. "We can't overwhelm the poor woman. Once she's regained consciousness, I'll let Mr. Hoffman, her father, in to speak with her. You two will have to wait."

Bernice persisted. "I have every right to see her—"

"Ma'am," the doctor interrupted, "I just finished telling representatives of the Federal Bureau of Investigation the same thing I am about to tell you. Mrs. Gordon's medical chart lists her father as her next of kin. I have no idea who you are, but in this hospital we play by my rules. Mr. Hoffman may see her for five minutes after I give him the green light. Everyone else, and I mean everyone, will wait until I decide her condition has stabilized."

"But—"

"I suggest you go home and get some sleep. I will have a nurse contact you when Mrs. Gordon is ready to receive visitors."

Bernice bristled. She was not used to getting no for an answer. "Very well," she snapped, barely civil. "I expect to be contacted *immediately* once she has stabilized."

"You have my word."

"And you"—Bernice pointed to Ryan—"I want you to tell me exactly how this happened. This is an outrage, subjecting a law-abiding citizen to this type of danger. What do you think she is, some kind of *spy*?"

Ryan stayed firm. "I'm afraid I can't give you any more information until I get permission from the FBI to do so. This is a highly sensitive investigation. We hope no one but the two dead members of the mafia knew that Mrs. Gordon was involved. If word gets out, then her life may still be in danger."

Bernice's mouth dropped open. She put a hand to her head. "I've had as much as I can take for one evening. But don't think for a minute you've heard the last of me." With this comment, she swept out of the room.

Dr. Hartstein waited until she was gone before he spoke again.

"Mother-in-law?" he asked Leo.

"My sister-in-law."

"Impressive lady. You may wait if you wish, Mr. Hoffman. It will be two more hours before the anesthesia wears off enough for her to be coherent."

"I'll wait."

"Very well then. I'm going home. She's being monitored, and guarded, very closely. These agents are a nuisance."

When the room was empty again Ryan practically pounced on Leo. "You have to tell her for me. You have to make her agree to say that I shot Gene Mandretti. It's the only way the story fits together. Otherwise, she'll be charged with murder. You have to help me save her."

"Don't worry about that. Why don't you go and get some rest?"

"I'd rather wait."

"As you wish."

The next hour and a half dripped by. By one o'clock the two men had fallen asleep, dozing off in their chairs. Leo snapped to attention when he heard a voice.

"Mr. Hoffman?" asked a nurse quietly. "You may see your daughter now. Five minutes. No longer."

He bolted out of his chair.

Maddy looked so small and helpless. Machines ticked and whirred around her. A tube in her wrist slowly replaced some of the blood she had lost. To Leo's relief, the two guards posted outside her room stayed outside.

He sat down next to his daughter and stroked her hand.

"Maddy? Princess?"

Her eyes opened slowly. She took a breath, and tried to speak. "Papa, is Ryan . . . do you know . . . is Mr. Sullivan—"

"He's fine, Maddy. He wasn't hurt."

"But the driver—"

"I killed him."

"You?" She moved, as if trying to sit up. He gently restrained her.

"Princess, listen to me. Ryan killed Mandretti. Do you understand that?"

Maddy looked puzzled. She shook her head.

"Trust me, please. Ryan Sullivan killed Gene Mandretti in self-defense. You were with him, and when you both tried to escape, you were shot by Gene's bodyguard. It's vital that you remember this, because people will ask you questions, and you must be able to answer."

"But Ryan—"

"Ryan's not in any trouble. He'll be okay." He paused. "You have to do this, Maddy. For Annie, and for me."

A glimmer of comprehension crossed her face.

"Promise me, Princess."

"I promise."

"Good. Now go back to sleep. You need rest."

He stayed with her until her even breathing convinced him that she had in fact gone back to sleep. Then he watched her for a long time, studying her face, every cell of his body reverberating with the force of his memories. He had never been there for her. He had never given her what she needed. But perhaps he'd been there when she needed him most.

The New York police, following instructions from the FBI, reported to the local press that Gene Mandretti, wealthy Manhattan businessman and landlord of the Blue Door nightclub, had been killed, along with his chauffeur, during a robbery attempt. The press also learned that Madeleine Hoffman, the club's owner, had been injured in the holdup. Papa Carbolo was suspicious of the story, and suspected that

Gene had been grazing in a forbidden pasture, but there did not seem to be any direct fallout from the boy's death. Then, in June, a mob trigger-man by the name of Joe Valachi started singing from his penitentiary cell in Atlanta. He began telling tales and naming names. The code of silence had been broken. The Five Families had more pressing problems to worry about.

It was a week before Maddy was released from the hospital. Her father, her aunt, and her friend Ryan came to see her every day. Fans from the Blue Door filled her room with flowers. When the tubes were withdrawn and the machines rolled away, Bernice brought Annie to visit. Maddy hugged her tightly, trying to reassure the frightened little girl that her mother would soon be home.

On the day Maddy was discharged Leo and Annie were there to escort her. She walked slowly through the glass double doors toward the car where Bernice waited to take her home.

"You're walking so slow, Mommy. It's like you just learned how," Annie sang out, mimicking her mother's measured pace.

"I guess I'll have to learn how to do it all over again," Maddy replied. Then she looked at her father. "There are a lot of things I have to learn how to do all over again."

"Me, too," he answered back.

She squeezed his hand. "I won't let go if you won't."

"Never again, Maddy. I'll never let go again."

And for the first time in a very, very long time, she believed him.

AUTHOR'S NOTE

One of the joys of writing historical fiction is the opportunity to blend real characters and historical events with their fictional counterparts. Below are some of the real people with whom Leo Hoffman interacts in *Heart of Deception*.

Colonel William Eddy, who had an outstanding service record in military intelligence during WWI, was personally tapped by William "Wild Bill" Donovan, founder of the American Office of Strategic Services, to head up the spy network in North Africa. In 1944 he went on to become minister plenipotentiary to Saudi Arabia, where he continued to serve as an important source for the Central Intelligence Agency.

Carleton Coon was a professor of anthropology at Harvard, who, along with his professional colleague Gordon Browne, worked closely with William Eddy in North Africa. They did in fact develop "mule-turd bombs," which were used effectively during the Allied campaign in Tunisia. There is still speculation about the level of Coon's involvement in the assassination of Admiral Darlan, the controversial officer who was to lead French military operations after the Allies won North Africa. The autobiography Coon wrote about his own activities at the time, *A North Africa Story* (Gambit, 1980), was a valuable source of information for this book.

Christine Granville was one of the most glamorous and successful undercover agents to work for the Special Operations Executive, the wartime British spy organization. Born Krystyna Skarbek, the daughter of a Polish count, she began her career as a spy by skiing from Hungary across the Tatra Mountains back into Poland to do reconnaissance. She evaded capture by the Germans multiple times, once by pretending to have tuberculosis by biting her tongue so hard that she "coughed up" blood. Among other accomplishments, she saved the life of Francis Cammaerts, who headed up SOE operations in Southern France. Fellow Polish expatriate Andrew Kennedy was her longtime friend and lover, although by all accounts fidelity was never her strong suit. After the war she had an affair with Ian Fleming, and he used her as the inspiration for Vesper Lynd, the double agent in his first James Bond novel, *Casino Royale*. In 1952 she was stabbed to death outside her apartment by a man she met while working as a cabin stewardess on a cruise ship. The most detailed biography available of this extraordinary woman is *Christine: SOE Agent & Churchill's Favourite Spy*, by Madeleine Masson (Virago, 2005).

Major Peter Wilkinson was for a time head of the British Special Operations Executive in Cairo. His completely unjustified belief that Chris-

tine Granville was a double agent caused her and her longtime par-
amour, Andrew Kennedy, to be sidelined in Cairo for nearly two years.

Darryl Zanuck, the famous filmmaker, did in fact show up in North
Africa to make a documentary film about the invasion, much to
General Eisenhower's consternation. The only conscious liberty
I have taken with the facts regarding the events described in this
book is the date of his arrival in Morocco, which I pushed up by a
few weeks.

DISCUSSION QUESTIONS
FOR READERS' GROUPS

1. What is your opinion of Bernice Mason, Leo's sister-in-law? Were her motives in separating Leo from his daughter altruistic, or deceptive? Similarly, when Amelia informs Maddy about her husband's infidelity, was she being helpful or vindictive?

2. What explains Leo's attraction to Christine, given that he knows she's not likely to be faithful? Is there anything about their respective characters that make them better spies?

3. What do you think of Leo's decision to go to France when his actions jeopardize his ability to reunite with his own child? Why do you think he decided to fight in the cold war rather than try to win back his daughter's affections?

4. Do you think that Maddy's decision to refuse further contact with her father was the correct one? Why or why not?

5. At Katherine's graduation celebration, Maddy is envious of her friend's ability to "never feel guilty about what she wanted, or to fret about the price she might have to pay to get it." What do you suppose makes her feel this way? As the novel progresses, does Maddy change in this regard?

6. Why was it so imperative that Maddy break off her relationship with Gene? Was it credible that she would rethink this decision later in life?

7. How are the decisions that Maddy makes in her life similar to or different from the decisions her mother, Martha, and her father, Leo, made? Do Maddy and Leo go about trying to correct their mistakes in the same way?

8. Maddy's piano teacher tells her that "artists are different." Christine Granville tells Leo that "some of us are just not suited to the rhythm of ordinary life." Do you agree that people with special talents ought not to be judged by what Gene refers to as "rules created for other people"?

9. The author makes substantial use of real historical figures. Do you think she did so effectively? Which was your favorite character (real or fictional), and why?

10. There's an old piece of advice for writers: "If your plot requires more than two coincidences to keep moving, start rewriting." Were there any such coincidences in *Heart of Deception*? Did they seem credible, or contrived? Has your own life or the life of someone you've known ever been dramatically affected by coincidence?

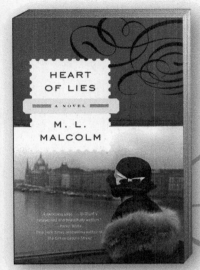
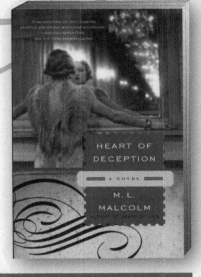